BEAR RAID

DeGoone Slickens hadn't made billions by being Mr. Nice Guy. That's why he had his office shielded by armed guards, and kept a loaded Winchester by his desk.

Now, though, his guards had been tossed through the air like footballs instead of ex-football players. That left Slickens alone with his Winchester in his hands to face the intruder, who happened to be a bear.

"Looks like it's just you and me," the bear said casually.

"Wait a minute," Slickens said. "You're not a real bear. You're just a guy in a mangy suit."

"I'm Bear-Man," Remo Williams said, jerking a thumb at his chest . . .

. . . which was exactly where Slickens aimed to plant a high-powered bullet. . . .

#81

The Destroyer

HOSTILE TAKEOVER

Created by
WARREN MURPHY & RICHARD SAPIR

A SIGNET BOOK

SIGNET
Published by the Penguin Group
Penguin Books USA Inc., 375 Hudson Street,
New York, New York 10014, U.S.A.
Penguin Books Ltd, 27 Wrights Lane,
London W8 5TZ, England
Penguin Books Australia Ltd, Ringwood,
Victoria, Australia
Penguin Books Canada Ltd, 2801 John Street,
Markham, Ontario, Canada L3R 1B4
Penguin Books (N.Z.) Ltd, 182-190 Wairau Road,
Auckland 10, New Zealand

Penguin Books Ltd, Registered Offices:
Harmondsworth, Middlesex, England

First published by Signet, an imprint of Penguin Books USA Inc.

First Printing, July, 1990
10 9 8 7 6 5 4 3 2 1

Copyright © Warren Murphy, 1990
All rights reserved

 REGISTERED TRADEMARK—MARCA REGISTRADA

PUBLISHER'S NOTE
This is a work of fiction. Names, characters, places, and incidents either are the
product of the author's imagination or are used fictitiously, and any resemblance to
actual persons, living or dead, events, or locales is entirely coincidental.

For that unregenerate anglophile S. T. Joshi.
And for the Glorious House of Sinanju,
P.O. Box 2505, Quincy, MA 02269.

1

The panic started in Hong Kong.

It was ten A.M. Hong Kong time. Trading was light on the floor of the Hang Seng Stock Exchange. Red-coated traders were shouting buy and sell orders in what was their normal controlled frenzy of trading. It was a day like any other. At first.

Loo Pak was the first to notice the news coming in over his pocket Quotrek computer.

Pak wore his Quotrek clipped to his belt, like an over-size pocket pager. He had just bought sixty shares of IBM and decided to check the black device. He pressed a button and the liquid crystal display came to life. The device was tied into an electronic subscription service provided by the British news agency Reuters. For a hefty monthly fee, Loo Pak had access to minute-by-minute news bulletins and stock transactions critical to doing busi-ness in the fast-moving world of global finance. It was news that as often as not would not see print for days—if ever.

To the average citizen, the Reuters bulletins were often fragmentary or meaningless. Not to Loo Pak. To him, the price of wheat in Chicago or the situation in Cambodia could have instant impact on his livelihood. The Reuters service acted as an early-warning device as important as radar.

Loo Pak blinked as he watched the black LCD letters form a headline. His eyes went wide. The headline was brief: "GLB DOWN 27 POINTS IN NIKKEI TRADING."

To Loo Pak that curt string of symbols held a world of meaning. It meant that the price per share of the hitherto fast-rising Global Communications Conglomerate had lost an unprecedented twenty-seven points on Tokyo's Nikkei Stock Exchange. It was dropping like a stone.

Loo Pak was heavily invested in GLB. He had already lost thousands of U.S. dollars in the four seconds it took him to absorb the bad news.

Loo Pak jumped up, waving both hands.

"Glob to sell!" he cried in English, the world-wide language of business. "Glob" was the pit term for GLB. "Any takers?"

A trader offered him fifty-five per share. He obviously hadn't gotten the news. Loo Pak took him up on it. In a twinkling, with no more than a staccato exchange of terse sentences and a few scribbled notations on their traders' books, Loo Pak had divested all his GLB stock and the other trader was positioned to eat a big loss. Unless GLB rebounded.

GLB didn't rebound. The new price hit the big electronic ticker tape. Word raced around the exchange floor that GLB, the world's largest communications conglomerate, was heading for the cellar. Anxiously, sweaty-armpitted traders conferred with their pocket Quotreks. Sell orders were shouted, and accepted. In the time that it took to execute them, the value had dropped another five points. The room began to heat up.

And on the electronic ticker overhead, the string of stock codes and numbers began to drop lower and lower. Not just for GLB, but for virtually every stock being traded.

It had begun. And once begun, there was no stopping it.

Within fifteen minutes, over two thousand professional traders were scurrying around the paper-littered floor of the Kabutocho Exchange in Tokyo, Japan. Their Quotreks were warning that Hong Kong's Hang Seng Index had dropped a stunning 155 points—dragged down because of heavy sell-offs of Global Communications Conglomerate stock by investors and mutual funds. Computerized trade programs kicked in. And were executed. In a twinkling, massive blocks of stock moved like ghostly juggernauts—impelled by the shout of a voice, the touch of a button. Not a coin was offered.

Not a single stock certificate was touched by a human agency. No securities physically changed hands. Nor would they. The exchanges might as well have been trading in air. Only abstract numbers changed. In traders' books. On computers and in international bank accounts.

But those numbers were all-important. For they represented more than mere gold or jewels. They represented man's faith in other men and the rules that governed international commerce.

And it was all about to unravel.

With the frenzy of sharks, Tokyo began unloading GLB holdings. And within ten minutes, Singapore and Melbourne were doing the same. Milan's Palazzo Mezzanotte trading floor buzzed with rumors as the opening bell was delayed twenty minutes. Frankfurt and Zurich markets started buying dollars, and then, realizing that the New York Stock Exchange was only hours away from opening, reversed themselves and sold.

By the time London's Financial Times Stock Exchange opened, it was a tidal wave. It washed over London's financial district like an invisible storm, beggaring major investors in a matter of minutes. And then, having wrought its soul-sickening carnage, it continued on, moving west, unseen, impalpable, unstoppable—but as devastating as a firestorm.

Overhead, orbiting recon satellites snapped photographs of a placid blue cloud-wreathed planet. The earth spun as it always had. Precision lenses recorded ordinary October weather—a sandstorm in the Sahara, a hurricane forming off Puerto Rico, rainstorms in the heart of Brazil, and the first snowstorm in upper Manitoba.

The lenses did not—could not—record the greatest upheaval in modern world history. Because it was panic, fueled by fear and kept alive by sentinel communications satellites as they squirted bursts of news back and forth between the continents.

And then the two-way message traffic changed ominously. The flow shifted west. Frantic telexes, cables, faxes, and transcontinental phone calls choked every line of communication known to modern man. Every one of them contained a single word.

It was a common word, but in the context it was being transmitted, it held the potential to plunge the world into an abyss of darkness and despair.

The word was "Sell."

2

His name was Remo and he held the clusters of varicolored balloons in front of his face as he entered Tallahassee, Florida's State House.

The guard at the door noticed the balloons immediately and called over to Remo from his security desk.

"I knew this was a bad idea," Remo muttered under his breath. He shifted his position so the balloons floated between him and the guard.

"What's your business here?" the guard wanted to know.

"Balloongram for the governor," Remo said. He didn't bother to disguise his voice. His voice wasn't the problem. It was his face. And his thick wrists. The wrists were, if anything, more of a giveaway than his high-cheekboned face. That was why his Chicken Wire uniform was two sizes too big for him. The cuffs bunched up around his freakish wrists, hiding them.

"I'll check with his office," the guard said, reaching for his station phone.

"You can't do that," Remo said hastily. A sea-green balloon bumped his nose.

"Why not?" the guard asked, looking up. He clutched the receiver in his beefy hand.

Remo thought fast. He didn't want to hurt the guard. The man was only doing his job. And Remo was here to hit the governor. No one else.

"Because it's a surprise," Remo whispered through the balloons. "It's his birthday."

"It won't hurt if I check with his secretary," the guard said, tapping buttons on the telephone keypad.

"Yes, it will," Remo said. "Trust me."

The guard hesitated. "How's that?"

"The governor's wife sent them."

"So?"

"I guess you haven't heard," Remo whispered conspiratorially.

"Heard what?"

"The governor and his secretary. They're, you know, intimate."

"No!" The guard breathed. "I hadn't heard that." He was looking at Remo through bubbles of elastic balloon. He saw a face that was broken up into distorted translucent coral-pink, ocher, and burgundy spheres. He wondered what had happened to primary colors.

"If you let the secretary know I'm coming," Remo went on, "she'll probably tell you it's not the governor's birthday or something. You know how jealous secretaries are."

"I wish," the guard said. "Still, I gotta call. It's my job."

"Suit yourself," Remo said. "But I warned you."

The guard completed his call and spoke quietly for nearly a minute. Remo heard both sides of the conversation, so he was prepared for the guard's response.

"She says it's not the governor's birthday."

"See! What'd I tell you?"

The guard rubbed his jaw thoughtfully. "I dunno. Maybe I shouldn't let you go up. You could be a nut."

"Do I look like a nut?" Remo asked sincerely through the soap-bubble cluster of balloons.

"Well, no . . ." the guard said. Nuts carried guns or knives, not balloons.

"Look at it like this," Remo suggested. "If you let me through, you might catch hell from the secretary, but she sure couldn't hurt you. But if you don't, the governor's wife is going to raise hell to the governor that her balloons didn't get delivered, and look where you'll be."

"You're right," the guard said. "I'm better off taking my chances with that hussy of a secretary. Okay. Go ahead."

"Thanks," Remo said, making a beeline for the elevator.

He got an empty cage and rode it up to the governor's floor. The hallway was polished and busy. Swift-moving government workers noticed Remo coming off the elevator. A suntanned blond asked, "For me?" and laughed as she disappeared into an office.

Remo frowned. He was attracting more attention than if he'd come in street clothes. But Upstairs had warned him to make certain that no one got a good look at his face. Not that Remo gave a hang about orders anymore.

He shifted the balloons in front of his face as he weaved between the workers, and backed into the governor's office, the balloons strategically positioned. Inside, he turned and spotted the secretary through the chinks between two blueberry-colored balloons.

"Balloongram for the governor," he announced in a bright voice.

The secretary was a sultry Latina, about twenty-three years old, her face already getting fleshy around the jowls. Her eyes flashed as she caught sight of Remo standing behind his balloons.

"What are you doing here!" she snapped. "I told that guard not to let you up."

"It's from his wife," Remo said, unperturbed.

"Oh," the secretary said, subsiding. Remo wondered if the governor *had* been carrying on an affair with his secretary, after all. Remo had no information on that—any more than he knew when the governor's birthday was.

"It's an anniversary balloongram," Remo said firmly.

"The guard said birthday."

"You know how guards are," Remo said with a shrug.

"Very well. Give them to me."

Remo backed away from the secretary's outstretched hands. She had long red nails that flashed like bloody daggers.

"No can do. It's a singing balloongram. Has to be delivered in person."

"I can't let you just walk in on the governor without an appointment."

"Tell that to the governor's wife." Remo said pointedly.

The secretary looked nervously from the governor's closed maplewood door to the balloon cluster.

"I'll announce you," she said tightly.

"It's *supposed* to be a surprise," Remo hinted.

"I've never had this happen to me before," she said, fidgeting with her hands.

"Trust me," Remo said. "I'm a professional."

"Very well," the secretary said. "What do you normally do?"

"You just open the door and I'll walk in. I guarantee that after I'm gone you won't hear a word of complaint from His Honor."

"Okay," the secretary said. She took the double doors' brass handles in her immaculately manicured hands and threw them open.

Remo breezed past her, shifting the balloons to hide his profile. This was a real pain, but so far it was working.

The governor of Florida looked up from his desk in surprise. His eyebrows jumped off his eyelashes as if pricked by pins.

"What?" he said in a startled voice.

"Balloongram," Remo sang off-key.

"We'll see about this," the governor growled, reaching for his intercom.

"It's from your secretary," Remo whispered. "I think she's sweet on you or something."

"Oh?" the governor said in surprise. Then, as the thought sank in: "Oh." It was a very pleasant "oh." It told Remo that the Florida governor was not having an affair with his gorgeous Latina secretary, but was open to the prospect. The governor's hand withdrew from the intercom and he leaned back in his chair.

"Well, go ahead," he prompted. "Sing."

"I hope you don't mind *a cappella*."

"Just do it."

"You have to hold the balloons. I'm Italian. I can't sing unless my hands are free."

The governor came out from behind his desk and took hold of the balloons.

"Use both hands," Remo warned, "or they'll get away from you. I think they cooked the helium too long or something."

The governor grabbed the knotted-together strings, and

when he had a firm grip, Remo fused his hands together with a sudden two-handed clap.

The governor winced at the unexpected stinging sensation. When he tried to pull one hand away from the other, it felt as if his hands had been welded together with Krazy Glue.

It was an absurd thought, but still it was the only explanation that presented itself to the governor's mind. And he voiced it.

"Krazy Glue?" he asked.

"Sinanju."

"But it's the same thing, right?"

"Wrong," Remo said, pushing the governor back in his high-backed brass-studded seat. The governor did not resist. The novelty of having his hands fused to a batch of bobbing balloons was overwhelming the natural fear response.

He looked up, for the first time seeing Remo's face. He took in Remo's dark, deep-set eyes, his thin, insolent mouth, and the full black hair topping an angry expression.

His eyes were attracted to the red stitching over the tunic pocket of Remo's Chicken Wire uniform. The stitching said: "REMO WILLIAMS."

"That name . . ." the governor began.

"Sounds familiar?" Remo prompted. "It's my name, although I haven't used it much in, oh, maybe twenty years or so."

"I can't quite place it," the governor admitted.

"You signed my death warrant last month," Remo said, his voice going from upbeat to flint-edged in a breath. "Come back to you now?"

The bone-white pallor that settled over the governor's face told Remo that it had.

"You got a call from a guy named Norvell Ransome," Remo went on. "He told you that unless you pulled the strings that bumped my execution to the top of the list, he'd tell the world that you were in bed with every drug trafficker north of Medellín."

The governor's response was so political that Remo almost laughed in the man's suddenly sweaty face.

"Of course, I know nothing about these baseless allegations."

"Yes, you do. And you know I escaped before they could strap me into the electric chair. You're probably wondering how I know all this."

"All what?"

"Norvell Ransome—the late Norvell Ransome, I should say—was temporarily in control of an organization called CURE. You probably never heard of CURE."

"I categorically deny ever hearing that name."

"Good answer. Pat. Saves me a lot of boring chitchat. CURE was set up back in the early sixties to take care of guys like you. Corrupt politicians. Crooked union bosses. Cops on the take. Judges on the make. The man who was selected to head CURE—never mind his name—ran it for years as a clearinghouse for domestic intelligence. CURE would tip off the authorities, and the bad guys would go to the slammer. But CURE wasn't enough. You see, there were too many guys like you. So it was decided to deal with them more directly. That's where I came in."

"If you have legal authority to arrest me," the governor of Florida said sternly, "I must insist on seeing your credentials."

Remo did laugh at that one. "Sorry, pal. I'm outside of legal authority. I'm what is known as an enforcement arm. Unofficially, I'm an assassin. I never liked my job description, but those are the cards I've been dealt."

"Assassin?" the governor said weakly.

"You see, when you signed my death warrant, here's what you didn't know: I was already dead. Not dead-dead. Officially dead. I was strapped into an electric chair up in New Jersey, about twenty years back. When I woke up, I wasn't dead. I was working for CURE. I didn't like it, but it beat going back to death row.

"Until, of course, I *did* go back to death row. That in itself is a long story. The short version is that my face was plastered all over the front page of the *National Enquirer*. My cover was blown. My superior saw the thing and keeled over into a coma. The President had to replace him. He picked your friend Ransome. Only Ransome was a bad apple. He sandbagged me in my sleep, wiped my memory clean back to my death row days and shipped me off to your charming little death row. It was his way of getting me out of the way."

"That story is so bizarre I cannot believe it," the governor said tensely.

"Actually, it wasn't Ransome's scheme," Remo said. "It was my superior's wacko idea of a retirement program. Send me back to where I came from. No one would know any different. Except while I didn't remember CURE, I did remember Sinanju."

"Krazy Glue?"

"I can see why you went into politics. You have the attention span of a pollster. Nope, not Krazy Glue. I already explained that. Sinanju is out of Korea. It's a martial art."

"Like karate?"

Remo frowned. "If it were like karate, your hands would be sacs of shattered finger bones instead of painlessly welded together. Comparing Sinanju to karate is like comparing your rubber ducky to a swan. Guess which one is the swan?"

The governor looked at his hands.

"You *can* separate them, can't you?"

"Search me," Remo said cheerfully. "No one I've ever done this to has lived long enough to request the operation. That's one thing about Sinanju. Even when you know it, you don't really know it. It taps into something inside you that you can't explain. You can only show."

Then it sank into the governor's mind.

"You're here to assassinate me."

"No," Remo corrected. "I'm here to execute you. Kennedy was assassinated. Gandhi was assassinated. You, you're a slimy crook who opened your state up to the scum of the earth. You take money so the cocaine kings can sell their junk on the streets you're supposed to protect. Nope. You get executed."

"I have money," the governor said quickly.

"Take it with you," Remo said coldly, reaching under the governor's blue jawline. He pressed with his thumb and forefinger and the governor's mouth locked in the open position.

"The thing is," Remo said, lifting the governor out of his

chair by the throat, "I've never done a governor. Judges, yeah. Foreign heads of state, from time to time. I think I did an assemblyman once for arson. Never a governor."

Remo looked around the room.

"You don't have a microwave around here, do you?"

The governor shook his head frantically. An "uh-duh" sound came out of his open mouth. Remo squeezed tighter and the sound ceased.

"Just as well," Remo said absently. "I hear they don't work unless the door is closed. Even if your head fitted inside, it wouldn't cook."

The governor tried to pull away. Remo transferred his hand to the back of the man's neck. With the other, he pulled the balloons from the governor's frozen grasp. They floated to the ceiling as they toured the room.

"It's too bad there isn't an electric chair in a closet somewhere," Remo said. "I think that would be appropriate, don't you? No answer. I guess you agree. Now, let's see. What are some of the popular methods of capital punishment? Hanging? No. Lethal injection? You'd need a syringe. Besides, I hate needles. Gas is out. This office doesn't look airtight. In fact," Remo added, noticing the windows for the first time, "it's kind of stuffy in here. What say we get some fresh air? Might help us think."

The governor's feet made tiny steps as Remo led him to one of the windows. Down below, traffic flowed noisily. Remo unlatched the window and shoved up the sash. A breath of lung-clogging humid air wafted in.

"Smells bracing, doesn't it?" Remo asked brightly. "Here, you look kinda pale. Suck down a good whiff."

Remo forced the governor's head out through the window. He rested the man's bobbing Adam's apple on the casement sill.

Holding it there, Remo continued speaking in a thoughtful voice. "Let's see. Firing squads are passé. I don't carry a gun, anyway. Or a knife. I think we're running out of options. Maybe you have an idea?"

The governor tried to shake his head. Remo felt the muscular spasms through his sensitive fingers.

"What's that?" Remo asked. "A guillotine? Now, where

are we going to get a guillotine? What's that you say? Improvise? With what?" Remo leaned closer.

"I can't hear you," Remo said. "Must be all this traffic." And Remo slammed the window shut so fast the glass cracked into an icy spiderweb, holding the governor in place.

Whistling, Remo retrieved the balloons from the ceiling and positioned them in front of his face as the governor's feet jerked and twitched. The pulpy sound of something heavy hitting the sidewalk several stories below was lost in the slam of the door as Remo left.

The governor's secretary looked up quizzically as Remo emerged, his face masked by a cluster of balloons.

"Is something wrong?" she asked.

"He vetoed the balloons," Remo said sadly. "Said he didn't like the color."

"Which color?"

"All of them. He wants black balloons next time."

"Oh, my God, am I in trouble?" She started for the door. Remo stopped her with his voice.

"I wouldn't go in there just now. I started singing and he lost his head. Between you and me, I think his marriage is on the rocks."

"Oh," the secretary said, returning to her seat.

Remo kept the balloons before his face all the way down to the lobby and past the guard.

"Wouldn't see you, huh?" the guard said smugly.

"He's not seeing anyone right now," Remo said solemnly.

Out on the sidewalk, Remo walked briskly up the street. He noticed that people were staring at him. Or rather, at his balloons. He ducked down a side street and almost stepped on the late Florida governor's head as it lay on the sidewalk. Remo looked at the dripping red stain oozing down from the governor's closed office window.

He looked around. There was no one in sight, so he knelt down and tied the balloon strings to the governor's hair. Returning to his feet, he let go.

Remo waved good-bye to the governor's head as it bobbed up past the State House, where a muggy breeze caught it, carrying it from sight.

As he walked away, Remo stripped off his uniform jacket, exposing a tight black T-shirt. He stuffed the jacket in a

dumpster after rending the nametag stitching to shreds, and wondered what the *National Enquirer* would say about this one.

Then he went looking for a taxi. There were a lot of them in the streets, but every one was occupied. Remo kept walking. He turned a corner and was surprised to see a knot of people in front of a window. They looked anxious.

Curious, Remo drifted up to the crowd. He read the sign over the window: "PRUDENT BROKERAGE." The storefront contained a small electric ticker tape.

"What's going on?" Remo asked of no one in particular. "Somebody famous die?"

A man in a gray flannel suit called back without turning around, "The stock market is crashing. Again." He had a frog in his throat.

"Really?" Remo said. "Oh, well, it's not my problem." He went in search of a cab.

3

Dr. Harold W. Smith wore his face like a wax mask.

He sat behind an oak desk, his face shiny with a thin film of perspiration. A tiny bead formed at the tip of his nose and clung there, held by static tension. Smith didn't notice it. His tired gray eyes were boring through rimless glasses at the computer terminal on his desk.

A green cursor raced across the screen, spewing strings of data. Sell orders being cabled to the New York Stock Exchange from all points of the globe.

They had been coming all morning, in waves like invisible missiles. Unlike missiles, they struck without sound or flash or concussion. Yet each hit wounded America as deeply as if they were rockets cratering the New York streets. Every strike landed in the vicinity of Wall Street.

But the damage would spread in ripples unless something happened to reverse it.

Smith tapped a key, and got an alphanumeric readout of the current Standard & Poor prices. They were not good. He tapped the key again and watched the cable orders. If anything, they were intensifying. The Dow had plunged over three hundred points since the opening bell. Trading had been halted once. It was now nearly noon—only two hours later.

Smith knew it would be only a matter of time. As the head of CURE, he could do nothing to affect the situation without presidential authorization. And he could not ask for that authorization until it was almost too late.

Smith leaned back and closed his eyes. He felt tired. The droplet of perspiration trickled down the notch under his nose.

The intercom buzzer sounded. Without opening his eyes, Smith keyed it and spoke.

"Yes, Mrs. Mikulka?"

"Dr. Smith. A call for you on line two," said Eileen Mikulka, who knew nothing of CURE. She was Smith's secretary in his position as head of Folcroft Sanitarium, a private hospital. Folcroft was the cover for CURE.

"Who is it?" Smith asked. His voice was strained. Ordinarily it carried a lemony New England tang; today it was as dry as a crisp graham cracker.

"A Mr. Winthrop. He's with the law firm of Winthrop and Weymouth."

The name sounded vaguely familiar, but Smith had no time to deal with Folcroft matters now.

"Take his number and ask the nature of his business. I'll return his call later."

"Yes, Dr. Smith."

Smith allowed his eyes another half-minute of respite, and when they snapped open again, they gleamed.

The computer screen continued revealing incoming sell cables. They were being transmitted to the Chicago Mercantile Exchange, the San Francisco Stock Exchange, and brokerage houses all over the country. The Toronto Stock Exchange began showing signs of uncertainty. And the Mexico City exchange was inundated.

It meant that Wall Street was unable to bear the load.

Smith clutched the padded armrest of his chair. He knew it was inevitable. The global economy was experiencing another meltdown. This one worse than the Crash of '87. Still, he could not act.

Smith opened the top-right-hand drawer and lifted out a red telephone. It was a standard AT&T model, except that there was no dial. He set it close to him and reached back into the drawer. It was a reflex, when he was under stress, to reach into that drawer. Some days it was aspirin. Other days, Alka-Seltzer or one of three other varieties of antacid.

Smith lifted out a tiny canister of foam antacid, returned it with a lemony frown, and lifted a bottle of children's aspirin he'd gotten as a supermarket sample. He hadn't even looked at the label. Now he noticed for the first time the trademark. It was a gold oval surrounding what seemed to be a black gap-toothed mouth with a pendulous uvula. Smith read the brand name. It meant nothing to him.

He set the aspirin in easy reach beside the red phone. He didn't need it—yet. He was simply too drained to feel anything. But he knew he would need it before the day was over.

Then it came. The cable traffic intercepts winked off as a warning program kicked in. The computer began beeping.

Smith's eyes flew open. For the first time, they reflected fear.

"It's started," he said hoarsely.

The system, which had surreptitiously logged onto mainframes in brokerage houses and financial institutions all over the nation, was picking up the next wave. The first warnings were coming from the East Coast, where the brokerage computers were reaching hysteresis. Automatic trading programs, set up to sell stocks when they fell below a certain price, were emitting warnings that the Dow prices were approaching those null points.

Smith reached for the red telephone. He waited as the ringing on the other end began. He felt so very tired.

"Smith?" a familiar nasal voice asked.

"Mr. President, you are undoubtedly aware of the situation on Wall Street."

"From what I understand, it's not just Wall Street. It's the whole world."

"I cannot affect the global market, but I may be able to arrest the dropping Dow. Before trading is halted again."

"You, Smith? How?"

"During the near-crash of '87 I worked out a system to counter the effects of computerized trading, which was approved by your predecessor."

"Correct me if I'm off base here," the President said, "but didn't they abolish computerized trading last year?"

"That's the popular belief. In fact, what was done was this: the computerized stock-trading programs were augmented with warning points. If a program was set to sell when a stock price dropped to sixteen and one-eighth per share, for example, the computers would flash a warning at sixteen and three-eighths."

"Then they would shut down, is that it?"

"No, Mr. President. They would not shut down. They simply flashed the warning. The sell-off would still kick in at the designated price."

"That's pointless."

"No, Mr. President. That's Wall Street."

"I don't understand. The problem is still there. We just get a warning. Is that it?"

"Precisely. And the first lag warnings have flashed to my computers."

"How much time do we have?"

"None," Smith said flatly. "In the time it has taken me to explain, several of those programs have already executed. If this continues, there will be more stocks being sold than there are buyers for them."

"Meltdown," the President said in a sick voice. Then, his voice rallying, he added, "You said something about a plan."

"After '87, I set up a shell corporation called Nostrum, Inc. It exists purely for this eventuality. Using CURE's financial resources, I can begin buying up large blocks of the afflicted stocks. It's a gamble. But the stock market is driven by rumor and trend. If Nostrum's purchases reach Wall Street ears in time, it might affect the panic psychology prevailing down there. Other buyers may jump in and help avert this rout."

"A rally?"

"That may be too much to expect. Arresting the decline is my hope."

"I can see why you had to ask me, Smith, even though CURE has autonomy in most operational tasks. If you fail—"

"If I fail," Smith said quickly, his eyes flicking to his watch, "the stock market will be no worse off. But the United States government will technically own all the depressed stock. I'll be buying it with the CURE operating budget. If that's not enough, I'll be forced to siphon funds from the Social Security Trust Fund. This is your choice."

"My God," the President said tightly. "I can't let the market fall apart like this, but if this goes wrong, we will have bankrupted the government on top of everything else."

"This is why the previous President approved oversight on this decision. You must decide now, Mr. President."

There was silence over the line. Harold Smith heard the President of the United States' shallow breathing. He said nothing. This was not his decision. He did not wish to influence it in any way.

"Do it," the chief executive said, and hung up.

"Thank you, Mr. President," Harold W. Smith told the dead line, and replaced the receiver. It was the decision he had hoped for but dared not ask. His fingers flew to the keyboard. The computer logged off its current feeds, and the words "Nostrum, Inc.," in ragged black letters on a green screen, flashed across the top.

Smith began transmitting buy orders to the headquarters of Nostrum, Inc., where its employees—none of whom had ever heard of Folcroft Sanitarium, never mind CURE— shook their heads and began buying up blocks of stock in quavering voices. They began with the most troubled stock, the rapidly declining Global Communications Conglomerate.

South of Rye, New York, nervous stock traders watched their overhead Quotron tubes with sick, shocked eyes. Every few seconds prices dropped another point or two. It was a rout.

Then, buy orders began coming in on Global Communications.

"GLB'S going up!" someone shouted above the roar. His voice was not heard. But the Quotron's silence spoke louder than any voice in the pit.

Global stopped dropping. Then other buy orders began coming in. The price stabilized at fifty-eight and five-eighths, climbed to sixty, and dropped briefly to fifty-eight and five-eighths again.

Back in Rye, Dr. Smith watched his Quotron window and allowed himself a dryish smile. It was a long way to the closing bell, but it was a start. He ordered Nostrum to buy another block of GLB and to pick up other bargains. He hoped that by day's end they would be bargains. He had spent most of his adult life serving his country. He didn't want to go down in history as the man who single-handedly bankrupted the United States of America.

4

P. M. Looncraft whispered old money, from the cut of his Savile Row suit to his tasteful Rolex watch. He lounged in the back of his white Rolls-Royce Silver Cloud as it turned the corner of Broad Street onto Wall. As the Rolls slithered past the statue of George Washington, its brass plaque commemorating the spot where, in 1787, he was inaugurated as the fledgling nation's first chief executive, Looncraft's prim mouth curled disdainfully.

Reaching into a leather cupboard, Looncraft lifted a pocket memo recorder to his long, lantern-jawed face.

"Memo," he said in a precise adenoidal honk. "When this is over, have that infernal statue taken down and demolished. Perhaps broken into pieces and turned into something useful. Such as a fireplace."

Almost soundlessly the Rolls whispered to the curb in front of Looncraft Tower.

"Call for me at seven sharp, Mipps," Looncraft said, alighting from the car. Briskly he strode into the marble lobby, pleased to see the uniformed guards posted by the elevators.

He nodded to them as one obligingly pressed the up button and reached in to hit the button marked: "LD&B."

The elevator was empty as it whisked P. M. Looncraft to the thirty-fourth floor. Two additional guards met him at the glass-walled foyer. They tipped their caps smartly, and Looncraft allowed them a curt nod as he swept past.

"No problems, I trust," he said smoothly.

"A few upset customers, sir. That's all."

"Carry on," P. M. Looncraft returned as he walked past the gold lettered wall that said "Looncraft, Dymstar & Buttonwood, Investment Brokers." He stepped onto the trading floor, where shortsleeved brokers worked their phones, banks of blinking buttons flashing insistently.

"Get off my back!" one shouted at another. "I don't have to take anything off you!"

Looncraft strode up to him and laid a reassuring hand on the man's shoulder. He turned, his face angry. His features quickly softened as he recognized his employer's dour face.

"Oh, sorry, Mr. Looncraft," he muttered. "It's pure pandemonium, sir. The Dow's off three hundred points. It's a bloodbath out there."

"Stay the course, young man," Looncraft said soothingly. "Stay the course."

"I will. Thank you, sir," the broker said, wiping his brow with a striped shirtsleeve.

Looncraft raised his long arms to call attention to himself, and called encouragement to his soldiers in finance.

"Take heart," he shouted. "By evening this will be over. Do not let fear rule you. Your jobs are secure. Looncraft, Dymstar & Buttonwood has a bright future, as have you all. We will survive this day."

The moment his voice fell silent, the brokers burst into heartfelt applause. Then, at a gesture from Looncraft, they returned to their phones, faces tight, fingers nervously testing the elasticity of their identical red suspenders. Not for nothing was P. M. Looncraft hailed as the King of Wall Street.

Looncraft marched to his office, his back ramrod straight, his long jaw jutting forward with determination, and glanced briefly over the pile of messages on his desk. None were important. He activated his Telerate screen and gave the current market quotes a brief glance. Global was hovering at fifty-eight and five-eighths. It jumped up, and then down, surprising Looncraft, who had expected a precipitous drop by this time. He wondered if he might have come in too early. He did not wish to subject his delicate nerves to the turmoil of a wildly gyrating stock market. It was enough to call for additional guards to be posted at opening, as a hedge against irate investors who might wish to settle their losses with handguns and other piddling weapons.

Looncraft looked away from the Telerate screen. Global had a long way to go before he needed to act. He picked up the two-star editon of *The Wall Street Journal*, neatly folded beside his telephone, and opened it casually, one eye on the frantic activity on the trading floor, visible through the glass inner-office wall.

An hour later he looked up from the paper and to his surprise, saw that Global was now at fifty-nine and three-eighths. He blinked, grabbed the telephone.

"Ask the floor manager—his name escapes me at the moment—to give me a report on the last hour's worth of GBL activity."

"At once, Mr. Looncraft. And his name is Lawrence."

"Whatever," Looncraft said dismissively. In fact, he knew the name of every employee on the payroll of Looncraft, Dymstar & Buttonwood, right down to the boy who had started working in the mailroom two days before. Some of the firm's best people came up from the mailroom. Looncraft had made it his business to know their names. He subscribed to the ancient superstition—it was actually more than that—that held that the ability to call a person or thing by its right name conferred power over that person or thing.

The intercom beeped.

"Mr. Lawrence on line one, Mr. Looncraft."

"Who?"

"The floor manager."

"Oh, of course." Looncraft pressed line one. "Go ahead."

"Global issues are rebounding from a low of twenty-one and an eighth," Lawrence said crisply.

"Who's buying?"

"DeGoone Slickens, for one."

"What!" Looncraft exploded. "That scoundrel! He wouldn't dare. Who else?"

"Nostrum, Inc., was the first. But others have jumped in."

"Nostrum! Never heard of them."

"I think they're venture capitalists. Their own stock trades on NASDAQ. Do you want me to look into it?"

"Later. Is this a rally, or just a short-term run-up?"

"The entire market seems to be stabilizing. Volume is at five hundred and eighty-nine million shares across the board. I think we're going to pull out of this tailspin. Could be the start of a dead-cat bounce."

"Blast," Looncraft said under his breath.

"Sir?"

"Buy Global," Looncraft snapped. "As much as you can get your hands on. Now. Then find out whatever you can about these Nostrum interlopers."

"Yes, sir."

"Damn," P. M. Looncraft said angrily. "This is the limit." He reached for the telephone, hesitated, and then, thinking that even his vice-chairmanship of the New York Stock Exchange did not exclude him from SEC investigation, moved his caster-wheeled chair to a personal computer on a gunmetal typewriter stand.

He logged on and got an electronic bulletin board. The legend across the top read "MAYFLOWER DESCENDANTS" in ragged block letters. His fingers keyed like twitching spiders.

"Knight to Bishop Two," he keyed. Then he logged off.

Within moments the Telerate screen began to show a dramatic rise in Global's selling price. Looncraft's undertaker's face frowned darkly.

It held that expression well into the afternoon, as the stock market rebounded slowly. Frequent calls from his secretary were met with a curt, "Take a message." Until her voice came over the intercom with even more hesitancy than usual.

"Ronald Johnson to see you, sir."

Looncraft's eyebrows lifted in astonishment.

"Who?" he asked, momentarily taken aback.

"He's one of your floor traders."

"Cheeky sort, isn't he?" Looncraft muttered. Only ten years ago a Wall Street trader would have been beneath his notice. But not these days. The whole financial world had been turned turtle after a decade of leveraged buy-outs and junk bonds.

"Show him in," Looncraft said. He did not say, "Show him in, Miss McLean." It was better if his employees thought he didn't know them by name, as if such minutiae were beneath his lordly notice.

Johnson stepped into Looncraft's spacious office like a nervous poodle. Looncraft silently waved him into a black leather chair and tented his long aristocratic fingers.

Looncraft waited for the young man to sit down, and then looked at Johnson with eyes that invited explanation rather than asked or demanded it. Looncraft had an inkling why a mere floor trader would leave his post at such a hectic time. Johnson handled the Global account.

Ronald Johnson cleared his throat before speaking. He wore the uniform of a broker—striped shirt, red suspenders, and a haircut that reinforced his poodlelike demeanor.

"Mr. Looncraft, sir," he said deferentially, "I realize that I may be out of line asking to speak with you at a time like this, but—"

Looncraft cut him off with a wave of his hand that made his Rolex flash in the late-afternoon sunlight coming through the thirty-fourth-floor window.

"But," the young man continued, "as you may know, I handled the Global transaction, and I'm puzzled by the buying we've done."

"Puzzled? In what way?"

"Sir, we liquidated our Global positions this morning at forty-six. Now we're buying back at fifty-eight. It makes no sense. We'll take punishing losses."

"Oh?" P. M. Looncraft asked, with just the right arching of his right eyebrow. Behind him, portraits of past owners of Looncraft, Dymstar & Buttonwood hung in massive gilt frames that could be considered tasteful only because of their great age. There were no Dymstars or Buttonwoods on the wall. Only Looncrafts. The Looncrafts had forced out the Dymstars and Buttonwoods generations before—keeping only their reputations. The Looncrafts looked down with imperious glares, making the young trader in the black leather chair even more nervous than he would have been. Just as P. M. Looncraft knew they would. That was why they hung along the walls of the office: so that wherever a visitor looked, he either stared at a Looncraft—living or dead—or kept his eyes on the floor.

"Yes," the young man said. "I wonder if in the heat of the meltdown—"

"There is no meltdown," Looncraft snapped. "The Dow is rebounding. The system is very resilient. We are merely experiencing a correction."

"Excuse me, sir. You're right, of course. But I couldn't help but wonder if in the excitement, the buy orders weren't miscommunicated."

"They were not," Looncraft said flatly.

"I see," Ronald Johnson said vaguely. He adjusted his neat blue tie.

"No, you do not see," Looncraft said. He knew that in trader's logic, a transaction was either profitable or unprofitable. In that way, they were as binary in their thinking as his computer. Buy cheap and sell dear was their prime directive. So when the chairman of LD&B sold low and rebought the same shares at significant cash losses, it simply did not compute. "And you would like to know why," Looncraft added.

Ronald Johnson leaned closer, his eyes almost feverish.

"Is this something new?" he asked hoarsely. Looncraft suppressed a smile. He knew that shine. It was greed. He had seen it in younger eyes than Johnson's—seen it grow brighter as the eyes behind it grew dimmer. He saw it in the mirror every morning.

"No," P. M. Looncraft said. "It is not a new market strategy."

Ronald Johnson's face fell. He was disappointed.

"As you know, we divested ourselves of all Global stock when the price reached forty-six points."

"Yes, sir. I executed that liquidation personally."

"While I was out of the office," Looncraft added pointedly. "Had I been in the office, my curious young man, I would have overridden that move. For I have heard rumors of an intended takeover of Global."

"By whom?" Johnson blurted out.

Looncraft shushed him with a wave. "It would be illegal if I were to tell you. But I heard it. I heard it *perfectly.*"

Ronald Johnson smiled. He knew that when P. M. Looncraft said he heard rumors of an intended takeover, it was gospel. And Looncraft knew that within minutes of leaving his office, Ronald Johnson would buy as many shares of Global as his personal portfolio could absorb.

"When I arrived at the office," Looncraft continued, "the damage had been done. I've been monitoring the situation with care. I first thought that I would wait until just before the closing bell and buy back Global at rockbottom prices. A happy accident—although I disliked not enjoying a solid position in Global for the brief hours that was true."

"But when the market rebounded . . ." Ronald Johnson said.

"I had no choice. Obviously, the takeover rumors I had been hearing had reached other ears. Thus the hasty and admittedly costly buy order."

"Yes, yes," Johnson said eagerly. "It makes sense. Those shares will be worth much more. But it's still a tremendous amount of stock. Too much. What if the price drops again?"

"There is no such thing as too much stock," P. M. Looncraft said severely.

"Perhaps you're right, sir. But it is risky."

"That is why it's called risk arbitrage, and why the term 'junk bond' was invented."

Ronald Johnson blinked. He realized his superior was not simply talking about acquiring soon-to-be-hot shares. He was hinting that LD&B might itself be involved in a takeover of Global Communications.

He cleared his throat. "I think I understand."

"You are a very bright young man."

"But our position is massive. If the stock falls again, we could be ruined. All of us."

"Negative thinking," Looncraft clucked. "I do not believe in negative thinking. I would appreciate it if you did not spread such sentiments around the trading floor—or at one of those watering holes you traders like to frequent after hours."

"No, sir. Count on me, sir."

"I will," said P. M. Looncraft, touching his intercom. "Send Lawrence in. Instantly."

Almost before Looncraft's gaze left the intercom, a tall management type stepped into the room. He wore conservative gray pinstripes and a gold silk tie. A complacent expression settled over his clean-shaven face as he said, "Yes, Mr. Looncraft?"

"Give Johnson your tie," said P. M. Looncraft.

The complacent expression fell apart. "Sir?"

"Your tie. Give it to Johnson." Turning to the floor trader, he added, "Johnson, would you please lend this man your tie for the remainder of the day so he will be presentable?"

Ronald Johnson came to his feet, beaming. "Yes, sir, Mr. Looncraft. Of course, sir. I appreciate this, I really do."

"But, Mr. Looncraft," Lawrence moaned, his face dropping like that of a man whose proposal of marriage has been rejected, "I am supposed to have this another three days."

"Let me remind you that the gold tie belongs to the firm," Looncraft said aridly.

"But, sir, I earned it. This is my month to wear the gold tie."

"It belongs to Johnson now," Looncraft told him. "He has earned it by his concern and ernestness during a most unsettling business day. Johnson has performed with great presence of mind, and LD&B wishes to recognize that service."

Lawrence stiffened. His hands stayed at his sides. He ignored the offered blue tie.

"I must remind you, sir," he went on hoarsely, "that

company policy expressly stipulates that the gold tie may be worn for thirty days before an employee is required to surrender it." Tears were streaming from Lawrence's eyes now. This was a humiliation. He was being degraded for no reason that he could fathom. "I must protest this in the strongest terms."

"I accept your protest," P. M. Looncraft said evenly. "Now, give Johnson your tie."

Lawrence whirled on Johnson like a cornered animal.

"Johnson! What is Johnson? A sniveling wet-behind-the-ears trader. I have been with LD&B for over twenty years, and the first time you call me by name is to ask me to surrender the tie. I have attained the gold tie seven times. That is an LD&B record."

"Duly noted. Now, give Johnson your tie," Looncraft repeated. His voice remained even.

Lawrence looked at the impassive face of his superior, then at the outstretched hand of the eager young trader, Johnson. "I won't have this," he sniffled. "I won't be treated like this. I quit!"

And Lawrence flung off the gold tie, throwing it in Johnson's shocked face before storming out of the office blubbering.

Ronald Johnson gingerly picked up the tie from the maroon rug, and after apologizing for his coworker's unfortunate outburst, began to tie it around his neck in a standard foulard knot.

"I can't tell you how much this means to me, Mr. Looncraft," Johnson said fawningly.

Looncraft rose from behind his desk. "I understand," he said, smiling humorlessly as he shook the trembling hands of his young employee. "Now, I want you to get back to work. You needn't trouble yourself with these well-intentioned concerns of yours. You have a bright future with us."

"I know," Ronald Johnson said, his eyes bright with that familiar gleam.

P. M. Looncraft returned to his desk, knowing he had chosen well. He had selected Johnson to manage the Global account because the man was, whatever else, conscientious. This was as it always was with conscientious men. Offer them mere money to ignore an irregularity and they would spurn it with ill-disguised distaste. But offer them recognition or glory, and they were your servants. It had worked since the early days of Looncraft, Dymstar & Buttonwood. It had worked for his ancestors, back in the days before there was a United States of America. His ancestors would simply wave a sword over a man's head and call him knight, and the man would give up his life for that title and those who conferred it upon him. It was the same with the gold tie. It was just a silk tie. Anyone could buy one. But when P. M. Looncraft dubbed it the company tie and forbade any employee to wear one like it, every man on the floor doubled his productivity to vie for the gold tie. Status-hungry traders who couldn't be bothered to earn raises because they were already earning obscene amounts in commissions were slaves to their desire to wear three feet of golden silk around their necks.

Still, Looncraft was disappointed in Johnson. He had not tied his tie with a full Windsor, and that was the mark of a slacker. Ah, well, the man was probably Scandinavian. Most Johnsons were.

Looncraft turned his attention back to the Telerate machine. The Dow Jones Industrial Average was holding just over nineteen hundred. He keyed in on Global. It remained unchanged at fifty-eight and five-eighths.

Looncraft cursed under his breath. The Dow would close significantly below opening quotes, but not as low as Looncraft had expected. Or wanted.

"Tomorrow is another day," he told himself glumly.

5

Remo Williams pulled his blue Buick coupé into the driveway of his Rye, New York, home. He got out and started for the back door, holding a newspaper in front of his face like a mafioso arriving in court.

"Ah, the hell with it," Remo said suddenly. He stopped, lowered the paper, and doubled back. "I'm sick of this." He paused at the front door, not caring who saw him, and boldly checked his mailbox.

He found only junk mail, which did not surprise him. The bills—what few there were—were made out to a James Churchward. That was the name on the box. There was no such person as James Churchward. It was a cover identity he'd used to buy the house.

Remo inserted the key in the lock and entered. The nearly bare living room greeted him with its slight odor of incense and candle wax. It smelled like a Chinese church.

Remo noticed that the only piece of living-room furniture—a large-screen TV—was a shambles of wood and electronics.

"Chiun! Are you at it again?"

A bedroom door opened like a book, framing a tiny figure in aquamarine silk.

"I found another of Smith's insects," said Chiun, reigning Master of Sinanju and Remo's trainer. He lifted a silvery disk between delicate fingernails. The nails were exceedingly long. His eyes were hazel almonds in the network of wrinkles that was his face. The puffs of white hair over his tiny ears were like thinning steam.

Remo accepted it as Chiun joined him, his aquamarine kimono skirts rustling.

"You mean a bug," Remo said. "This is a listening

device. And this is getting ridiculous. We find them, and he plants new ones."

"He has gone mad."

"You've been saying that for years," Remo said, rubbing the bug between compressed palms until he got a sound like gravel in a sifter. He walked over to a wastebasket and spanked his hands together. What remained of the listening device sprinkled into the receptacle like powdered aluminum.

"We're going to have to talk to him," Remo said fiercely.

Chiun cocked his head. "I understood you vowed never to speak with Smith again," he said.

"I did. But I'm going to make an exception, just this once."

"You are still angry with him over the unfortunate incident?"

"You bet I am. After all these years of working for that old tight-ass, I find out he's got my house rigged with listening devices and a gas-delivery system so anytime Smith wants, he presses one of his damn computer keys and I'm anesthetized in my sleep. It would have happened to you too, you know, if you hadn't been in Korea when Smith lowered the boom."

"Smith did not lower the boom, as you call it," Chiun corrected. "It was that villain Ransome."

Remo threw up his hands. "Smith. Ransome. Who cares? It was Smith's boom. Ransome lowered it. And I'm retired to death row with my memory wiped clean back to Johnson's presidency. I don't even know if I have all my original memories back."

Chiun's wrinkled face started.

"I had not considered that possibility," he said slowly. His child-bright hazel eyes refocused on Remo.

"Do you remember that illustrious day when I saved your life?"

"I remember a couple of times that happened. What of it?"

"And the promise you made to me of your own free will?"

Remo's eyes narrowed. "What promise?" he asked warily.

"That you would not rest until Cheeta Ching became my bride."

"Cheeta? You mean the TV anchorwoman?"

Chiun took an involuntary step backward. He sucked in his parchment-dry cheeks with mock horror.

"No!" he cried. "It is true. That fiend Smith deprived you of your most treasured memories. Come. We must confront him with this latest proof of his perfidy. We will demand that he restore you to your full faculties."

"I never made any such promise," Remo said evenly.

Chiun stopped halfway to the door. He whirled, his kimono skirts swirling. The pattern was carnation. It looked like a bathrobe purchased from a Ginza street stall.

"Worse than your memories, he has absconded with your gratitude," Chiun proclaimed in a bitter voice.

"I never promised you Cheeta Ching. Even if I had, how do you expect me to deliver? Abduct her?"

"No, entreat her. Tell her of the riches that will be hers if she becomes my bride."

"You're twice her age," Remo pointed out. "Besides, she's married."

"To become the consort of the Master of Sinanju, she would gladly divorce that unworthy person. I would shower her with gold and jewels. She would spend her days basking in the reflected glory of my awesome magnificence."

"She makes a cool three mil a year. She doesn't need your gold, and she's famous all by herself."

"This is an impossible country," Chiun spat. "The women are paid fabulous sums for looking into the TV camera and reading unimportant words."

"Can it, Chiun. If you have a crush on Cheeta Ching, do your own courting. Now, let's go. We're having a showdown with Smith."

The Master of Sinanju watched his pupil storm past him, his face a mask of elemental rage. He tucked his hands into draperylike sleeves and padded after Remo on silent feet.

As they got into the car, Chiun put a quiet question to Remo.

"What do you intend to say to Smith?"

Remo started the engine and threw his arm across the

back of his seat as he backed out of the driveway. He shifted to forward gear and sent the car slithering down the street.

"I've had it," Remo said after a long pause. "Ever since that *Enquirer* story broke, my life has been an open sore. It was bad enough being dumped onto death row again. But to find out that Smith hadn't mellowed over the years—just gotten better at hiding his cold-bloodedness—that's it. No more."

"It was not Smith's nature that was hidden. It was that you allowed yourself to become blinded to it. All emperors are cruel."

"Smith's no emperor. He's just a bureaucrat. And let me finish, will you?"

Seeing the intensity of his pupil's words, the Master of Sinanju swallowed his planned rebuke.

"My house has been violated," Remo went on tightly. "All my life I've wanted a home of my own. I get one and now it's filled with Smith's low-rent spy-movie junk. He's been watching us all along. For Christ's sake, we live next door to him. I knew it was a mistake to move into his neighborhood."

"I agree. But I do not hold it against you," Chiun said levely. "We all make mistakes."

"Against me!" Remo flared, taking a corner on screeching whitewalls. "I don't remember that being my idea."

"Perhaps it is another lost memory," Chiun sniffed as he absently arranged his skirts.

Remo fell silent. They had left the city behind and turned onto a wooded road. The salty fresh tang of Long Island Sound, occasionally visible through breaks in the treeline, filled their nostrils.

"You still have not told me what you intend," Chiun said at last.

"I don't know yet," Remo admitted. "I told him months ago I was through with the organization. But you're still under contract, aren't you?"

"Technically, yes," Chiun admitted. "But I too am disappointed in Smith. He claims that he is helpless in the matter of Cheeta Ching. He swore he would arrange a private meeeting between us."

"Then we walk. It's that simple. We don't need Smith, or America. We're the top assassins in the world. We can write our own ticket. Go anyplace. Live high. Be appreciated."

Chiun's eyes shone with pride. "I have longed for you to speak those words for many years, Remo."

"Then you're with me in this?" Remo asked.

"Yes," Chiun said. "No matter what entreaties Smith makes, no matter the quantity of his blandishments. We will stand together on your decision. *Our* decision."

"Done," Remo said firmly. His lips thinned as the austere stone lion heads mounted on either side of the Folcroft Santitarium gate came into view like dim beacons of hopelessness.

He pulled through the open wrought-iron gates, handed the guard an ID card that said "Remo Mackie," and parked in the administrative parking area.

"Well, this is it," Remo said as he got out of the car. "The showdown."

"Fear not," Chiun said, floating beside him as they entered the spacious Pinesol-scented lobby. "We are resolute."

"Smith is going to have a fit when he sees us," Remo muttered as they rode the elevator to the second floor. "I've been trying to lie low ever since that *Enquirer* thing. Coming to Folcroft will really upset him.

"No more will we hide our faces like common executioners," Chiun said loudly. "In China we will have an honored place beside the throne."

Remo looked down at Chiun. "China? Who said we're going to China?"

"There is need of us there. The population is restive. There are whispers of plots, treasons, even open revolt."

As they stepped off the elevator, Remo hushed Chiun. "I got a problem working for the Chinese government, but we'll talk it over later."

Mrs. Mikulka looked up from her file cabinet as they approached the anteroom outside Dr. Smith's office.

"We're here to see Smith," Remo said sharply.

"Dr. Smith left express orders that he's not to be disturbed," said Mrs. Mikulka. She knew Remo as a one-time groundskeeper of Folcroft and Chiun as a patient, now cured of delusions of grandeur.

"Too bad," Remo said, going through the door anyway.

"Pay no attention to him," Chiun whispered to Mrs. Mikulka. "He is overwrought. A cruel accident has robbed him of his most precious memories."

"Amnesia?" asked Mrs. Mikulka sympathetically.

"Worse. Ingratitude."

Ignoring Mrs. Mikulka's protests, Chiun went in and closed the door behind him. Remo stood inside the door, his fists clenched. Chiun drifted up to his side.

Across the Spartan office, Dr. Harold W. Smith's coat-hanger-thin shoulders showed on either side of his desktop terminal. The top of his head was also visible, the hair white and crisp as frost. The tapping of his fingers on the keyboard came like the beginning of a rainstorm.

"He is engrossed in another of his follies," Chiun said softly. "He is not aware of us."

"I'll change that," Remo said tersely. He raised his voice. "Smith!" he said coldly.

"What?" Smith's worn face poked out from around the terminal like a bespectacled gopher peering from its hole. It retreated instantly. "Not now," Smith said querulously. "The stock market is in danger of collapsing."

"What is he babbling about now?" Chiun asked Remo.

"Stocks and bonds."

Chiun nodded. "Oh, the tulip-bulb mania."

"Tulips?" Remo asked.

"Before it was stocks and bonds, men gambled in other illusions. The Dutch had tulips. The Japanese bartered rice. The Indians, dung."

"Dung? Really?"

"It was very important to them. They used it to cook their food. That is why you should always avoid Indian foods. There is no telling what filth enters the cooking process."

"Good point," Remo said, advancing on Smith's desk.

"Smith, I want a word with you," Remo said sharply.

Smith was hunched over the terminal so far that it seemed as if his spine would crack. He didn't look up. He was keying furiously now.

Remo looked at the screen. He saw three-letter stock symbols and numbers marching in parallel lines like alien creatures in a video game.

"The stock market can get along without you," Remo said, hitting a key at random. To his surprise, the screen winked out.

"My God!" Smith said hoarsely, inputting furious commands. "Five minutes. Just five more minutes."

"No. Now!"

Smith whirled his chair around, crying, "Stand back. The nation's future is hanging in the balance."

Remo blinked, shocked by the vehemence of his superior's voice—but even more shocked by the realization that Smith wasn't seated in his usual leather chair. He was in a wheelchair. Smith gripped the wheel rims tightly as if he were prepared to run Remo down.

Remo raised his palms in surrender. "Okay, okay," he said, taken aback. "Five minutes."

"Thank you," Smith said crisply. His hands returned to the keyboard. He leaned into the machine as if looking through a portal to some horrifying world.

Remo drifted back to Chiun's side.

"You didn't tell me he was still in a wheelchair," he whispered.

"He has been very ill," Chiun confided. "When that toad Ransome took over the organization, he denied Smith medical treatment. He is recovering. But his legs are still weak."

"There's nothing wrong with his nerve," Remo said. "He acted like he was going to bite my head off." The anger had seeped from his face. He watched Smith in thoughtful silence.

Finally Smith withdrew his hands from his keyboard.

"Thank God. It's four o'clock."

"Quitting time?" Remo asked.

"The stock market has closed. At last."

"I heard it crashed. Again."

Smith rubbed his tired gray eyes. "Not quite. But it was a near thing. I did everything in my power to reverse it. The Dow lost over five hundred points, but it had been down as low as one thousand."

"Tough."

"It was nearly economic ruin," Smith said. His eyes began to focus on his surroundings. He looked at Remo as if seeing him for the first time. "Remo! What are you doing here! You are not supposed to be seen in public. If someone should recognize you . . . !"

"Tough. I'm here. I got tired of staring at the walls. By the way, I got the governor."

"You went to Florida?"

"Yeah, I was sick of waiting for you to give Chiun the green light. So I took care of him."

"My God," Smith said, hoarse-voiced. "You assassinated the governor of Florida! Without authorization?"

"Authorization, my ass. It was personal. And he was a legitimate target. He was in bed with half of the coke importers in the hemisphere. He tried to have me executed. Remember?"

"We were building a case against him. One that would stand up in the courts," Smith said coldly. "What will I tell the President?"

Remo folded his lean strong arms. "Whatever you want. I don't care anymore. I've had it with you, and with America. You, for rigging the so-called retirement plan that landed me back on death row, and America for electing governors like that jerk who signs death warrants without regard for due process."

"Remo, I can understand your feelings. But you know how it is. CURE doesn't exist. Officially. You don't exist. When your face was made public, it was a crisis—made doubly troublesome because I was in a coma. The retirement program was meant to take you out of the public eye until the situation stabilized. Were it not for my replacement's lust for power, you would have spent, at most, a few inconvenient weeks in prison."

"Inconvenient!" Remo came around the desk like a man possessed. "I got news for you, Smith. Prison isn't inconvenient. It's pure hell. Let me remind you, I was a cop before all this. CURE framed me the first time. Walking the last mile to the chair once was enough for one lifetime. I've had it. I'm leaving America."

"Actually, that may be a good idea," Smith said slowly.

"For now. Perhaps after a few more months, memories will dim. No one will recognize you as the face from the newspapers. I was going to suggest plastic surgery as an option."

"No chance," Remo said bitterly. "And I'm not talking about a freaking vacation. Get it through your head: this isn't a temper tantrum. I quit!"

Smith's lips thinned. He looked past Remo to Chiun, who had been standing silent and impassive, his hand hidden in his joined sleeves.

"And you, Master of Sinanju? What have you to say about all this?"

"I am letting Remo do all the talking," Chiun said stiffly.

"I see," Smith said. He took hold of his chair wheels and rolled out from behind his desk. He looked up at Remo with unflinching eyes. "You have chosen a difficult time to abandon your country."

"You mean the stock market?" Remo asked. "There's nothing I can do about that. I'm an assassin, not a stockbroker."

"No? What if I told you that CURE just prevented the worst economic collapse since the Great Depression?"

"CURE? You mean you and your computers?" Remo said, pointing at Smith's silent terminal.

"What if I further told you that the near-collapse was no accident?" Smith added. "But a deliberate action taken to wreak economic hardship?"

"Who would do that? Who *could* do that?"

"That is what I intend to spend the weekend learning. For even though I helped avert a catastrophe, at nine-thirty Monday morning the cycle could begin again."

"Just a minute ago, you wanted me to leave the country," Remo pointed out.

"I still do. According to my computers, this crash originated on the trading floor of the Hong Kong Stock Exchange. It began with a panic selling of shares in the Global Communications Conglomerate, which is considered the IBM of this decade. It's in everyone's investment portfolio—which is why when it tumbled, everything else came down with it. Hong Kong claims that they were responding to a panic on the Tokyo market. Tokyo said it began with Hong Kong. And it *did* begin in Hong Kong."

"Remo and I are willing to go to Hong Kong," Chiun said quickly.

Remo turned to Chiun. "We are?"

"We can look into the employment situation in China," Chiun whispered, "and Smith will have to pay our air fare."

"Not me. My career ends here."

"As you wish, Remo." The Master of Sinanju faced Smith. "Emperor, I withdraw my offer. Remo will speak for us."

"Thank you," Remo said. He looked back at Smith, who was trying to get the childproof cap off a bottle of children's aspirin. Impatiently Remo reached out and took the bottle from Smith and opened it with a simple upward motion. Tiny spurts of burned plastic sent out an acrid stink. Remo looked at the label. It said "Free Sample" on the front—just under the yellow oval that seemed to frame a snaggletoothed mouth.

"I thought this was aspirin," Remo said, puzzled.

"It is," Smith said, taking the bottle. He popped two pills down dry. He started coughing and Remo went to the water dispenser and came back with a paper cup of spring water.

"Here," he said. He noticed the same openmouthed symbol on the cup. "What is this thing?" Remo asked, holding up the cup. "The Folcroft crest?"

Chiun craned his neck to see.

"It is a bat," he said. "Anyone can see that."

"I don't," Remo said. "Does this look like a bat to you, Smith?"

"No," Smith said, his cough subsiding.

"Anyone can see that it is a bat," Chiun said peevishly. "A bat inside a yellow circle."

Remo looked again. "Oh, yeah. I see it now. It's kinda like an optical illusion. I see it as a yellow oval with a black mouth in the middle."

"And I see it as a bat within a golden circle," said Chiun.

"I see a black blob in a yellow disk," Smith said, lemon-voiced. "Now, may I have my water? I assume it is for me."

"You know, Smith," Remo remarked, handing over the cup at last, "you have the imagination of a snail."

"Thank you," said Harold W. Smith, who had been picked to head CURE for precisely that reason—among others. He drained the cup and lifted bleary gray eyes. His face was pale, with an undertinge of grayishness. He looked as healthy as a beached flounder.

"Are you certain you intend to leave?" Smith asked gravely.

"My mind is made up. Chiun's too."

"Remo speaks for both of us," Chiun said firmly.

"I cannot stop you. Especially in my present state. But perhaps I can stop these people from ruining our economy without you."

Remo frowned skeptically. "You? How?"

"When you were interrupting me, I was running a CURE offshoot, a shell corporation called Nostrum, Incorporated. It was something I created after the so-called Wall Street meltdown of 1987. You see, I suspected that that crash was engineered, but I could not prove it. So I created Nostrum. It was designed to shore up the market by buying key blue-chip stocks during a future panic—such as today's. I am pleased to say that it worked. Nostrum employees, of course, have no idea they work for CURE."

"I know exactly how they feel," Remo snapped.

Smith cleared his throat. "Today's panic seems to have some of the same earmarks of having been engineered," he went on. "I mention the confusion over who started the initial sell-off—Tokyo or Hong Kong. They happened almost simultaneously, but my analysis is that Hong Kong started it, and Tokyo followed the trend. The difference is less than fifteen minutes, but is there. Hong Kong claims that they received a Reuters report of the Tokyo sell-off fifteen minutes before it actually began."

"I don't follow," Remo said vaguely. "High finance isn't my strong suit."

"The Reuters report was false," Smith said firmly. "Possibly even fabricated. My task—the task I was about to give you—is to follow up on that. Find out how Reuters could have reported an event that did not begin until fifteen minutes after it transpired."

"I get it now," Remo said suddenly.

"You do?" Smith asked in surprise.

"Sure. It's from that dippy movie. *Batman*."

"What is?"

"The cup. The aspirin. They're Batman merchandise. Like the T-shirts and caps I see everyone wearing these days. I hear they've made a couple of billion in merchandising bucks on this little design alone."

"They did?" Chiun asked, suddenly interested.

"Sure. They slap this thing on everything from baseball caps to soft-drink cups and they get a royalty each time. A nickel here, a dime there, but it adds up."

"Billions?" Chiun's voice was awestruck.

"Yeah. Now that we're unemployed, maybe you can figure out a way to merchandise Sinanju the same way. We'll never have to work again."

"Billions!" Chiun said feverishly. "Think of it, Remo. The symbol of the House of Sinanju on every coin in the world. We will be billionaires."

"Forget it, Little Father. The sign of Sinanju is a trapezoid bisected by a slash. It just doesn't cut it."

"And this does!" Chiun shrilled. "A mere bat, which, if you look at it wrong, looks like a broken-toothed mouth?"

"It's not the bat that people are buying, it is what it symbolizes. Batman. He's a guy who goes around—"

"Yes, yes. I have seen that insipid TV show."

"The TV show is history. This is the new Batman. He kicks ass. Kids love him."

"How anyone could love a man who dresses like a winged rodent is beyond me," Chiun said dismissively.

"Trust me. Or better yet, rent the video. But enough of all this. Smitty, this is it. I'd say it's been fun, but that was before you booby-trapped my house."

"I do not share Remo's bitterness," Chiun said loftily. "I forgive you for such minor transgressions. It is your failure to bequeath me Cheeta Ching that I find unconscionable. But this sad ending to our association lies on your head.

Had you fulfilled the terms of our last contract, I would be bound to service."

"I understand," Smith said, spinning his wheelchair toward a green file cabinet. He pulled a folder from a lower drawer. "Before you go," he added, pulling a sheaf of stapled papers from the file, "there is one last bit of unfinished business to transact."

"Yeah?" Remo said sourly.

"I must have the Master of Sinanju sign a document. It is a mere formality."

"What is this document?" Chiun asked, approaching Smith.

"The firm I mentioned eariler," Smith said. "Nostrum, Inc. For security reasons, neither I nor any Folcroft employee could be listed in its papers of incorporation. I took the liberty of using your name, Chiun."

"My name?" Chiun asked, accepting the papers.

"Yes. Simply sign this release, signing over control of Nostrum to me, and you are free to leave. I will attend to all the legal details."

"One moment. I wish to read this document," Chiun said.

"Come on, Chiun," Remo said impatiently. "We've wasted enough time here."

"Speak for yourself, Remo," Chiun snapped.

"I thought I spoke for both of us," Remo retorted.

"That was before I discovered I was the president of an important corporation.

"It's a shell corporation," Smith explained. "Of course, it does own an office building and has assets of over seven million dollars."

"Seven million?" Chiun gasped. His wispy beard trembled. "Mine?"

"Technically, yes," Smith admitted.

"Oh, no, you don't!" Remo said, snatching the documents from Chiun's clawlike hands. "I can see where this is going. You're going to dangle this under Chiun's greedy nose, and he's going to take the bait. Nice try, Smitty, but we quit."

"*You* have quit, Remo," Chiun said, snatching the document back. "I have *not*."

"What happened to I-spoke-for-both-of-us?" Remo demanded hotly.

"You spoke for Chiun, CURE employee. Not for Chiun, CEO of Nostrum, Inc."

"CEO?"

"It means chief executive officer," Smith supplied.

"I knew that!" Remo snapped.

"But I did not," Chiun returned. "Emperor Smith, I cannot sign away my rights without conferring with my attorney."

"Oh, here we go!" Remo wailed. "You don't even *have* an attorney."

"This is true," Chiun admitted, lifting a long fingernail. "Therefore I must remain in Smith's employ until I can find one and this matter is settled with correctness and fairness."

Remo groaned an inaudible word.

"Emperor," Chiun asked Smith, "am I correct in assuming that I have an office in this Nostrum entity?"

"Yes, it has never been used, but your name is on the door."

"Then I wish to inspect my office and my building. I must know that it was not being run into the ground during my unavoidable absence."

"I can arrange that. But if the stock market crashes on Monday, it won't matter. All of Nostrum's assets are tied up in stocks and other securities."

"Sell!" Chiun cried. "Sell them immediately. Buy gold. Everything else is mere paper. Gold is eternal. It cannot be burned, or lost, or made worthless by manipulative men."

"We cannot sell until Monday," Smith explained. "The market is closed. Your best protection is to help me uncover these unknown stock manipulators."

"I will crucify them on their own worthless paper," Chiun raged. "The baseness of them. The perfidy. Attempting to ruin my wonderful company."

"I'm not hearing this," Remo said weakly.

"Shall I book you on the next flight to Hong Kong?" Smith inquired.

"At once," Chiun said, furling the Nostrum documents and slipping them up one sleeve for safekeeping.

"And you, Remo?"

Remo was leaning into the wall, his eyes closed in pain.

"Okay, okay, I'm going to Hong Kong. But don't count on me coming back."

"I know you'll do the right thing."

"Come, Remo," Chiun said imperiously floating from the room.

Remo started for the door, then doubled back. He advanced on Smith with such purposeful violence that Smith reached for his wheel rims and sent the chair retreating to the wall.

Remo leaned over.

"You've gotten very clever at manipulating him," he said in a chilly voice.

"I need him," Smith said simply. "And you."

"Just don't try to manipulate me anymore. Got that?"

"Yes," Smith croaked. He watched Remo leave the room with tired eyes. He wondered how much longer he could keep the organization together. It was falling apart.

Then, as he sent the chair rolling to the safety of his desk, he caught a glimpse of his wasted face reflected in the one-way picture window that looked out over Long Island Sound. He wondered how much longer he could hold up.

He looked over to his cracked leather office chair, sitting forlorn and forgotten in one corner of the room, and abruptly stood up. He pushed the wheelchair aside and dragged the chair back to its rightful place.

When he sat down, he felt immensely more comfortable. He made a mental note to remember to be back in the wheelchair when Remo returned.

6

Remo Williams endured the flight across the continental U.S. in smoldering silence. He spoke not a word to Chiun during the Pacific crossing. He now stood with his lean arms folded outside Hong Kong's Kai Tak Airport as Chiun disdained the taxicabs in favor of a bicycle-powered pedicab.

Remo climbed into the rickshawlike rattan pedicab seat silently. The driver, who straddled the bicycle front, listened as Chiun rattled off incomprehensible directions, and started off.

Remo kept his mouth shut as Chiun hectored the driver, who nearly collided with a red-and-cream double-decker bus during the congested ride.

As they passed the junk-littered waterfront, the stink of the harbor invaded Remo's sensitive nostrils. Even Chiun sniffed. Remo suppressed his breathing so that the atmosphere-borne pollution particles didn't trigger his olfactory receptors.

But the stink was stronger than his self-control. The harbor stench mingled with the ever-present odors of rotting cabbages and sweaty human bodies.

Finally Remo could stand it no longer.

"China," he said in a brittle voice, "is definitely out!"

"Did you say something, Remo?" Chiun inquired in a disinterested voice. There was no point in allowing Remo to come out of his funk without having to work at it. A little.

"I said we're not moving to China. It stinks here."

"This is not China. This is Hong Kong."

"I've been to China. It smells exactly like this. It's congested like this. Look at these streets. There are more people than pavement."

49

"The same as New York," Chiun said coolly.

"I don't want to live in New York either. China is out."

"We could live in the countryside. Inner Mongolia is much like my village of Sinanju."

"Great. A clam flat decorated by barnacle-encrusted rocks. No, thanks."

"Your tone is bitter," Chiun said, not looking at Remo. The sea of Chinese faces passed by like unbaked rolls. "Could it be you are unhappy with me?"

"I'm unhappy with everyone," Remo said.

"Ah," said Chiun.

"Especially you," Remo added. "Smith I can understand. You sandbagged me back in his office." Remo snorted. "I-spoke-for-both-of-us, my foot."

"This is business," Chiun said. "You have no head for business. It is up to me to safeguard our financial security."

"Smith conned you."

"I own an important company. It is my duty to protect it. When this assignment is done, we will be done with Smith."

"Promise?"

"Promise."

The tension stayed in Remo's face, but he unfolded his arms. Chiun rearranged his skirts. He was wearing a simple gray traveling robe, unadorned but for three red roses across the chest—which for the Master of Sinanju was dressing plainly.

The pedicab pulled up before a modern office building in the heart of Hong Kong's Central District, near the monolithic China Bank with its guardian lions.

The sign outside said "REUTERS NEWS SERVICE."

"This must be the place," Remo said, alighting. Chiun paid the pedicab driver in American dollars.

"Not enough!" the driver protested in English.

Chiun fired back a stream of singsong Chinese. The driver's face broke out into a sick-eyed grin. Remo recognized that grin. It was universal throughout Asia. It masked anger, fear—sometimes hate. The driver tried to protest, but Chiun cut him off in his own language.

Finally the driver mounted his pedicab, stone-faced, and scooted away.

As they entered the glass lobby of Reuters' Hong Kong branch, Remo asked, "What was that all about?"

"He overcharged us."

"How do you know that?"

"I refused to pay his demands and he only protested twice. The certain mark of a cheat. Remember that if we go to China."

"We're never going to China," Remo said flatly.

"Remembering will cost you nothing."

"Forgetting even less," Remo said, looking around.

The Reuters branch was all glass walls and computer-equipped cubicles. It hummed with ringing telephones and men and women scurrying from desk to desk like, it seemed to Remo, mice in a laboratory maze.

Remo grabbed a tweedy British-looking man as he hurried by.

"Excuse me, pal," Remo started to say. "I'm looking for the head of Reuters."

"See the clerk," the man said in a thick British accent, pronouncing it "clark." He pointed back over his shoulder. "And it is pronounced 'Roiters,' not 'Rooters.' " He disappeared through a blank door.

Remo looked back at the beehive of activity. He cupped his hands over his mouth.

"Which one of you is Clark?" he called.

Eighteen out of a possible twenty-seven hands went up.

"Must be a popular name," Remo muttered. He pointed to the nearest upraised hand. "You. Come here."

The man came up to him, saying, "May I be of assistance?"

Remo flashed an ID card. "Remo Farris. SEC. I'm investigating rumors that the stock-market problem started in this office."

"Highly improbable, sir. But you'll have to speak with Mr. Plum about that matter. I'm only a clerk."

"What do you mean, only?" Remo asked. "And what does your name have to do with anything?"

Chiun stepped in.

"Please excuse Remo," he said. "I am Chiun, his interpreter. I will translate your words for him."

"What do you mean?" Remo said. "I speak English."

"No," Chiun corrected. "You speak American. It is not the same. This man is a clerk. The British pronounce it 'clark.' It is not his name."

Remo turned to the man. "Is that true?" he asked.

"Quite so, sir. Sorry for the inconvenience. Shall I tell Mr. Plum that you wish to see him?"

"Sure."

"Come this way."

They followed the clerk to a cluttered desk, where he opened a file in a computer.

"State your business," the clerk said to Remo, his fingers poised over the keyboard.

"I already did."

"Again, please. For our records."

Remo sighed. He explained again his SEC cover story, his purpose, and his fictitious name.

"Will there be anything else, then?" the clerk asked.

"Not unless you give out prizes for waiting," Remo said in a bored voice.

"Very good, sir." The clerk pressed a button marked "Send" and waited.

"Where did you send that?" Remo wanted to know.

"To Mr. Plum's office. Naturally."

"Where is that?"

"In the office across the hall."

Remo looked. The clerk was pointing to the office where the tweedy man Remo had first accosted had disappeared.

"This Plum," Remo said. "Is he about six feet tall, sandy hair, and built on the lean side?"

"I believe he is, sir. Ah, here comes the response now."

A block of text appeared on the screen. Remo tried to read it over the clerk's shoulder, but the man had already digested the text and was erasing it by holding down the delete key.

He turned in his swivel chair and expressed his regrets with a pointed smile.

"I'm sorry, sir. But Mr. Plum is not available to callers at this time. If you'd like to leave your name . . ."

"I already did. Remember?"

"I fear I no longer have that particular information on

my terminal. I shall have to take it again." His fingers lifted over the keys. "Mere formality. It shan't take long."

"It's already taken too long," Remo grumbled. "Come on, Little Father."

Remo skirted the profusion of desks and went through the unmarked door. Chiun floated after him, serene of face.

Clive Plum, manager of Reuters' Hong Kong branch, was in the middle of a phone conversation, his eyes on the interoffice computer transmission, when the office door opened with a bang. Remo appeared before him as if teleported there.

"My dear man," he said, rising involuntarily. "I don't believe you have a proper appointment."

"The name is Remo," the man said curtly in a rude American accent. "And I'll settle for an improper appointment. Just so long as we get this done."

"I see," Plum said. His eyes went to the phone clutched in his hand.

"I won't be a mo," he said. Into the phone he said, "Knight to Queen's Bishop Three." And then he hung up.

"I play chess by phone," he explained self-conciously.

"I'd be embarrassed to admit it too," Remo said casually. "And you're holding up my retirement with small talk. You people reported a Hong Kong stock sell-off fifteen minutes before it happened. Where did that report come from?"

"I must tell you, my dear fellow," Plum said, "that the SEC does not have jurisdiction here. This is Hong Kong, a crown colony. We are subject to British authority. And British authority only."

Remo leaned over and took the telephone receiver in one hand. He squeezed. The plastic creaked. When Remo replaced it on the cradle, it resembled a dog's chew bone.

Remo smiled without humor. "Right now," he said, "you're subject to American intimidation."

"I see," Plum said weakly. "Well, all reports such as this go through our computer room. Perhaps it was a computer malfunction."

"Perhaps you'd better show me," Remo said in the same too-polite tone. He gestured toward the door.

Plum stood up, adjusting the cut of his charcoal-gray Edwardian suit. "I really must protest—"

"Protest all you want—after we're done. Call the SEC. Call the President. Just don't waste my time. Got that?"

"I believe I do," Plum said, coming around the desk.

Remo followed him with his eyes, noticing for the first time that Chiun wasn't in the room. On the way out of the room Plum picked up a silver-headed cane from a wooden rack by the door.

Remo followed him into the hall, where Chiun was engaged in conversation with a pair of white-gloved Hong Kong police officers. They were speaking in Cantonese, so the trend of the conversation was lost on Remo.

"I say . . ." Plum began, lifting his stick in the direction of the police.

Plum broke into a relieved smile as the police surged toward him. The smile went south—along with the faces of the two officers. As they passed the Master of Sinanju, they inexplicably tripped over their own feet.

It was one of the oddest sights Plum ever recalled seeing. Not only did both men trip, but they tripped in perfect synchronization, without having encountered any impediment in their path.

Most remarkably, they did not rise again.

"Ready, Little Father?" Remo asked.

"I would watch this one," Chiun said, drawing near. He nodded in Plum's direction. "He signaled for police in some fashion. But they will not bother us for a while."

"Meet Chiun," Remo told Plum.

"Charmed," Plum said through a frozen polite smile. It stayed on his face like a 3-D tattoo all the way to the computer room, six floors above.

"Where is Ian?" Plum asked a white-coated technician.

"I believe Ian is in the loo, sir."

"What's a loo?" Remo asked Chiun.

"The lavatory."

"Now that I know what a loo is, what's a lavatory?"

"I believe Americans call it the bathroom," Chiun said.

"Tell you what," Plum offered. "As Ian's superior, why don't I fetch him?"

"Just make it snappy," Remo said sourly.

Plum did. He came out almost as quickly as he went in.

"Summon the police," he said, aghast. "Ian has been murdered."

"What!" Remo went into the rest room like a rocket. He found a young man seated on the toilet, his pants down around his knees, his forearms clutching his stomach and his eyes staring into eternity.

Remo smelled the blood before he saw it. It was dripping from the man's crossed forearms. Remo separated the arms. There were a dozen puncture wounds in Ian's naked abdomen.

"Damn," Remo said, stepping back into the computer room. He accosted Plum. "Who do you think did it?"

"Obviously it is a plot of some kind," Plum said. Remo looked past Plum and noticed Chiun's nose wrinkle distastefully.

"I smell blood," Chiun squeaked.

"I'm not surprised," Remo told him. "The dead guy is bleeding like a stuck pig."

"The blood I detect is not coming from that room, but from this man."

"I believe I may have touched him," Plum said. "Possibly got a spot of blood on my hands. Nasty business, murder. It offends the sensibilities."

Plum shifted his walking stick to his other hand and pulled a handkerchief from his breast pocket. He used it to give his hands a brisk rub, his stick tucked under his arm. Remo noticed a drop of blood spatter from the knob. Another drop joined the first on the immaculate floor.

"Your stick appears to be bleeding, sport," Remo said.

"Ah, so it is," Plum said. "Thank you for pointing it out to me. I shall have to give it a thorough cleaning."

"He must think we're both idiots," Remo told Chiun.

"He is half-right," Chiun said.

"I don't quite follow," Plum said looking about his person for a place to put his bloodied handkerchief.

"Follow this," Remo said. "You killed Ian."

"Preposterous!" Plum sputtered. He took the other end of his stick in hand, twisting it anxiously. Remo could tell by that, that his guess had struck home. So he was prepared for what happened next.

Plum was twisting the walking stick nervously. Suddenly the stick slid apart, revealing a rapierlike blade. It was red for a third of its gleaming length.

"Watch it, Chiun!" Remo warned. "He's got a sword."

The blade came up in Remo's face. He didn't flinch as Plum slashed the air menacingly. The fine blade made the distinctive flutter and swish sound only the best swords produce.

"Give it up, Plum," Remo warned. "Or I'll get rough."

"Stay back. I am a master swordsman, I will have you know. Sandhurst and all that."

"Hey," Remo said, lifting both hands as if to surrender. "I'm unarmed."

"Capital. Then I shall run you through."

Plum lunged. Remo let the blade slide between his arm and rib cage. He clamped the blade with his armpit and twisted at the waist.

The tempered steel snapped. Plum withdrew, staring at his maimed blade.

"I say," he said stupidly. "This is quite unsporting. This sword cane has been in my family for generations."

"Sorry," Remo said in a mock-contrite voice.

"I demand satisfaction."

"Demand all you want," Remo said, plucking the tip of the sword from under his arm and breaking it into bite-size shards with quick finger movements, "but you're going to volunteer answers."

"I think not," Plum said stiffly, his eyes darting all around the room. He started to retreat, his broken sword still raised defensively.

"Shut the door, Chiun," Remo said. The Master of Sinanju closed the computer-room door. He stood there, his hands disappearing into his sleeves.

Remo advanced on Plum, who edged back toward a bank of windows.

"You killed him to cover up something, didn't you?" Remo said evenly. "Whatever it is, you're part of it. Wince if I'm getting uncomfortably close."

"I have only one thing to say to you, rebel!"

"Rebel?" Remo asked.

"Rule Britannia!" Plum shrieked, and threw himself into the window glass.

"Damn!" Remo said, leaping for the man. He had been prepared for another attack, not suicide. Plum went through the window headfirst. His polished shoes were going over the windowsill when Remo grabbed one. The shoe came off in Remo's hand. He recovered and got the silk-stockinged ankle.

"Give me a hand, Chiun," Remo barked. "He's fighting me."

The Master of Sinanju was already sweeping across the room at full sail.

Remo stuck his head out of the shattered panel. Below, the ant-farm congestion of Hong Kong traffic blared and hummed.

"Come on, Plum," Remo said. "You don't want to go this way."

"Let go of me, you blighter!" Clive Plum was kicking at Remo's free hand. Remo transferred his grip to Plum's other ankle.

Plum started kicking with the other foot, his face turning red as the blood rushed to it. A vein on his forehead was swelling as if about to burst.

Chiun took hold of the other ankle.

"Okay, let's reel him in," Remo said.

Plum abruptly stopped struggling. He hung limp as Remo and Chiun pulled him up over the sill.

"Watch the broken glass," Remo cautioned. "Don't want to cut him."

They pulled Plum's shoulders to the casement, and then he started to fight again. He held on to the casement, heedless of the glass slicing his fingers.

"Grab his hands!" Remo said. "He's cutting them to ribbons."

A spurt of blood went past Chiun's wrinkled face. It came from Plum's punctured wrists.

"He is doing this deliberately," Chiun said, reaching for a flailing wrist.

"I got him," Remo said. He captured Plum around the waist in a bear hug. Plum went limp. His head still hung out the window. Remo pulled, and felt a stubborn resistance.

"I thought you had his hands," Remo complained.

"I do," Chiun insisted.

"Then what's he holding on with—his teeth?"

"I will look."

Chiun leaned his head out to see Plum's face.

He came back solemn-faced.

"You may let go."

"Why?"

"Because this man is dead," Chiun explained quietly. "He has impaled his throat on a glass tooth."

"Damn," Remo said, letting go. He put his head out the window.

Clive Plum was staring out at the Hong Kong skyline. He had the same glassy-eyed stare that Ian had had on his face. The main difference was that Ian was tight-lipped in death. Plum's mouth was open. That was because the glass shard that had punctured his throat had also impaled his tongue and forced itself all the way to the roof of his mouth.

Blood was filling his mouth, reddening his teeth—a thick blood-and-saliva river that started to overflow at the corners of Plum's mouth.

Remo came back into the room.

"Great. Now they're both dead."

"You are not doing well today."

"Me? You're not exactly Johnny-on-the-spot with help."

"I am only the interpreter," Chiun sniffed.

"Let's see what we can salvage out of this debacle," Remo said. Off in one corner, two computer technicians cowered. Remo crooked a finger in their direction. They looked at one another.

"Both of you," Remo called.

Obediently they approached, trembling like beaten dogs.

"I take it all the Reuters bulletins go through this room," Remo said.

"That is correct, sir."

"Who was in charge of it?"

"Ian."

"Is he the dead guy?"

"That is correct."

"Know anything about the rumor that rocked the market earlier today?"

"Yesterday. It was yesterday, our time."

"Just answer the question."

"No. Neither of us does. That was Ian's province."

"Who does he take his orders from?"

"Mr. Plum, sir."

"Who's Plum's boss?"

"The home office."

"Where's that?"

"London, sir."

"The London stock market took a big beating too, didn't it?"

"The entire global market is in a sorry condition. As you know."

Remo turned to Chiun. "What do you think?"

"I think we have accomplished little enough here," Chiun said. "We must go elsewhere for our answers."

"Sure, but where?"

"Smith will tell us."

"Just as long as you handle Smith," Remo said in disgust. "I'm sick of him, invalid or not."

7

Dr. Harold W. Smith didn't consciously hear his intercom buzz. His face frowned when the buzz came again, but it still didn't intrude upon his concentration as he watched the lines of green data scroll up on his computer terminal.

The third time did.

"What is it?" Smith snapped into the intercom.

"They're here to see you, Dr. Smith," Mrs. Mikulka said imperturbably.

"Who is?" Smith asked, not taking his eyes from the screen.

His secretary's voice dropped to a near-whisper. "You know. Those two."

"Show them in," Smith said curtly. He knew exactly whom his secretary meant, and so he was not surprised when the Master of Sinanju breezed into the room. Remo followed him, lugging a red-and-gold-lacquered trunk. Smith recognized it as one of Chiun's traveling trunks and for a moment feared that he was about to lose the Master of Sinanju.

"Greetings, Emperor Smith!" Chiun proclaimed. "I come bearing the solution to all your worries."

"You found something in Hong Kong?" Smith said hopefully.

"That's the bad news," Remo said sourly, dropping the trunk onto the bare floor. "No."

"What happened?" Smith asked anxiously.

"A minor setback," Chiun said, casting a sharp glance in Remo's direction.

"The guy in charge of Reuters' computers was skewered by his boss. Obviously a cover-up."

"My God. Then it *is* a plot. What happened to the murderer?"

"He committed suicide."

Smith's eyes went sick. "This is bigger than I thought. They have plants in Reuters."

"How do you know this isn't a Reuters plot?"

"Don't be ridiculous, Remo. Reuters is a renowned and respected international news service."

"And Wall Street in an American institution," Remo said acidly. "And it almost went belly-up because of a wild rumor."

Chiun clapped his hands sharply. "Enough of this trivia. It is time to speak of important things."

"What could be more important than the threat to the world's economy?" Smith asked, blank-faced.

"Nostrum, Inc.," Chiun said loftily. "I wish to take possession of it." Chiun drifted up to Smith's desk, one hand held palm-up. "The keys, please."

"Keys?"

"You *do* have the keys?"

"You don't need keys to enter the building."

"What! You have left my precious corporation unguarded!"

"No, of course not. Trusted employees take care of security matters."

"We will see how trustworthy they are after I have met them," Chiun said harshly.

"The door to Nostrum is open to you at any time," Smith assured the Master of Sinanju. "You have only to walk in the front door."

Chiun frowned.

"In fact, I would like you to take possession of Nostrum immediately."

"You would?" Chiun said suspiciously.

"Sounds too easy, Chiun," Remo called out mischievously. "I'd be careful if I were you. Could be a trap."

"Nonsense," Chiun said. "Do not listen to him, Emperor. He does not speak for me."

"And never has," Remo muttered, sitting on the trunk.

"While you were in Hong Kong," Smith said, "I have been monitoring the fallout from the meltdown. As you know, it began with rumors regarding Global Communications Conglomerate, the largest multimedia group in the world."

"Don't they own that cable network?" Remo asked. "The one that's all-news?"

Smith nodded. "The Global News Network, as well as a movie arm and several newsmagazines. They own some newspapers involved in an FCC effort to force divestiture."

"I do not understand any of this," Chiun sniffed.

"It does not matter," Smith told him. "What does matter is the redistribution of Global stock. It has been concentrated into the hands of a small group of corporations and investment houses, including our own company, Nostrum."

"*My* own company," Chiun corrected.

"Ahem. Yes," Smith went on. "Putting aside the small amounts of stock that appear to have been snapped up by bottom-fishers, five investors now own large blocks of Global. Aside from Nostrum, there are P. M. Looncraft's brokerage firm, his financial adviser, the Lippincott Mercantile Bank, DeGoone Slickens, the corporate raider, and an offshore company I have never before heard of, Crown

Acquisitions, Limited. Each one of these investors has been heavily involved in the troubling hostile-takeover and junk-bond mania of the last decade. It's probable that one of these people, at the very least, is after Global, and the others are simply grabbing up stock because they have inside information that Global is a takeover target. Clearly something is in the wind, because Looncraft and Slickens are bitter business enemies."

Chiun looked to Remo in perplexity. Remo just shrugged, as if to say: It's Greek to me too.

"It stands to reason that since Global was the primary target of this rumor, and of the market-meltdown accidental fallout from the maneuver, then one of these companies is responsible for the plot."

"Then Remo will descend upon them and shake the truth from these devious curs," Chiun shouted.

Remo jumped up. "Me?" he asked hotly.

"I would do it myself, but I will be overseeing my vast financial empire," Chiun said importantly.

"No way," Remo said.

"I would like to go along with your idea," Smith said sincerely, "but Remo's intransigence aside, we still have the problem of his face. CURE security demands that we keep him out of the public eye."

"Which brings me to the solution I spoke of earlier," Chiun said brightly. He turned to Remo, who was still seated on the lacquered trunk. "It lies in the trunk you see before you."

"Really?" Smith asked. His eyes went to Remo.

"Search me," Remo admitted. "I don't know what's in it either. But I wouldn't get your hopes up. It smells like a taxidermist's footlocker."

"Silence," Chiun said. "You will open the trunk, Remo."

Reluctantly Remo got up and undid the brass latches. He lifted the lid.

Smith leaned forward, then, remembering that he was in a wheelchair, sent it rolling out from behind his desk.

With a flourish, the Master of Sinanju dipped both hands into the trunk and raised a shaggy brown patch of hide.

"Behold," he cried, beaming.

"It looks like a bearskin," Smith said, puzzled.

"Smells like one too," Remo put in.

"This is not ordinary bearskin," Chiun said. "For it was the hide of the terrible brown bear slain by my ancestor Master Ik."

"Named, no doubt, by the smell his kimono gave off after he returned from the hunt," Remo said smugly.

"Ik is a proud Korean name," Chiun said huffily. Smith rolled up to the skin. He fingered the hide carefully. It felt rough and scratchy. In places the fur was matted. The head was attached by a tube of skin. It lolled over the hide drunkenly, its eye sockets empty. Feet and paws hung from the main portion by furry flaps.

"What is this?" Smith asked, pointing to a beaten gold oval to which a string of bear teeth was attached in joined arcs.

"That is the symbol that will soon make the evildoers quake in their boots," Chiun said proudly. "I made it myself."

Remo came around to the front, curious.

"That looks kinda like—" he started to say.

"Correct! The dreaded emblem of Bear-Man."

"Bear-Man?" Smith whispered. Remo started edging for the door.

"Yes!" Chiun cried. "Soon to be a registered trademark of Nostrum, Inc."

"I fail to comprehend," Smith said blankly.

Remo called back from the half-open door, "You two sort this out."

"Hold, Remo," Chiun shouted. "For this concerns you."

"No, it doesn't," Remo said quickly. "And there's no way you're getting me to put on that rug."

Sudden comprehension broke over the craggy features of Harold W. Smith.

"Ah," he said.

"You understand?" Chiun asked Smith hopefully.

"Yes, and I'm afraid I must agree with Remo. The problem with his doing investigations has to do with his conspicuousness. His face could be recognized by anyone."

"That's settled," Remo said, coming back from the door.

"Exactly," Chiun continued. "This mighty costume will

convert that from a problem into a solution. And incidentally, make us all billionaires. Think of it, Smith. If Americans can believe in the fearsomeness of the lowly bat, what will they think of the awesome Bear-Man, scourge of Wall Street?"

"They will think the circus is in town," Remo said quickly. "Right, Smitty?" Smith didn't answer. His brow was furrowing in thought. Remo started to edge back toward the door again.

"It *could* work," Smith said slowly. It was almost inaudible, but the words reached Remo clear across the room.

Chiun turned his head. "Remo. Put this on. Show Smith how formidable a figure you cut as the mighty Bear-Man."

"I am not—repeat, not—putting on that flea-bitten thing," Remo insisted. "It looks ridiculous."

"In my homeland," Chiun explained, "the bear is the most formidable animal. Unlike the bat, which flutters like a mere rag in the wind."

Smith looked up from his thoughts.

"It's absurd," he said, "but it *could* get us through the weekend. Until the stock market opens again."

"No," Remo said firmly.

"Remo, listen to me," Smith said fervently. "We have only the weekend in which to work. It may be all over by then if the stock market tumbles once more. I've a three-pronged attack in mind. I will conduct an investigation of this Crown Acquisitions, Limited by computer. Chiun will manage Nostrum, which I believe may be the target of a hostile takeover because it owns significant Global stock, without which Global cannot be merged or absorbed."

"Have no fear, Smith," Chiun said sternly. "There is no threat that I cannot fight."

"This one may be different. You've never gone up against a hostile takeover."

"I spit upon those who dare try."

"The third line of attack is to investigate those who bought up large blocks of Global stock. Remo is the perfect person to do this."

"Not me. I don't know anything about stock."

"But you do know about persuasion."

"So does Chiun. He can persuade paint off a fence."

"I must be at my desk to fend off those who would assault my office building," Chiun inserted.

"And I am bound to my desk as well," Smith said. "I would go into the field myself, but as I am now in a wheelchair, I'm afraid my effectiveness is limited. And I am still subject to weak spells. I really shouldn't be under this strain."

Chiun turned on Remo.

"Remo!" he shouted loudly. "How dare you imperil your emperor's health by your stubbornness."

"He's not my emperor," Remo said flatly. "Never was."

"Yet he needs you," Chiun said.

"Your country needs you," Smith added. "And the world. For that is what lies in the balance."

Remo's unhappy expression wavered. He looked from Chiun to the bear suit to Smith and back to the suit again. Chiun held the suit higher so that its dangling-bear-tooth emblem rattled like an Indian talisman.

"All right " Remo said at last. "I'll pitch in. For the world. Not for Smith or the organization."

"Excellent," Smith said.

"But I'm not wearing that cockamamie suit," Remo added firmly. "And that's final."

8

Douglas Lippincott was in banking. His father had been in banking, and before that *his* father had been a banker.

The difference between Douglas Lippincott and his ancestors was, as Douglas Lippincott saw it, that he never foreclosed on widows and orphans.

Douglas Lippincott, president of the Lippincott Mercantile Bank, foreclosed on corporations. Douglas Lippincott was an investment banker. When he lowered the boom, individual families weren't put out on the street. Instead, entire towns went on welfare.

As a result of foreclosures, Douglas Lippincott presided over a multinational corporation that cut timber in Alaska, raised minks in California, processed shale in Kentucky, and made money everywhere else.

He was seated in his plush office sixty floors above lower Manhattan, contemplating his moral superiority over his widow-abusing forebears, when there came a crashing noise outside his office. Lippincott, of the Providence Lippincotts, was old-money. He loved old things. Although the Lippincott Building was barely a decade old, he eschewed the glass and steel of its ultramodern exterior for maple paneling and a solid oak door which shielded him from the eyes of his underlings. Thus he could not see what had caused the commotion, any more than his employees could see into the sanctity of his well-appointed office.

Lippincott ignored the crashing sound. If it was important, he knew, one of his assistants would bring it to his attention. He went back to picking his nose with a personalized silver tool handed down through generations of Lippincotts so they needn't sully their hands pursuing everyday personal hygiene.

The crash sound was repeated, causing Lippincott to cut his septum with the scraping edge.

"Blast it!" he said, reaching for a silk handkerchief to stem the blood.

He forgot all about the handkerchief and his nose when an office worker opened the door with his skull. The door banged open and seemed to catapult the man into a bookcase. The books came out of the shelves like quarters from a slot machine. They struck the man on the head. Lippincott winced. Not for the man, but for the books, which had been in the Lippincott family since before the Revolution. Many were first editions.

Lippincott reached for his intercom and then forgot about that too.

His widening eyes went to the towering hairy apparition that lumbered into the room. It stood upright on two hind legs and had a bear's head mounted on its forehead. The face under the bear's head was enveloped in a bearskin helmet with two ragged holes excavated to expose the eyes.

The eyes were mean.

"Who . . .what are you?" Douglas Lippincott demanded uncertainly. Miss Manners had never, to his knowledge, written on the subject of conversing with bears.

"You've heard of the bear market?" the apparition rumbled.

"Of course."

"I'm the bear."

"Is this a joke?"

"I wish."

"Come again?"

"Your company brought up over nine thousand shares of Global," the bear said, pointing an accusing claw directly at Lippincott.

Lippincott clutched the edge of his desk. He got a grip on his voice before he spoke again. "Possibly. What of it?" he asked quietly, his eyes going to the door. He hoped that some brave loan officer would rush to his rescue, but all he saw were frightened sheep running for the doors. A few did not run. They sprawled across untidy desktops. A head stared out from over the top drawer of a file. Lippincott wondered where the rest of the man was.

"Someone is up to no good," the bear said. "And I'd better not learn it was you."

The bear turned to go.

"Wait," Lippincott called after him. "Is that all?"

"That's the message."

"This is most unbusinesslike," Lippincott said. "What is your name?"

"Just call me Bear-Man, cleaner-upper of Wall Street."

"I don't suppose you have a card?"

"Thanks for reminding me," the bear said, lumbering back into the office. He reached up and yanked a bear tooth off his chest shield. He clapped it into Lippincott's open palm.

"What is this?" Lippincott demanded, looking down at the discolored tooth.

"A warning tooth. Don't screw up or you get the next one through the brain. Bear-Man warns only once."

Lippincott looked up at the retreating creature and demanded, "My God, man, couldn't you have just faxed this?"

Bear-Man didn't answer.

Douglas Lippincott closed the door to his office and waited an hour. When no one came in or called, he ventured out again. The outer office was empty, except for poor Peabody, whose head was sticking up from a file cabinet. His eyes were closed.

Lippincott approached carefully, and hearing the sounds of breathing, went in search of a glass of water. He came out of his private washroom carrying a full glass and threw it in Peabody's face.

Presently Peabody opened his eyes. They blinked, focused, and then went stark.

"Is it gone?" Peabody demanded anxiously.

The file cabinet shook with his agitation, which reassured Lippincott that Peabody was not merely a disembodied head in a drawer. He was worried about the company insurance premiums.

"What happened?" Lippincott demanded.

"The . . . the bear . . ." Peabody said shakily.

"Yes, yes, I saw it. Don't fret. It's gone now."

"Thank God," Peabody said. "I tried to stop it, sir, but it insisted upon seeing you."

"Did it state its business?"

"It refused. And when I told it to make an appointment, it . . . well, you can see for yourself what happened."

"Precisely how did you get into this . . . predicament?" Lippincott demanded curiously. He pulled on the top drawer and looked in. Somehow, Peabody's body had been forced into the cabinet, so that the lower drawers had been forced out to make room for his imprisoned body.

"I don't recall, Mr. Lippincott. One moment I was speaking to that . . . bear. The next I was . . . stuck. I don't remember any intervening action."

"I see," Lippincott said. "I suppose we shall have to get you out of this."

"I can't move my arms or legs."

"I'm afraid a blowtorch may be the only solution," Lippincott said. "Wait here."

"Where else would I wait?" Peabody said without a hint of humor or irony. His eyes still stared anxiously. He had never been filed bodily before.

DeGoone Slickens had made his money in Texas oil. With a two-hundred-dollar stake he had started an oil company in partnership with two other wildcatters. Slickens waited until the company started to get into debt—as all new companies invariably did—before he announced that he had been diagnosed as suffering from liver cancer.

"The doc gives me three years," Slickens had informed his ashen-faced partners that day in the Amarillo office. "Three and a half, tops."

"What you gonna do, De?" one of them asked.

"Make the best of my remaining days," he told them sincerely. "I want out of the company. My buy-out price is a quarter-million."

The other two swallowed and looked at one another with expressions even sicker than those that had greeted the news of Slickens' impending demise.

"You know we can't carry that kind of debt, De. We're in hock as it is."

"Those Hidalgo wells will pay off in time," Slickens assured them in his aw-shucks voice. "You can haul the debt fine. I'll tell you what—sign a two-year note, and if it gets sticky here and there, I'll let you slide on a few payments."

The men signed eagerly. But when problems with a dry hole made it necessary to ask for an extension, DeGoone Slickens didn't return their calls. Instead, he issued a demand letter calling for the whole note, adding at the bottom how his condition had worsened and his three years were now only two.

His partners defaulted and DeGoone Slickens ended up owning the entire company. Out of the profits, he paid his doctor a six-figure hush-money payment. For DeGoone Slickens had never had cancer of the liver. His true medical condition was his lack of a heart.

DeGoone Slickens made so much money in oil during the 1970's that he started buying up other companies. Whether they were for sale or not. The maneuver was called risk arbitrage, and DeGoone Slickens was its apostle.

By the time the Texas oil boom went bust, he was known across the nation as a corporate raider, operating out of Manhattan, where his country-boy twang made other CEO's dismiss him for some kind of cowboy idiot. Which was exactly what DeGoone Slickens wanted. He had built his career on being underestimated by business adversaries.

More than one of these CEO's ended up on the street with DeGoone Slickens sitting in their saddles.

Nobody liked DeGoone Slickens, which was why he had two bodyguards sitting outside his office at all times. They were former Dallas Cowboys whom Slickens had hired because, in addition to being a two-man Berlin Wall, they were nice status symbols. And when he was stuck sitting with them in traffic, they regaled him with football yarns.

DeGoone Slickens considered them an excellent investment.

Until one of them came charging into his office unannounced. He slammed the door behind him, putting his broad back to it, huffing and puffing for all the world like he'd just been sacked at the ten-yard line.

"What's the matter?" DeGoone said, seeing the look of horror on the former linebacker's flat face.

"Bear!" he cried, struggling to catch his breath.

"What?"

"There's a bear out there. It got Tomaski."

"What're you handing me?"

"Really, Mr. Slickens. It's a bear. Big as life."

"You have a gun," Slickens pointed out in a no-nonsense voice. "Go out there and shoot the varmint."

"Can't. It took my gun from me."

"A bear?"

"A *talking* bear."

"Are you drunk?"

"I know it sounds crazy, but it was asking for you."

"Me?" said Slickens, startle-faced. "What would a talking bear want with me? I'm a coon hunter."

"I don't know, but I wouldn't recommend letting him in. He pulverized Tomaski."

Then there was a loud knocking on the door.

"Open up," a rumbling voice warned, "or I'll huff and I'll puff and I'll blow this door down."

"What should I do, boss?" the ex-linebacker asked.

"Get ready," Slickens said, taking a Winchester off the wall. He jacked a shell into the breech and pointed it at his linebacker bodyguard.

"Open it," Slickens said. "And jump out of the way."

The linebacker unlocked the door and flung himself to one side.

The bear came through the door, claws raised high.

DeGoone Slickens fired.

The bear kept coming, its matted fur untouched.

Slickens whacked another shell into the chamber and fired again.

The bear bounced to one side, unhit.

"Dang it!" Slickens roared. "I can't draw a bead on him. You, Barker. You played football. Tackle him."

"Not me!" the ex-linebacker said, diving out the open door. "I quit."

"Looks like it's just you and me," the bear said casually.

DeGoone blinked. His jaw dropped. He looked at the bear carefully.

"Wait a minute," he said. "You're not a real bear. You're just a guy in a mangy suit."

"Obviously you're smarter than the average bodyguard. They thought I was a real bear."

"They're ex-football players."

"Too much steroids, I guess. Now, let's get down to business. And put that thing down. I can get pretty rough when my fur is rubbed the wrong way."

DeGoone hesitated. He brought his Winchester up to eye level again and squinted down the barrel. He did it quickly, but with the practiced care of a backwoods hunter.

In the time it took him to shut one eye, one of the pseudo-bear's paws swiped out and relieved him of his rifle.

DeGoone Slickens stood behind his desk holding empty

air. His trigger finger tightened on nothing. That's when he realized he had been disarmed. It had happened that fast.

As DeGoone watched, the bear took his rifle in both paws and bent it double against his chest. Then he threw the horseshoe-shaped rifle at a moosehead, scoring a ringer on its antlers.

"I'm Bear-Man," the bear said, jerking a thumb at his chest. "I'm the spirit of Wall Street. Every time there's a crash, I come out of hibernation. And my message this time is: it had better not happen again."

"Why tell me?"

"Someone's screwing around with Global stock. You bought a carload of it. If you're responsible, Bear-Man comes back and shreds your face. *Rowwrr!*"

Bear-Man's claws lifted in the air in warning. DeGoone Slickens backed away until he fell into his chair.

"I don't know what you're talkin' about," he said. "And if you know I bought Global stock yesterday, you should also know that I trade in blocks of stock like that every damn day of the week."

"Just remember my warning. Here," the bear added, ripping something off his chest and tossing it onto the desk.

DeGoone caught it. It was a bear's tooth.

"What's this for?" he demanded.

"It's a magic bear tooth. Put it under your pillow. And if you're pure of heart, I won't visit you again."

And with that the bear lumbered out of DeGoone Slickens' office. Slickens waited until he heard the hum of the descending elevator clearly before picking up the telephone. He started to dial 911. He never dialed the second 1.

"Shoot, what am I doin'?" he muttered. "Who's gonna believe a walkin' tall tale like that?"

He put the phone down and walked to the corner of the room, where a computer sat draped under a plastic cover. He removed the cover and fired it up. When he got a bulletin-board logo that read "MAYFLOWER DESCENDANTS," he attacked the keyboard with two stubby fingers.

Wall Street runs on rumor and speculation. After the first two sightings of the so-called Wall Street Bear, phone lines and faxes hummed with further news of the grizzly apparition as it made its way along New York's financial district. Wall Street, ever sensitive to its image of fiscal sobriety, circled the wagons at every media attempt to obtain a printable quote. But among themselves, Wall Street's movers and shakers buzzed about the phenomenon known as Bear-Man.

They also took precautions, under the guise of preparing for possible investor backlash over the near-meltdown that *Business Week* had christened "Dark Friday."

So it was that when Remo Williams approached the Looncraft, Dymstar & Buttonwood Building, he could see the sentinel security guards stationed throughout the lobby.

He shifted the formaldehyde-scented paper-covered bundle under his arm and changed plans. The phone booth outside the building was out. It was one of those alcove-style stations. Remo had no stomach for changing in a glass booth anyway. He had never understood how Clark Kent avoided getting hauled off to the can for public exposure.

Remo found a narrow alley between two buildings and undid the package. He stepped into the bear suit like a boy climbing into his Dr. Denton's through the seat trap. His loafers fitted snugly into the attached bear feet. His fingers slid into the dangling bear paws. That left only the hard part.

Remo reached back to the flap of bear hide that was supposed to go over his head. The weight of the hard bear's head mounted on top pulled it halfway down his scratchy back. The bear paws didn't make grabbing it any easier.

"Damn Chiun and his wild hairs," Remo grumbled.

Finally he snagged the bear's head by its black nose. He pulled the whole rig up and over his head, positioning the ragged eye holes so he could see clearly. Or as clearly as it was possible to see with stiff bear hairs sticking into his field of vision.

Now garbed as the ferocious Bear-Man, Remo jumped out of the alley and padded for the Looncraft Tower. Startled passersby fled. One offered him five hundred dollars for his autograph. Remo ignored him.

Remo went up the side of the building like a bear after a honeycomb. But the honey Bear-Man wanted was on the thirty-fourth floor.

Remo clung to the thirty-fourth floor and slipped along the tiny ornamental ledge with extra care. Not only were the attached claws getting in his way, but the thought of taking a thirty-four-floor nosedive to his death while dressed as a bear created vivid images in his mind.

He found the trading floor on the north side of the building.

Getting in presented a problem. Not only was the window glass fixed, but a crowd was gathering inside. Laughing traders gaped at him like they were at a zoo. One separated a honey-and-peanut-butter sandwich and slapped one slice, honey-side-out, against the glass in front of Remo's snout.

That did it. Bear-Man reared back with one paw and punched the glass.

It cracked like so much ice. Remo leaned in. He took the pane in with him in one crunchy shatterproof section.

As Remo got off the floor and brushed himself off, the LD&B traders shrank back, their laughter turning nervous and gaspy.

"Oh, my God!"

"It's true!"

"He's for real."

One trader approached cautiously. "Are you a bull or a bear?"

"Are you blind or just stupid?" Remo snapped back.

"It's true!" a woman gasped. "It *does* talk!"

"I meant are you bullish or bearish?" the trader pressed.

"*Definitely* bearish," Remo growled. "And I'm looking for your boss, Looncraft."

"Oh, he just stepped out," someone said. "Why do you want to see him?"

"Bear business," Remo said, lumbering forward.

The knot of traders separated before him like water beading on a hot skillet. Remo stumbled around the trading room, his clumsy bulk knocking over phones and Rolodexes, and once, a computer terminal.

Every eye followed him. A few pointed out that when

the bear passed certain computer screens, the phosphorescent letters swam like water disturbed by a stick.

P. M. Looncraft's office was clearly labeled. It was also constructed of glass—walls and door. Remo put his big black nose to the glass because his vision was obscured by hair.

The desk was unoccupied. P. M. Looncraft was definitely not in.

"Okay," Remo said, facing his wide-eyed audience. "When's he due back?"

Glances were exchanged. Shoulders jumped in unknowing shrugs.

"No one knows," a woman volunteered.

"Okay" Remo, said snapping off a bear claw and tossing it to the woman who spoke. "You tell him I was here. I'll be back."

A shaky male voice lifted above the crowd, warning, "No, you won't."

Remo tilted his bear helmet doggy-style, the better to see the source of the warning.

A blue-uniformed security guard stepped through the crowd, a gun held before him. The gun was as shaky as his voice, maybe shakier, Remo saw.

Remo rested defiant paws on his furry hips.

"You got a license to hunt bear?" he demanded of the guard.

The guard crept forward.

He sneered. "You're no bear."

"That's no bull," Remo shot back. "Okay, you got me. I surrender," he added, throwing up his paws.

"Good," the guard said, lifting out of his careful half-crouch. "Do as I say and you won't be hurt."

"Exactly what are you going to do?" Remo wanted to know.

"Handcuff you," the guard said firmly.

Remo's paws dropped together, outstretched. "My wrists are yours," he said.

Reaching behind his gunbelt, the guard pulled out a clinking pair of handcuffs.

Remo waited patiently. He didn't want to spook the nervous guard into any wild shooting. When one wristlet flopped into his arm, Remo swiped the gun from the other's grasp. The paw tangled up in the trigger guard, and the gun fell to the floor.

The guard reached down.

Remo stamped on the weapon, thinking the guard was going for it.

Unfortunately, the guard was going for his ankle-holstered backup gun. He brought it up and snapped off a hasty shot.

Remo sidestepped to the left. The bullet passed to his right, striking an acoustical ceiling panel. The guard corrected his aim. Remo slid aside so fast the guard was aiming at the spot where his eyes told him Remo was. But he wasn't there anymore.

The guard snapped off a shot he never heard. Remo's paws took him by the face and squeezed his nose and mouth shut. The guard fainted long before he would have lapsed into unconsciousness from asphyxiation.

Remo let him drop to the floor, and lifted quelling paws.

"Don't worry," he called out. "He just fainted. And I'm outta here. But keep watching the windows. I'll be back. "

Remo crawled out the window as a Polaroid camera flashed, capturing his buttoned-up rear end for posterity.

After he had vanished, the employees on the trading floor of Looncraft, Dymstar & Buttonwood took a hasty poll.

The consensus was that they would clean up the mess and not breathe a word of any of this to humorless P. M. Looncraft when he returned. There were no dissenting votes, not even from the security guard after he woke up screaming.

9

Remo Williams was surprised that the address of Nostrum, Inc. was a modern twelve-story chrome-and-bluedglass building near Wall Street. He stopped in front of the building, thinking that he had misremembered the address Smith had told him.

"Smitty's too cheap to own a nice place like this," he muttered, going through the revolving door.

Remo went to the lobby directory. A maintenance man had the glass front open and was replacing white plastic letters.

"Say, buddy," Remo asked him, "is there a Nostrum, Inc. in this building?"

The workman finished what he was doing and closed the glass before answering.

"That's the old name," he said. "Now it's Nostrum, Ink."

"What's the difference?" Remo asked.

"Take a look for yourself," the man told him, jerking a thumb at the directory.

Remo looked. He found a "NOSTRUM, INK" listed on the eighth floor.

"I hate to tell you this, but 'Ink' is misspelled."

"That's a matter of opinion. When the chief says to change it, I change it. We don't question the chief around here."

"This chief," Remo inquired. "Would he be about five feet tall with the complexion of an eighty-year-old walnut?"

"That's the chief, all right. 'Cept he doesn't look a day over seventy-five."

"I guess I've got the right address after all," Remo said, catching an upward-bound elevator.

On the eighth floor, Remo walked down a very long corridor, at the end of which a woman squatted on the rug under a brass plaque that read "NOSTRUM, INK." A fax telephone, Rolodex, and open appointment book lay before her crossed legs. The nameplate by her knee read "FAITH DAVENPORT."

"Someone steal your desk?" Remo asked, giving her the benefit of a friendly grin.

The grin was returned as a polite smile. She was a clean-scrubbed ash blond in a charcoal Lady Brooks pantsuit. Her eyes were the same blue as the sky, but Remo decided her uptilted nose was her best feature.

"The chief has liberated us from the tyranny of chairs and desks," she told him in a crisp voice. "We're very close to the earth here at Nostrum, Ink. Do you have an appointment?"

"Actually, no," Remo admitted.

The smile stayed in place but the warmth in Faith's eyes went cool. "I didn't think so," she said, eyeing Remo's T-shirt and chinos.

"I'm a friend of Chiun's," Remo explained. "You can tell him I'm here, and I'm sure it'll be all right. The name's Remo."

"Last name?" the blond said, picking up the phone.

"He'll know who it is," Remo assured her.

"Mr. Chiun," Faith said after a pause. "There is a gentleman here who claims to know you, Remo. He won't give his last name."

Faith looked up. "He insists upon having a last name."

"Oh, give me a break," Remo said. "Tell him it's Remo . . . Stallone."

"Remo Stallone," Faith said into the receiver. She listened briefly. "I understand." She hung up. "He asks that you make an appointment," she told Remo.

"He what?"

"The chief is a very, very busy man."

"All right, I'll play along. When's he free?"

"Actually, he's free right now. He hates appointments." Faith looked at her watch. "It's eleven-thirty-two now. Why don't we pencil you in for, say, eleven-thirty-three?"

"Are you serious?"

"Please take a seat," Faith said, gesturing to a bare spot by the wall.

Remo settled on the spot. In his head, he counted off the seconds until Faith called to him. Her watch was five seconds late by Remo's internal clock.

"I'll announce you now," she said, picking up the phone. "Mr. Chiun, Remo Stallone to see you. Yes, he does have an appointment."

Faith hung up. "Go right in."

"Thanks," Remo said, shaking his head in disbelief.

"I thought you looked Italian," she called after him.

Remo walked into a large room where suspender-festooned young workers sat behind banks of computer screens. The screens were on the floor. So were the telephones and other office impedimenta. Not to mention the workers. They looked uncomfortable, and a few could be heard complaining about their backs.

Remo breezed past them to a door on which the word "CHIEF" was painted in black lettering. He entered without knocking.

Inside, the Master of Sinanju looked up from his tatami mat on the bare floor.

"Remo!" Chiun said brightly. "Welcome to Nostrum, Ink."

"I see you've got everyone dancing to your tune," Remo said, closing the door.

"Why not?" Chiun returned proudly. "I am their chief. My employees are very loyal to me. It is all very tribal."

"I'm glad you're settling in so well."

"It is not all easy," Chiun said. "I have had to fire some of them already."

"Embezzlers?"

"Poor spellers. They could not properly write a simple word such as 'ink.' It was unbelievable, Remo. Everywhere I look, the signs said 'Nostrum, Inc.' With a 'c.' "

"Pitiful. The U.S. educational system is to blame."

"I blame Smith," Chiun sniffed. "He hired cheap help. But I am well on my way to setting things right."

"So what does Nostrum do, anyway?"

Chiun looked to the closed door. He leaned closer.

"It makes money," he said low-voiced.

"No kidding?" Remo said, suppressing a smile.

"No, really. Look." Chiun picked a sheet of paper from a pile and handed it to Remo. Remo took it.

It was a stock certificate in the name of Nostrum, Inc.

"I think you'll have to reprint these," Remo said. "It still says 'Inc.' With a 'c'."

"This is an old one," Chiun said. "We sell these."

"Yeah, that's how it works, all right."

"You do not understand, Remo. We also print them. In this very building. We print them, and people pay vast sums for these worthless things."

"Maybe they like the design."

"I thought of that too," Chiun said, taking the certificate back. He looked at the face. "But in truth it is an ugly design. I am having that changed as well."

"Well, maybe Smith can explain it. I've been running around town all morning and came up goose-eggs."

"You wore the suit?" Chiun asked anxiously.

Remo sighed. "Yeah, I wore the suit."

"Where is it now?"

"I stashed it in a locker in Grand Central."

Chiun looked hurt. "What?"

"Hey, take it easy. I'm in my civilian identity."

"Ah, I understand," Chiun said. "I watched the video. I know how these things work. After terrorizing the villains, you have assumed your true identity, the better to safeguard yourself from their cowardly attacks upon your person."

"Something like that," Remo agreed.

"You *did* terrorize them?" Chiun asked in concern.

"They'll have bear nightmares into the year 2000," Remo promised. "But I don't know what good it will do. Nobody broke down and confessed or anything. But all Smith wanted was for me to shake them up. Maybe one of them will make a move."

The intercom buzzed. Chiun touched a button with a delicate finger.

"Yes?"

"Mr. Chiun—"

"I told you to call me 'Chief,' " Chiun said querulously.

"I am your chief executive officer. You must use the proper form of address."

"Sorry, Chief," Faith said.

"That is better," Chiun said importantly as Remo rolled his eyes ceilingward. "Now, what is it?"

"Two messengers just arrived with shipments."

"I will be right out," Chiun said.

He stood up. "Come, Remo. I will show you how to run a business. Someday Nostrum may be yours."

"This ought to be good," Remo said, following him out through the busy workroom, where suddenly every worker sat up straight and began talking in a loud voice about how comfortable the floor was, and into the reception area—such as it was.

A pair of uniformed armored-car messengers stood there, arms resting on hand trucks stacked with wooden crates. They were breathing hard. One of them rubbed a sweaty brow with a green bandanna.

Chiun drifted up to the two, his arms tucked into his kimono sleeves, saying "I am Chiun, chief of Nostrum."

The man with the green bandanna finished with his forehead and puffed, "Delivery from Goldman Sachs. Two hundred and fifty ingots."

"Ingots?" Remo said.

"Hush, Remo," Chiun told him. To the messenger he said, "Open the crates and I will count them personally."

"Sure thing." The guard pried the lid off the top crate with a short prybar. One by one, he counted out fifty small gold ingots, stacking them in neat piles. The other man waited his turn until all 250 ingots lay open for display.

Chiun counted them three times before he turned to Faith at her reception mat.

"Issue this man three hundred shares of preferred," he said.

"Yes, Chief." Faith picked up the phone and began talking.

"Who is next?" Chiun asked.

"I am. Salomon Brothers. One hundred ingots."

"You know, Little Father," Remo said as the second set

of ingots was brought forth, "I don't think this is how they normally do it on Wall Street."

"It is the way I do it. Do you know that when I arrived this morning, they were selling my obviously priceless stocks for mere money? Often credit. It was unbelievable. I asked to see the Global stock we owned, and my hirelings told me that although we owned it, we did not have possession of it. I asked when we would take possession and they told me that was not how it was done. The stocks would remain in the hands of a third party. We owned it in name only. It is a ridiculous system these people have. The money changes hands, but not the property. I put a stop to that at once."

"I'll bet you did."

A green-suspendered clerk came out of the office with a sheaf of stocks. He handed them over to the Goldman Sachs messenger, who went away just as Chiun finished counting the second gold shipment.

After the other messenger had left with his stock, Remo put a question to Chiun.

"Does Smith know how you're running this place?" he asked.

"I have not spoken with him all day," Chiun admitted. "But I am certain he will be delighted. I have sold more Nostrum stock today than in the previous month."

"Really?" Remo asked.

"I will let you in on a secret," Chiun said conspiratorially as clerks came out to gather up the gold in mail carts and wheel them into a side room. "Men will pay incredible sums if they believe a thing is valuable. Smith offered Nostrum stocks for mere credit, and few bought. I insisted upon gold, paid in full upon delivery, and they are beside themselves to own it."

"Little Father," Remo said sincerely, "I think you've got the hang of how they do business on Wall Street."

10

P. M. Looncraft came into his office late. This time, it was not considered unusual by his employees. It was a Saturday.

On the way to his office, Looncraft stopped to lay a firm hand on the pink-striped shoulder of Ronald Johnson, who wore the gold tie of Looncraft, Dymstar & Buttonwood proudly.

"How are we today?" Looncraft said, low-voiced, knowing that every man on the floor would notice the personal interest he was taking in Johnson. He made a point of not calling Johnson by name—the better to keep the man in line.

"Excellent, sir."

"And Global?"

"I've acquired over five thousand shares for the company. They will execute Monday morning at the opening price."

"Hmmm. Only that?"

"I did buy some for myself," Johnson admitted.

"Good man. How many shares?"

"One thousand, sir. It will empty my bank account."

"Brave soul," Looncraft said in sympathy.

"Sir?"

"We may have to divest. I hear rumblings about Global."

"What kind?" Johnson squeaked. Catching himself, he lowered his voice. "I mean—"

"I know what you mean," Looncraft whispered. "It seems Global may be having FCC difficulties. And they are overleveraged. They may have to divest. Possibly downsize significantly.

"But . . . but my entire savings is in Global," Johnson croaked.

Looncraft clapped a hand on Johnson's shoulder. "You are a loyal employee, Johnson," he said magnanimously. "I value you. LD&B can absorb losses better than you. The firm will buy your shares at market, if you wish to sell."

"Yes!" Johnson said fervently, tears coming into his eyes. "I'll execute it immediately."

"Wise man. No sense being long and wrong, as they say."

"Thank you, sir."

Looncraft started to walk away. Johnson's voice brought him up short.

"Mr. Looncraft. One moment, please."

"Yes?" Looncraft asked, making sure to suppress the greedy grin on his cadaverous face before he turned around.

"Nostrum. You asked me to look into them."

"So I did," Looncraft said. "In my office, Johnson."

"Certainly, sir. Let me execute the Global transfer first."

Looncraft started to object, but caught himself. "Do that, by all means."

Looncraft went to his office, telling the secretary, "Johnson will want to see me presently. Keep him waiting ten minutes."

"Yes, sir."

That will teach the upstart, Looncraft told himself as he placed his briefcase beside his desk. He hung his chesterfield coat on an old-fashioned wooden rack. He went to his deskside computer terminal and logged onto a bulletin board that bore the legend "MAYFLOWER DESCENDANTS."

His lantern jaw fell when he saw the message on his screen "CHECK," it said. There was a number next to the message, along with the notation: "MADE REDUNDANT. CAUSE UNKNOWN." It told Looncraft that they had lost the Reuters connection. It was distressing news.

He sat back to ponder the matter. A new element had apparently entered the game. He would have to be prepared. Then his secretary announced the arrival of Johnson.

"Has he been waiting a full ten minutes?" Looncraft asked. When the reply was affirmative, Looncraft said, "Send him in."

"Here is the signed contract," Johnson said, placing a

sheet of paper on Looncraft's spacious desk. Looncraft's glance flicked to it, and seeing that it was properly and irrevocably executed he waved for Johnson to sit.

"Tell me about Nostrum," Looncraft said, steepling his fingers. He was looking, not at Johnson, but off toward his great-great-great-great-grandfather, H. P. Looncraft.

"They're a NASDAQ stock," Johnson said, reading from his notes. "Very difficult to dig up information on."

"But you did."

"Some, sir. It's very odd. They went public only a year ago, and I had a tip only this morning that their stock is heating up."

"Really?" Looncraft said, swiveling in Johnson's direction.

"I don't know what you make of this, but their stock has been selling like crazy all morning."

"Today? Today is Saturday. The market is closed."

"That's the crazy part. They've bypassed NASDAQ. They're selling it from their offices. No credit, no trading. Strictly cash-and-carry."

"Preposterous!" Looncraft sputtered, leaning forward.

Johnson had his full attention now and pressed the point home. "They accept payment in gold only," he said. "And the price has jumped six times just this morning. They're trading at one-ten a share and upticking."

"Gold?"

"Yes, sir. The rules are, if you deliver the cash equivalent in gold, you come away with the stock."

"The physical stock? Sold over the counter like yard goods? Absurd. No one trades in the physical stock anymore. It's not practicable."

"As I say, they're selling quite a bit of stock in this manner. Rumors are sweeping the street that they're hot. I can't imagine what will be the reaction when the market opens Monday."

"This Nostrum, who runs it?"

"The CEO is a mysterious person named Chiun."

"Just Chiun?"

"I understand he's Korean."

"Hmm. The Koreans are no slackers," Looncraft mused. "Everybody thinks the Koreans will be the next Japanese."

"That remains to be seen," Looncraft said disapprovingly. "What do they produce?"

"That's the part that's fuzzy, sir. I'm unable to develop any information on their product line—if any."

"Well, they must *do* something."

"They do generate a healthy bottom line. And it looks like they plan on going places, if traders have to deposit gold in return for their stock."

"How many shares of Global did they acquire yesterday?"

"Quite a bit. My estimate is between seven and eight thousand. Which reminds me. Since acquiring my Global stock, LD&B now owns over five percent of that firm's outstanding stock. As you know, according to SEC rules, you must declare your intentions in the matter."

"I intend to tender an offer of eighty per share, and I would like you to handle it."

Ronald Johnson jumped up, dropping his notes. "Sir!" he said. "But I just sold you a thousand shares at fifty!"

"Which you were perfectly delighted to do less than fifteen minutes ago," Looncraft said pointedly.

"But I understood . . . I mean, you told me that Global was in trouble."

"It is. It is also the largest communications conglomerate in the world, and I mean to have it."

"I must protest, sir. I believe you've taken unfair advantage of me as an employee."

P. M. Looncraft's eyes narrowed until they resembled the steely eyes on the banks of Looncraft family portraits on the wall behind him. Ronald Johnson suddenly felt as if he were under the multiple gaze of some many-headed hydra.

"Fifteen minutes ago, my good man," P. M. Looncraft said in a voice as steely as his eyes, "I had intended to divest myself of all Global holdings. But your information about Nostrum leads me to deduce that they know something about GLB I do not. Possibly a takeover by that Texas brigand Slickens. I have changed my mind. Had you not panicked, that stock would still be yours."

"I know that, sir, but—"

Looncraft lifted a placating hand.

"And had I not, in my generosity, offered to relieve you

of the burden of your position, you might just as easily be sitting on stocks worth far less than what I offered you. You know how this game is played. Timing is everything. A man can sometimes suffer great losses or realize tremendous riches on just a fraction of a point if he buys in at noon and sells by four."

"May I point out, sir," Johnson rejoined, "that it was my information that brought you to this conclusion?"

"So noted."

"Might I not be allowed to share in the investment potential?" Johnson suggested hopefully.

"Of course. Feel free to purchase any shares you can lay hands on come Monday morning. That is how the market functions. One investor feels a stock is overvalued and sells it to another, who feels it is undervalued. It is all calculated risk, magnificently realized."

"But—"

"It's a man's game, Johnson," P. M. Looncraft lectured. "If you're going to play it, be a man."

"Yes, sir," Johnson said unhappily.

"Now, let's get a tender together on this Nostrum. Say, one hundred and thirty a share. No more, no less."

"Nostrum? What about Global?"

"I will need to take over Nostrum's shares if I am to acquire Global, thanks to that Slickens person. He currently holds more of Global than I do. The rotter."

Johnson stood up. "At once, Mr. Looncraft."

"Keep me updated."

Ronald Johnson turned to go, his shoulders slanted twenty degrees from the horizontal lower than when he had entered the office.

"And, Johnson?" Looncraft said.

"Sir?"

"You have a spot on your tie. Have it cleaned. It is company property."

Johnson's smile was wistful. He was thinking of how much money that tie had cost him.

"Thank you, sir," he said meekly as he left the room.

Looncraft waited until the door had shut before allowing a broad satisfied smile to spread over his angular face. These affected young fogies, he thought. All wanting to

play the game. Every one bound and determined to win.
And all so very terrified of losing.

It was their fear that always worked against them. And
for P. M. Looncraft.

He returned to his computer terminal.

11

"It's true!" Faith Davenport was saying. "Rumors are flying up and down the street about it."

"A talking bear?" Remo Williams said in a skeptical
voice. "Imagine that." He sat on the rug in the reception
area of the newly rechristened Nostrum, Ink. He had
come out to strike up a casual deskside conversation with
Faith, but the lack of furniture made that difficult, so he
sat down on the rug with her.

"They say he demolished Lippincott Mercantile Bank
and frightened DeGoone Slickens' staff right into the street,"
Faith said, spooning peach yogurt into her delectable mouth.
Remo watched every mouthful disappear, thinking he now
preferred her pretty mouth to her uptilted nose. "They
say he's a mass hallucination, but a lot of traders think he's
a harbinger of a coming bear market."

"Makes sense," Remo said soberly. "A bear ushering in
a bear market."

"Don't smirk, Remo," Faith said, shaking a plastic spoon
at his nose. "The street is very superstitious. Something
like this could make the traders even more jittery than
they are. Besides, it really wasn't a talking bear. It was
someone dressed in a bear suit. Called himself, of all
things, Bear-Man."

"Is that so?" Remo said, his eyes narrowing. "You know,
I'd like you to tell Chiun that."

"The chief, you mean."

"He lets me call him Chiun," Remo said, knowing it would impress Faith. He was having trouble impressing her, which was a rare experience for him. Usually Remo had to fight to keep women away. Most sensed his animal power and followed him around like puppy dogs. It intrigued him.

Remo was about to ask her if she was free for dinner when Chiun burst out into the hall.

"Remo!" Chiun squeaked excitedly. "Quickly! Bar the doors. We are under attack!"

"We are?" Remo said, jumping to his feet.

"One of my minions informs me that forces are massing to conquer us."

"What forces?"

"A conspiracy consisting of a cabal known as Looncraft, Dymstar & Buttonhead."

"The brokerage house?" Faith asked.

"You know these villains?" Chiun asked suddenly.

"I worked for them before I came here. I hated the place. Too stuffy. No one even knew my name."

"Then I hereby promote you to my aide-de-camp," Chiun announced.

"Aid-de . . . ?" Faith said, her yogurt forgotten.

"Your salary is hereby doubled. Now, come, we must plan a counterattack. Remo, see to the doors. Let no one enter who is not known to us."

"Hold the phone, Chiun," Remo said.

"You will address me as 'Chief,'" Chiun said huffily.

"That's *not* funny," Remo said sharply.

"It was not meant to be," Chiun returned. "These are perilous times. My precious Nostrum is under attack."

"If you'll listen to me a freaking second," Remo retorted, "maybe I can put this in perspective before you go completely off the deep end."

"What do you know about business matters?" Chiun asked skeptically.

"Enough to know that Looncraft Et Cetera isn't a secret cabal of plotters," Remo shot back. "They're an investment house. And they're not going to send in an army to loot and pillage. They're mounting a hostile takeover."

"Yes, that is what my hireling called it. The dastards!"

"A hostile takeover isn't what you think. They just make an offer to buy your company."

"I will not sell," Chiun said firmly.

"You may not have any choice in the matter," Faith put in.

"Right," Remo said. "You explain it to him, Faith. He'll listen to you."

"I am listening," Chiun said, tucking in his chin like a wizened old turtle facing danger.

"Well, Chief, it's—"

Call me 'Chiun,'" the Master of Sinanju said, throwing a smug look in Remo's direction.

Remo frowned.

Faith launched into her explanation. "The way a hostile takeover works is that the raiders—"

"Raiders!" Chiun squeaked.

"It's a business term," Remo said.

"Go on," Chiun said.

"The raiders make a public tender," Faith explained. "Say, Nostrum stock is selling for a hundred dollars a share."

"That was twenty minutes ago. I have since raised it to a hundred and ten."

"Okay, it's a hundred and ten a share. Well, the raider is saying he'll pay fifty dollars above that price to anyone who will sell to him."

"He will?" Chiun cried. "Then *I* will sell to him."

"Uh-uh," Faith said, shaking her head. "Better not. Because if he acquires enough outstanding stock, he can gain a controlling interest in the company. Don't you know that?"

"Chiun's new to this country," Remo explained.

"Silence!" Chiun said loudly. "I do *not* understand. I own Nostrum. How could persons who have bought my stock take control? It is merely paper."

"Try reading the certificates sometime," Remo inserted.

Faith added, "To own stock is to have an interest in a company."

"Their interest I can accept," Chiun snapped back. "Let them regard my magnificent building with envious eyes from afar if they so wish."

" 'Interest' is a business term," Faith said firmly. "It means 'ownership.' They are buying shares in the company's ownership."

Chiun's wrinkles smoothed in his astonishment. "You mean when I have been selling my stock, I have been selling my company?"

"What's the problem?" Faith wondered. "You *do* retain controlling interest. How much stock do you own?"

"I do not know," Chiun admitted. "I have been selling it so quickly, unaware of its true value."

"Here we go," Remo said. "Congratulations. You're about to go down in corporate history as the CEO who sold his own company out from under him."

"Wrong!" Chiun said triumphantly. "I have the gold."

Remo turned to Faith. "Do you want to tell him or shall I?"

"What? What!" Chiun squeaked.

"That gold is the *company's* gold," Faith said gently. "It doesn't belong to you."

"But Nostrum is mine."

"It also belongs to the stockholders," Faith told him, "the ones who bought up your shares."

"Which will belong to Looncraft if he succeeds in a takeover bid," Remo added smugly.

Chiun took hold of the puffs of hair over his ears in exasperation.

"What madness is this!" he shrieked. "I have been tricked by that deceiver Smith!"

"Who is Smith?" Faith asked Remo.

"Minority stockholder," Remo said quickly. "Chiun took his advice. Always a big mistake."

"Oh." Faith touched Chiun's shoulder. "It's not too late, you know," she said gently.

"That's right," Remo added. "He may not want Nostrum."

"That's true. These raiders often buy a company just to sell off pieces for profit. Unless Nostrum owns something LD&B wants."

Remo snapped his fingers. "Global! Maybe he wants your shares of Global. Smith said it could happen."

"Then I will sell Global!" Chiun trumpeted.

Remo took Chiun by the elbow and drew him out of

Faith's hearing. "Not a good idea. Check with Smith first."

"This is not Smith's company," Chiun said brittlely. "It is mine."

"Weren't you listening to anything we just told you?"

"Let them sue," Chiun spat. "I will never give up Nostrum, which I built with my own two hands."

"In one morning after you had it handed to you on a silver platter," Remo pointed out. "So let's talk to Smith before this gets any worse."

"I no longer trust Smith. He did not prepare me for the duplicity of corporate life."

"Join the club," Remo said archly. "Look, we gotta call Smith anyway. We've been looking for a nibble. This may be it."

Chiun looked toward Faith, who stood with her arms folded, trying not to overhear the conversation.

"Perhaps there is another way," Chiun said. "Perhaps this is a job for—"

"Don't say it!"

"Bear-Man," Chiun whispered. "Consider coming to work for me, Remo. Nostrum, Ink, can use a house assassin. I am the best, of course, but as the chief, I cannot stoop to such lowly work."

"What, have we joined the ranks of royalty?" Remo asked.

"Some have greatness thrust upon them—" Chiun began.

"And others have it slip between their fingers because they get greedy," Remo finished.

Chiun's face was stung. "I am still the Master of Sinanju."

"Who's in a dither because some brokerage house is about to buy the rug out from under him."

"This is my castle," Chiun said firmly.

"Not if you've sold most of your stock and Looncraft can buy it up."

"Maybe you should buy it back," Faith interjected. "Top his offer."

"What? Buy back all that worthless paper?"

"It's not worthless if you lose ownership because of it," Remo countered. "I may not know a lot about high finance, but I know that much."

Chiun considered. "Perhaps I will speak to Smith after all," he said.

"Can't hurt," Remo said in a reasonable tone.

Moments later they were in Chiun's bare office. Remo put the call through because it was a secure line which couldn't be entrusted to Faith, who waited outside the office.

"Smith, Remo. Chiun wants to talk to you." Remo handed the phone to the Master of Sinanju.

"Smith! Nostrum is under siege."

"Excellent. Who is it?" Smith asked eagerly. His voice was amplified by a speakerphone attachment.

"A cabal who call themselves Looncraft, Dymstar & Buttonhead."

"Wood," Remo interjected. "Buttonwood."

"I was hoping something like this would happen," Smith said.

"*What?* You admit betraying me, Smith?"

"No, of course not. But obviously Looncraft is interested in the Global block Nostrum holds."

"Maybe not," Remo put in. "Chiun's changed the rules. He's been selling his stock above the market price. No cash, no credit. Investors have to plunk down gold and they walk off with stock."

Smith groaned. "Oh, no. A move like that is like blood in the water to those sharks. They'll think you're up to something. No wonder Looncraft has become interested in Nostrum. They must believe you're an up-and-coming company."

"So maybe they don't want the Global stock after all," Remo said in disappointment.

"It's very, very likely," Smith replied dispiritedly.

"We will find out," Chiun said. "We will offer them Global and see if they go away."

"No," Smith said quickly. "Global is our bait. It's the only thing we have that will draw out the plotters. Under no circumstance must you sell that stock. Or any of your other holdings. We have a responsibility to the world economy to show faith in the marketplace."

"You cannot stop me, Smith," Chiun warned.

"Perhaps you should call a meeting of the board of directors before you begin," Smith said after a tight pause.

"Who are they?"

"The co-owners of Nostrum. Majority shareholders."

"And who are these people?"

"Remo is one. I believe he's secretary."

"What? Remo owns Nostrum too?"

"I do?" Remo said, surprise on his face.

"And there are others," Smith added. "It's standard corporate organization. Before Nostrum can make any major decisions, such as selling off Global stock, a full board meeting must be convened and the matter voted on."

Chiun fumed. His hazel eyes squeezed into slits of bitterness.

"There will be no need for that," Chiun said in a distant voice. "And since you know so much about these matters, what do you suggest I do?"

"Looncraft wants Nostrum," Smith explained. "That much we know. Why don't you meet with him? Take his temperature."

"Is he sick?"

"It's an expression," Smith said. "See if his interest is in Nostrum or your Global holdings. The Asian stock markets will open at eight o'clock Sunday night, our time. We must be prepared for a rout. Every moment is precious. There is still time to head off another crash."

"Very well," Chiun said, hanging up. He turned to Remo with smoldering eyes. "Why didn't you tell me you were secretary of Nostrum?"

"Because I didn't know," Remo answered. "And if you want to know the truth, I don't care. This is just another Harold Smith snow job. I don't own anything. And neither do you. This place is a house of cards, and when this job is done, Smith is going to light a match to it. Count on it."

"And Smith will rue the day," Chiun said levelly.

"Okay, so what's our next move . . . Chief?"

"Your next move it to take your rightful place at the reception area."

"Me?"

"Did you not hear Smith? You are secretary. Then you will do a secretary's job and earn your pay."

"I get paid?"

"Two dollars an hour."

"No chance. I gotta have, let me see . . . two dollars and eighty-nine cents."

"Two sixty-nine. And not a penny more."

"I'll take it," Remo said, grinning. "Is that what you pay Faith?"

"No," Chiun said seriously. "She has seniority over you. Besides, she is now my aide-de-camp in the bitter conflict to come."

"Anything to keep me out of that itchy bear suit," Remo said fervently.

12

P. M. Looncraft drained the last of his afternoon tea before responding to his secretary's intercom buzz. It was nearly six P.M., the end of a busy day. He was in no mood to be interrupted.

Looncraft spoke into the intercom. "Yes?"

"A Mr. Chiun on line two."

Looncraft blinked. "Chiun, of Nostrum?"

"That is what I understand, Mr. Looncraft."

"Tell him I am at a meeting," Looncraft said instantly. "Let the beggar cool his heels."

"Yes, Mr. Looncraft."

P. M. Looncraft leaned back in his black leather executive's chair. He was surprised. This Chiun was contacting him. Imagine. Well, let him stew in his own juices. There was no reason to speak with him, although Looncraft had a tickle of curiosity about this new Wall Street genius who could command gold ingots in return for his stock.

Looncraft attended to a few minor business details and placed all important papers in his briefcase. Before leaving his office, he went to his personal computer and logged onto the Mayflower Descendants bulletin board. It was quiescent, which surprised him. He had expected an update on the Reuters matter.

Gathering up his briefcase, he left Looncraft, Dymstar & Buttonwood with not so much as a good-night to his secretary or any of his employees, who would toil at their desks for another hour. He especially ignored Ronald Johnson.

Looncraft's Rolls-Royce Silver Cloud was waiting for him at the curb thirty-four stories below, his liveried chauffeur standing stiffly by the open door.

"Home, Mipps," Looncraft said. The door closed behind him and Looncraft settled back into the plush interior.

He noticed the smell first. Like a wild animal's scent.

The Rolls started from the curb, pushing Looncraft into the hairy figure seated beside him in the dim limousine interior.

Looncraft recoiled from the unexpected scratching of rough hair as if from a cactus.

"My word!" he said in horror.

"How's it going?" a rumbling voice asked conversationally.

Looncraft touched a light switch. The overhead light revealed a hulking figure swathed in brownish fur.

"Who the devil are you?" Looncraft sputtered.

"You've heard of the Waltzing Bear?"

"Vaguely."

"Well, I'm the Wall Street Bear. We're cousins."

"Balderdash. I know Wall Street and everything there is to know about it, and I've never heard of you."

"I came by earlier today. Don't tell me you didn't get the message."

"What message?"

"That I came by."

"Are you daft?"

"Are you English?" the bear asked suddenly.

"My ancestors helped to build this country while yours no doubt were living in dripping caves. The Looncrafts were among the first to settle in Plymouth."

"Your accent doesn't sound English, but your lingo does."

"I am a proud descendant of H. P. Looncraft, who came

to this country when George Washington was a mere
back-alley drabtail."

"You're also the one who wants to take over Nostrum,
Ink. With a K."

"There is no law against acquiring a company such as
that one. And I've taken a fancy to it."

"Well, unfancy it," the bear told P. M. Looncraft in
serious tones. "The CEO of Nostrum doesn't appreciate
your interest. And he definitely does not take kindly to
interference."

"Chiun sent you?"

"Actually, I'm the spirit of Wall Street. I guard good
companies against bad ones. You're the bad one. Nostrum's the good one."

"Rubbish. In business there is no good or bad. Just
profit and loss."

"Spoken like a true business pirate. So what's your
interest in Nostrum?"

"If you wish to discuss this," P. M. Looncraft sniffed,
"see my girl about an appointment."

"Don't need an appointment," the bear said, grabbing a
fistful of Looncraft's shirtfront in a formaldehyde-scented
paw. "Not while I have you."

"Unhand me, you . . . you cur."

"You've got me confused with the Hound of the Garment District. And are you sure you're not English?"

"I have told you, my forebears—" Looncraft began.

"Forget your forebears. I'm the only bear you have to
worry about right now. You didn't accept Chiun's phone
call. Big mistake. Now he's mad."

"I do not care. And do you mind releasing my shirt?
These are custom-made by H. Huntsman & Sons."

"Sorry. I get excited when no one takes me seriously,"
the bear told P. M. Looncraft. He let go, his bear paws
brushing imaginary dirt from Looncraft's shirtfront. One
claw snagged his tie, shredding it.

"Sorry," the bear said again. "Keep forgetting to trim
my nails. I just crawled out of hibernation, you know."

"You do not fool me," Looncraft said stiffly. "You are
not an actual bear. You are only a man in a ratty suit."

"I guess that's how you got to be a big wheel, huh? I

admit it. Under this rug is a live human being. But no one must ever see my face. That's why I had to become Bear-Man."

"Bear-Man?"

"It's a nasty job, but somebody's got to protect the small investor. So let's get down to brass claws. You're after Nostrum. I'm telling you Nostrum's off-limits. It has nothing you want—unless you like investing in trouble."

"That is for me to determine," Looncraft said acidly.

"That's the answer I expected, so I'm going to ask you straight out. Are you after Nostrum or just its Global stock?"

Looncraft's prim mouth tightened into a bloodless band.

"No comment, huh?" Bear-Man said. "I think you just answered my question."

"I do not have to speak with you. Return to your master—"

"Chief. He likes to be called 'Chief.' "

"Very well. Return to your chief and inform him that P.M. Looncraft intends to acquire as much Nostrum stock as he can lay hands on, and then he will take very personal pleasure in firing Mr. Chiun as CEO on the day he walks in the door as its new owner. Will you be good enough to deliver that message to him?"

"I will. But believe me, you don't want me to."

"I would appreciate it if you would convey the message, just the same."

"Okay," Bear-Man said. "Have your driver let me off at the next corner and I guarantee your words will be caressing his ears within a half-hour."

"Delighted," Looncraft said through a thin smile. He picked up the speaking tube. "Mipps, pull up at the next convenient intersection. I have a passenger who wishes to alight."

"Excuse me, Mr. Looncraft. You're alone back there."

"Precisely what I wish to speak to you about after we have discharged our passenger," P. M. Looncraft said in a frigid voice.

Remo Williams stepped from the Rolls-Royce and lifted a paw to hail a cab. Or attempted to. Three cabs mistook him for a costumed street mime and ignored him.

The fourth was only too happy to give the newly famous Bear-Man a ride when he jumped on his hood at a red light and climbed in through a window, saying, "Nostrum Building."

"You got pockets in that suit?" the cabby asked suspiciously.

A heavy paw settled onto the driver's shoulder. Claws dug into his flesh with relentless pressure.

"Now, that's a very, very personal question to ask a bear," Remo said.

The driver ran the light in his hurry to get Remo to his destination.

Bear-Man strolled into the Nostrum lobby and bounded into an elevator. But it was Remo Williams who stepped off at the eighth floor. He had the Bear-Man costume rolled tightly under his arm as he slipped into the men's room. He pushed it into a covered trash receptacle and forced the lid irrevocably into place with a quick slap. Unless someone physically removed the receptacle, the suit would be there when Remo next needed it, which he fervently hoped was never. He felt like he needed a shower.

The Master of Sinanju sat on his executive mat in his otherwise bare office. It was growing dark outside.

"You gave Looncraft my warning?" Chiun demanded.

"Yep. And he gave me a message in return. He says he's looking forward to tossing you out on the street when he takes over."

Chiun shot to his feet. His cheeks puffed out like an angry blowfish. "Then it is war!" he raged, shaking a tight fist.

"So what's the battle plan?"

"We will descend on him and smite him for his temerity."

"That will take care of Looncraft," Remo pointed out in a reasonable tone, "but not Looncraft, Dymstar & Buttonwood. Someone will just take his place as the head of that company, and the problem will be the same."

"Then we will kill his successor and every successor thereafter until no one will dare take his place."

"I admire your persistence, but Smith won't like that,"

Remo said. "Besides, Looncraft as much as admitted that he's really after your Global stock."

Chiun's shaking fist dropped. It disappeared into his joined kimono sleeves. "He did?"

Remo nodded firmly. "He did. And you can't get him off your back without getting Smith's permission."

"I am through with Smith," Chiun announced.

"Good. Let's go to Mexico. Both of us."

"Not until I have seen to this trouble. Get Smith on the line for me."

"You know," Remo said, dropping to the floor and dialing the special number, "this isn't what Smith meant when he told you I was the corporation's secretary."

"No?" Chiun snapped. "Then why are you doing as I bid?"

"Never mind," Remo growled. "Smith? It's Remo. We had a break. Looncraft as much as admitted he's after Nostrum's Global stock."

Remo listened for a while. Then he looked up.

"Smith wants a meet."

"Inform Smith that I have pressing business matters I must first attend to," Chiun said distantly.

"Did you hear that, Smitty?" Remo asked into the phone. He listened some more. To Chiun he said, "Smitty said if the market crashes on Monday, Nostrum won't be worth the concrete it sits on. His exact words."

"Inform Smith that I will attempt to fit him into my busy schedule," Chiun said grudgingly.

Remo passed on the message as "We're on our way, Smitty."

Remo hung up and asked, "Shall I call a travel agency?"

"It will not be necessary," Chiun sniffed. "The Nostrum corporate jet is at our disposal."

"We have a corporate jet? Really?"

Chiun started for the door. "All important personages have corporate jets. Come, Remo."

Remo followed the Master of Sinanju through the trading room. On their way through, Chiun called out in a loud voice, "Toil harder, minions."

Their chorused "Yes, Chief" sounded like the Mormon Tabernacle Choir on a bad day.

"My corporate tribe loves me," Chiun said as the elevator door closed after them.

Dr. Harold W. Smith waited until the Folcroft lobby guard flashed the warning that Remo and Chiun had entered the building before switching from his leather chair to the wheelchair. He rolled back into place behind his desk.

Remo and Chiun entered shortly thereafter.

"Master Chiun, Remo," Smith said in his colorless voice.

Chiun's "Emperor" was distant. Remo slouched onto a sofa and folded his arms unhappily.

"I'm afraid this strategy session is necessary," Smith said, unperturbed. "In another twenty-four hours the Tokyo and Hong Kong markets begin trading. Already there are reports of nervousness in the overseas markets. It bodes ill for Monday."

"So what?" Remo said carelessly. "Everyone knows that the little guy dived out of the market in eighty-seven. It's just big companies trading now. Besides, all my money is in cash."

"And mine in gold," Chiun added.

"Please," Smith said. "Let's be adults about this."

"You've got Chiun here—who doesn't know a Rolodex from a Rolex—playing the big wheel, and me running around Wall Street dressed like a bear, and now you want us to act like adults. Sorry, Smith. That train left the station this morning ."

Smith fiddled with a pencil.

"We have made progress," he said. "Up until now we couldn't be certain if this was a general slump or if Global stock was the goal. I believe the latter now. Looncraft would appear to be our best suspect, although it is difficult to believe. Looncraft Dymstar & Buttonwood is one of the premier investment houses in the world. Surely a man as seasoned in high finance as Looncraft would not cause such a financial upheaval merely to obtain a company, no matter how desirable. LD&B are heavily invested across the board. They stand to lose more than they gain."

"Since the junk-bond market went belly-up last year, maybe he's gotten desperate," Remo suggested.

"Possibly. But in order to take control of that company, he would have to wrest away not only the Nostrum holdings but also those of the Lippincott Mercantile Bank and DeGoone Slickens. Slickens and Looncraft were bitter enemies all during the takeover mania of the eighties. Once Slickens learns that Looncraft is after Global Communications, he will attempt to hold him up for the moon. Hmm. This would explain why Looncraft hasn't made an overt move for Global. He may be counting on a Monday stock collapse to depress the prices enough that the other holders will be forced to sell."

"I do not understand any of this," Chiun complained.

"Neither do I," Remo admitted. "If Looncraft is willing to wait for a panic sell-off, why is he after Nostrum? He could wait Chiun out too."

"He knows I am cannier than that," Chiun insisted. "My reputation has preceded me."

"No," Smith said slowly. "Remo is exactly correct." Remo shot Chiun a Chesire-cat grin. Chiun flounced around, presenting his colorful back to Remo.

"This requires more thought," Smith muttered half to himself. "There must be more to this business. And where does Reuters fit into this? Looncraft has no connection with them, so far as I know."

"You know," Remo said, "Looncraft struck me as being very English."

"Looncraft? Nonsense. His family has been in America almost as long as my own. Looncrafts helped build this country. Wall Street lore says that when the stock market was first formed in the shade of a tree near what is now Wall Street, a Looncraft was part of the agreement. Today P. M. Looncraft is hailed as the King of the Street."

"Funny," Remo said. "He told me almost the exact same thing—except he didn't mention the part about the tree."

"Looncraft is as American as I am," Smith said firmly. "Whatever he is up to, he is an American."

"He talked like a Brit," Remo insisted. "Except for his accent. That's the part that threw me. He sounded kinda like a Hollywood actor trying to pass for English. He had the slang down pat, but not the sound."

"His family predates the Revolution. Perhaps he is proud of his lineage."

"Yeah, he did seem pretty smug about the whole thing," Remo admitted.

Chiun spoke up. "A Korean is a Korean," he said sagely.

"What's that?" Smith asked, his brow furrowing.

"I have lived in this country for many years," Chiun explained, "but I have not lost my Koreanness. I have had ancestors who dwelt in Egypt and Siam and Tibet, standing guard at thrones for most of their adult lives. Yet when they returned to Sinanju, to retire or to die or to be buried, no one questioned their Koreanness simply because they had dwelt apart for a span of time."

"What are you trying to say, Master of Sinanju?" Smith asked, interested.

"I am saying that where one dwells does not change what one is," Chiun said. "I have noticed in this country that if one is white, one is considered an American after but one generation. But a Korean or a Chinese or a Turk is considered a Korean or a Chinese or a Turk in his heart, regardless of the number of years he had spent here."

"I still do not get your drift," Smith said, mystified.

"If Remo felt that this Looncraft person was English, perhaps he is," Chiun answered. "In his heart."

"Looncraft is no more English than I."

"You know," Remo put in, "that was the other thing about him. Now that I think of it, he kinda reminded me of you, Smith."

"Hush, Remo," Chiun admonished. To Smith he said, "You hail from the province called New England, Smith?"

"I grew up in Vermont and New Hampshire," Smith admitted. "But New England is just a name now. It has no political meaning. If you mean to suggest that this matter may have British origins, I'm afraid you have a great deal to learn about American culture."

"And you have much to learn about human nature," Chiun retorted.

"I will accept that," Smith said thoughtfully. "Now, this is what I think we should do. If Looncraft's goal is Global Communications, there is no reason, now that we know he's in back of this problem, not to sell him Nostrum's shares. He should back away from Nostrum. Perhaps that will take the pressure off the stock market as well. If Looncraft can consummate a successful takeover of Global, by whatever public means, the market might be encouraged by that transaction."

"Are you sure?" Remo asked. "We could be playing into his hands."

"Above everything else, we must avoid a Monday-morning crash. If Looncraft is our stock manipulator, there will be time enough to deal with him. The stock market comes first. Are you agreeable, Master of Sinanju?"

"Why ask me?" Chiun said in a dry voice. "I do not own Nostrum alone. There is Remo, my secretary, who keeps secrets even from me."

"I told you," Remo said wearily. "I had no idea I had stock in Nostrum."

"And the bored directors," Chiun added, "who are aptly named, for I have never seen any of them."

"Board of directors," Smith said. "And I will obtain their proxy votes. They are just straw men."

"Did you hear that, Remo?" Chiun growled. "I am co-owner of an important corporation with a bear and scarecrows."

"Hey, I warned you this was a snow job all along," Remo shot back. "Don't complain to me. Complain to Smith."

"I will do as you suggest, Smith," Chiun said at last. "But only to protect my corporation from this duplicitous raider."

"It is for the best," Smith said. "And I suggest you make the arrangements tonight. The sooner the better."

Remo stood up as Chiun turned on his heel and padded from Smith's office.

"One moment, Remo," Smith called after him.

"Forget it, Smith," Remo called over his shoulder. "I don't work for you. I'm officially on Chiun's payroll now. I pull down a cool two sixty-nine an hour."

"Actually, Remo, I was hoping you might push me to my car," Smith said, rolling out from behind his desk.

Remo stopped. "Oh, I forgot about the chair. Well, why not? It's on the way."

Remo got behind Smith's wheelchair and started push-ing. He joined Chiun in the elevator and guided Smith out to the parking lot.

"Open the car door, will you, Chiun?" Remo asked.

As the Master of Sinanju opened the driver's door, Remo carefully picked Smith up in both arms—Smith felt surprisingly light—and deposited him behind the wheel.

"Thank you, Remo," Smith said quietly.

"Can you really drive like this?" Remo asked solicitously as he slammed the door closed.

"My legs will not support me just yet, but I can manage the pedals." Smith started the car up. "Please keep me informed," he said, and pulled away.

Remo watched him go, his face sad.

"I feel sort of sorry for him, you know. Even after all he's put me through."

"And me," Chiun said. "Do not forget his base trickery."

"That's Smith for you," Remo said. "Okay, let's get a move on. The corporate jet awaits. . . ."

13

The private estate of P. M. Looncraft was a two-story manor in the Great Neck section of Long Island. Designed by a Welsh architect, it was built of firebrick inside and out so that in the event of a fire the ashes could be hauled away, the indestructible walls hosed down, and the old furniture replaced with new literally overnight. The house was also as earthquake-proof as it was possible to make a house. It was built to withstand hurricanes, tornadoes and any other natural cataclysm short of a direct nuclear strike.

A lead-lined fallout shelter fifty feet below the basement awaited that eventuality.

P. M. Looncraft had no more fear of fire than any

homeowner, but he treasured his orderly, well-regimented life. He saw no one and engaged in no activity that would inhibit his six-day work week. And in its baronial splendor, his home was designed to shield him from outside intrusion.

Time was money to P. M. Looncraft. But his privacy was sacred.

So when the soft wind-chimelike tinkling of his front doorbell filtered into his cheery living room, P. M. Looncraft's long face collapsed in a disapproving frown. He detested visitors—especially unannounced ones.

Looncraft's butler padded out of the pantry and said in precise Oxbridge English, "I shall see who it is, master."

Looncraft said nothing. That in itself signaled that he neither expected nor welcomed whoever was at his door.

Taking a pinch of snuff from a monogrammed box, Looncraft put the unwanted visitor out of his mind as he delicately inhaled it through each nostril. His butler, Danvers, was a product of the finest English butlering school. No one entered Looncraft's firebrick castle unless Danvers allowed him in.

Danvers' low-pitched voice drifted in from the foyer, politely and precisely informing the visitor—whoever he might be—that Mr. Looncraft was not in to callers.

Danvers' voice repeated the sentence in a slightly more insistent voice, and then again in a kind of high girlish skirl.

"Gentlemen, please! You are tresp—"

The abruptness with which Danvers' voice was cut off shocked P. M. Looncraft to his feet. He started for the fireproof safe that occupied one corner of the room. It covered a trapdoor that connected to the bomb shelter with a fire-pole. P. M. Looncraft was keenly aware of the threat kidnappers presented to the modern businessman.

Looncraft got halfway across the room before a cool and casual voice asked him a question.

"Where do you want him?" the voice said.

Looncraft turned. A lean young man of indeterminate age was coming into the room. He carried Danvers, all six-foot-one and 211 pounds of him, under one arm as if carrying a goose-feather pillow.

Even more remarkable, Danvers did not resist. He simply hung there, his arms and legs and neck frozen as if from sudden rigor mortis.

"Danvers! Good God, man! What's happened to you?" P. M. Looncraft called in his precise New England voice.

Danvers' mouth was locked in the open position. His tongue squirmed as if trying to make consonants, but the only sound came from his nose. It buzzed. Rather like a fly.

"What have you done to Danvers?" Looncraft said coldly.

"Long story," the intruder said unconcernedly. "So where do you want him?" He was dressed in his underwear, Looncraft saw to his horror. He wore a white T-shirt and chino pants. "C'mon, I haven't got all night."

"On the divan," Looncraft said. And because he pointed, Remo Williams, who didn't know a divan from Saran Wrap, knew enough to put him on the sofa.

Danvers settled on the cushions in a kind of upended-beetle position. He didn't move, even when he started to tip over. The man pushed him back with a casual if contemptible gesture.

"What is the meaning of this?" Looncraft asked stiffly. He took a step backward. The intruder appeared to be unarmed, but Looncraft knew that certain kinds of men, like other predators, would chase you if you ran from them. Looncraft would not run. He was a Looncraft. Except, of course, to preserve his life.

"Someone wants a meet with you."

"I am going nowhere with you, you interloper."

"That's fine. Because he's come to you."

Then a fantastic figure stepped into the room. He was a little man, of doubtful Asiatic heritage, Looncraft saw. He wore an outlandish blue-and-gold ceremonial garment. His hands were linked like an old-fashioned postcard Chinaman's in his touching wide sleeves.

"I am Chiun," he said formally, his hazel eyes glittering. "Chief of Nostrum, Ink."

"You have some nerve intruding upon my home," Looncraft said, curling his thin upper lip disdainfully.

"I will overlook your impertinence in not accepting my calls, white," the one called Chiun said as the other man folded his arms like some skinny eunuch in a high-school production of *The King and I.* "For I have come to make peace with you."

"Peace?"

"You covet Nostrum," said Chiun, stepping closer. His sandals made no sound on the bare brick flooring. "Yet I have reason to believe that it is not Nostrum you truly desire, but these."

The joined sleeves parted like a train uncoupling, to reveal a sheaf of folded papers clutched in one ivory claw. Looncraft recognized them as stock certificates.

"And what, pray tell, are those?" Looncraft wanted to know.

"I told you he sounded almost English," the lean man put in suddenly.

"He does not sound at all English," Chiun retorted, not looking away from Looncraft's gaze. "But he speaks like an inhabitant of Gaul."

Looncraft emitted a barking laugh. "Gaul! My dear heathen."

"Do not call me that," Chiun said coldly. "My ancestors were known throughout the civilized world when yours were painting themselves blue and wearing animal skins."

Looncraft's disdainfully curled upper lip almost disappeared as it locked with his lower lip.

"I offer these stocks to you," Chiun continued, "because I have been advised that it is the prudent thing to do."

"At market or—?"

"In gold," Chiun returned. "No checks."

"I'm afraid I have no gold on hand," Looncraft said in an amused voice.

"Take cash," the man in the T-shirt put in.

Chiun hesitated. His clear eyes narrowed, and Looncraft wondered if he was some kind of half-breed. He detested people of diluted heritage.

"Very well," Chiun said unhappily.

"One moment," Looncraft said, going to his safe. He knelt and twirled the tumblers. Opening a box, he withdrew a stack of hundred dollar bills, broke the bank's paper band, and counted out a precise number of bills.

"If you are surrendering your entire holding," Looncraft

said after he closed the safe, "this should cover the transaction."

The two men exchanged sheafs of paper. Chiun ran his fingers along the top of the stack of bills, his eyes focused.

"Not going to count it?" Looncraft said. "Trusting sort, eh?"

"You are right. I should recount," Chiun said. He fanned the bills again and, satisfied, tucked the money in one sleeve.

"These certificates seem to be in order," Looncraft said after going through the surrendered stock. "I trust that concludes our somewhat unorthodox transaction."

"You have what you covet, businessman," Chiun intoned coldly. "Now you will leave Nostrum alone."

"I am a businessman, as you say. I do only what is good for business. And I see you are very serious in your own way."

"So be it," Chiun said, turning on his heel and leaving the room. He called over his shoulder, "Come, Remo."

"Wait! What about Danvers?" Looncraft demanded.

Remo paused at the door. "Stick him next to the fire for a while. His muscles should soften up in no time."

"But—"

The outer door closed and P. M. Looncraft walked over to his arthritic nightmare of a butler.

"Danvers," Looncraft said shortly. "I expect a full explanation of this dereliction of duty from you."

Danvers only buzzed.

Outside, Remo held the car door open for Chiun, who settled into the passenger side like blue smoke rolling into a cave.

"What do you think, Chiun?" Remo asked as he climbed behind the wheel.

"I think that man is not to be trusted."

"He's got what he wants."

"Such men as he never get what they want. Their appetites are too large."

"Takes one to know one," Remo said, pulling away from the palatial estate. "If you don't mind, I'm going to drop you off at the hotel."

"And where are you going?" Chiun squeaked.

"I got a date. With Faith."

"I am not certain I approve of my employees fraternizing."

"Who are you, Simon Legree?" Remo asked. "She used to work for Looncraft. I'm just going to get the inside story. In case we have more problems with him."

"Very well," Chiun sniffed. "Just remember—no fraternizing."

"Scout's honor," Remo said.

Remo Williams felt good as he entered the lobby of Faith Davenport's upper Manhattan apartment house. He had showered, shaved, and changed into a fresh T-shirt and chinos.

As far as he knew, he didn't smell at all like a bear, but the pickled expression that came over the blue-blazered lobby guard's face as he approached the reception desk made him wonder.

"Remo Stallone to see Faith Davenport," Remo said with a straight face.

"Is she expecting you?"

"None other," Remo fired back confidently.

"One moment." The guard went to a typewriter and rattled the keys. Pulling the sheet from the roller, he inserted it into a copier-type device and pressed a button that said "Send."

"Computer?" Remo asked, curious.

"Fax machine."

"Isn't that a phone next to it?" Remo asked, pointing to a desk phone.

"You are very observant," the guard said coolly.

"I happen to be corporate secretary to Nostrum, Ink," Remo told him smugly.

The guard looked at Remo over his glasses wordlessly. His expression was a supercilious: Oh, really?

As they waited for a reply, Remo asked, "Why not just pick up the phone and announce me?"

"We do not intrude upon our guests in this building," the guard sniffed.

The fax machine hummed and a new sheet of paper

rolled out. The guard read it and looked up, disappointment writ large on his face.

"You may go up," he said. "It's the twenty-first floor. Apartment C. That's Twenty-one-C," he added smugly.

"Thanks," Remo said, glad to get away from the distasteful look on the guard's face.

On the twenty-first floor he buzzed twice. Faith Davenport opened the door, a smile on her face and a gleam in her blue eyes.

Almost at once her face fell, matching almost line for line the downstairs guard's expression.

"Oh," she said in a disappointed tone.

Remo blinked. "Something wrong?"

"I thought you were taking me out."

"I am. My car's downstairs."

Faith's gaze raked his fresh T-shirt. "Which did you have in mind—McDonald's, or were you going to splurge and take me to Charley O's?"

Remo forced a smile. "We'll go wherever you want."

"I'm used to eating in places that require proper dress. And ties."

"I don't wear ties," Remo said, feeling his mood sink.

"Or shirts either," Faith said, stepping back with studied reluctance so Remo could enter.

Remo was surprised at the elegance of Faith's apartment and said so as the door closed behind him.

"How do you afford all this on a secretary's salary?"

"I play the market. I'm hoping to go back to school. Can I fix you a drink? Some Zinfandel or Grenache?"

"Actually, I don't drink," Remo admitted.

Faith used tongs to clink ice into two glasses, and looked over at him.

"You don't drink or wear business clothes," she wondered, "so what are you doing working for Nostrum, Ink?"

"What's with you?" Remo asked, suddenly annoyed. "I was dressed like this when you first met me."

"When I first met you, I didn't know you were an employee. And it is Saturday. We sometimes dress down on Saturdays. Evian water okay?"

"Sure," Remo said, suddenly feeling like he'd shown up at a formal affair in Halloween costume.

Faith came over and handed him a drink. She sat down and took a sip of Scotch. When her mouth came up, it reeked of alcohol fumes. Remo's eyes left her no-longer-quite-delectable lips and shifted to her eyes. They were veiled.

Faith took another sip. "Maybe we could order out."

"If you want," Remo said, thinking that he had hoped to end up back at this apartment, and not going out turned that possibility into a certainty.

"I know this wonderful Italian place," she said, putting down her drink. "Their pesto is superb." She twisted around and picked up the phone. She dialed as she put a pencil to a piece of paper and began checking off boxes.

"Want me to order for you?" she asked. "Everything's good."

"Actually, I have a lot of food allergies," Remo said quickly. "I'm on a strict rice-and-fish diet. Sometimes rice and duck."

"I never heard of an Italian restaurant that served duck," Faith said, frowning, her pencil poised. "I guess we'll have to go with fish."

"Fine with me," Remo said, noticing the chilliness creep into her voice.

Faith inserted a slip of paper into a fax and pressed "Send."

"I don't know what I did before the fax," she said as the machine hummed.

"I usually made do with the telephone, primitive as it is."

"But with phones you have to actually talk to people. This is so much more efficient."

"It *is* quieter," Remo admitted.

Faith retrieved her drink. "Well, what shall we talk about while we're waiting?"

"Tell me about Looncraft," Remo suggested. "You worked there once."

Faith made a face. "Don't remind me. It was a cold place. I had to get out or I was going to go crazy."

"I hear Looncraft is called the King of Wall Street."

"Make that Prince," Faith said, making quote marks with her fingers. Remo hated it when people did that.

"The chief is already being touted as the new King of the Street."

"No kidding?" Remo said, ignoring his mineral water. "Where'd you hear that?"

"It's all over the street. Everyone is talking about him. Before that, everyone was wondering why Looncraft sold off his Global holdings."

"He did?"

" 'Did' is the word," Faith said, making quote marks again. "I hear that during the early hours of the meltdown he liquidated his position. Hours later, he bought it all back, and more, at a higher price than he'd first sold it."

"I don't know the market, but that doesn't sound logical to me."

"It's not. Even if Looncraft had suddenly gone contrarian."

"What's that?" Remo said, relieved that her fingers didn't dance with the unfamiliar word.

"A contrarian is an investor who swims against the tide. When everyone is selling, he buys. And vice versa."

"Sounds fishy."

"Enough of Looncraft. Tell me more about the chief. I find him fascinating."

"What about me?" he said, flashing his best boyish grin.

"Oh, you're nice too," Faith said dismissively. "But men in authority have always fascinated me."

"Is that so? Well, Chiun is eighty years old, grew up in a fishing village in Korea that smells like a thousand-year-old dead clam, and has a major crush on Cheeta Ching."

"He does?" Faith's voice dropped like a stone.

"Absolutely," Remo went on, warming to the subject. "He hates white people. Especially women."

"Oh," Faith said, taking an extra long sip from her drink. Then, deep in thought, she drained it and went back to the wet bar.

She returned with the tumbler filled almost to sloshing over. Her eyebrows knit into one slim unhappy eyebrow.

Son of a gun, Remo thought. She has a crush on Chiun.

The food came while Remo was attempting to revive the conversation.

Faith let the deliveryman in, paid him by credit card,

and set the Styrofoam package on the dining-nook table. Her face was pouty as she set plates.

"Help yourself," she called to Remo as she gathered together silverware.

Remo opened the package, and his sad expression turned to revulsion.

"I think they made a mistake," he said. "Unless you ordered squid over rice."

"It's supposed to be octopus. And it's yours."

"Yeah," Remo said, looking again, "the eyes do kinda look octopussy."

"You *did* say fish," Faith reminded him as she sat down.

"I said fish, not octopus. Octopus is something else."

"Octopus is very chic this season."

"Fine," Remo said, pushing his plate away. "Give mine to the sheiks. I don't eat octopus."

"Must be terrible to be allergic to food," Faith said unconcernedly. "I don't know what I'd do without good food and drink—and excellent sex."

Remo looked up from the mess on his plate, his face hopeful. But Faith was looking out the window at the Manhattan skyline, not at him.

He decided to take a shot at salvaging the night. "Excellent sex is my specialty," he said through his best smile.

"Mmm? What's that?" Faith asked, her eyes refocusing as they swept back toward him.

"I said excellent sex is my specialty."

"Is that so?" Mild interest came to her face. "What kind of visualizations do you use?"

"None," Remo said, surprised at the question.

"I think of money," Faith said dreamily. "Actually, power *really* makes me horny—but how do you visualize power? I mean, it's an abstract, right?"

"Not to me," Remo said in a sincere voice. "To me, power is very, very concrete."

"What do you mean?" Real interest showed in Faith Davenport's expression this time.

"I could show you, say, after you're finished eating," Remo suggested.

"Show me now," Faith insisted. "If it gets cold, I can nuke it in the microwave."

Remo shrugged and got up. "Give me your wrist," he said, putting out his hand.

Faith lifted her hand. Remo took it in one of his own. With the other, he found her wrist pulse with the tip of his forefinger.

"What are you doing?"

"I'm going to show you the power of my forefinger."

And Remo began tapping. Faith frowned in perplexity. But as the tapping finger found a rhythm, her features smoothed. Her eyes got dreamier, and she licked her lips at the corners. Her mouth grew redder and delectable once more.

"What . . . what are you doing?" she asked nervously. But she didn't attempt to pull her wrist away.

"When I'm done," Remo promised her, "you'll never look at a forefinger without getting incredibly aroused."

"Honestly?"

"After I'm done, a forefinger will represent power. You can visualize it and get instant results."

"I love instant results," Faith said, beginning to squirm in her seat. Her breathing picked up. Her eyes squinched shut. She moaned. It was a tortured but pleased moan. It told Remo that she was ready for him.

He stopped tapping.

"No! Don't stop!" she cried. "Not now."

Grinning, Remo resumed his tapping. And Faith resumed her tormented squirming. Her eyes closed completely now. Her free hand clutched the table edge.

In the years since Remo had learned Sinanju—learned it fully—he had found that the techniques through which he could master the physical universe could also tap into female sexuality. Unfortunately, the full power of Sinanju was too much for most women. Remo had to hold back. Right now, he was just giving Faith a taste. When he was through, she would, as Remo had promised, never be able to look at a male forefinger without becoming violently aroused. What he didn't tell her was that it would be his own finger that would never fail to arouse her.

Then it happened. Faith Davenport began to shiver uncontrollably.

"Oh," she cried. "No!" she cried. "Oh, no," she added.

"No No No. Yes Yes Yes!" And when her shivering subsided, her smile was dreamily goofy.

She began to slide off the chair and under the table. Remo pulled her back by her flutter-pulsed wrist.

"How was that?" he asked, grinning.

Faith Davenport didn't reply. She didn't hear the question. She had orgasmed into blissful unconsciousness, a frequent but not always inevitable side effect of Remo's technique.

"Damn!" Remo said bitterly. "I thought I had that passing-out stuff under control."

Sighing, Remo lifted her up in his arms and carried her into an immaculate white bedroom. He set her on the shiny brass bed and wondered what she would say if she woke up with him lying patiently beside her.

Then he got a sudden whiff of Scotch on her breath and had to suppress the gag reflex.

Remo decided the effort wouldn't be worth it.

He left the apartment, his face dejected. He could bring a woman to orgasm simply by touching her wrists. But keeping her conscious after foreplay was something he had yet to learn.

Down in the lobby, the guard smirked. "That was quick."

"Quicker than you think," Remo returned darkly, and stepped out into the cold night. As he stood on a street corner trying to remember where he had parked his car, a matronly woman in a floor-length mink coat offered him a dollar from her purse.

"Here, you poor homeless thing," she said. "It must be terrible to be without decent clothes on a cold night like this."

Remo stuffed the dollar back into the surprised woman's purse. "Keep it, lady," he snarled. "I happen to be a Wall Street tycoon. And I've got a fur that makes yours look sick."

The matron walked off in a huff.

14

Harold W. Smith arrived at his Folcroft office at six o'clock on the Sunday evening following Dark Friday. He laid his well-worn briefcase beside the desk and, settling into his cracked leather chair, pressed a concealed stud under the desk edge. Up from the left corner of the desktop a nondescript computer terminal rose like a glass-orbed Cyclops.

Smith logged on. He scanned domestic-news digests that were automatically culled from satellite newsfeeds and processed for him by the huge CURE mainframes concealed behind a false wall in the Folcroft basement. The country was awash in speculation about the coming trading day. Already the Israeli stock market—the only one in the world that operated on Sunday—was trading. It was down ten percentage points—significant, but not telling.

In another hour or so, at eight o'clock, the Tokyo, Singapore, and Hong Kong stock markets would open. They would give the first warning of a replay of the Friday financial air pocket and a foretaste—if it was to be—of another Black Monday.

Smith paged through the digests carefully. Already there was a flurry of rumors about planned mergers and acquisitions, now that stock prices had dropped so sharply. There would be a lot of bargain hunting available to investors brave enough to take the chance. And excellent opportunities for the few surviving corporate raiders who could muster financing.

He looked for any news concerning the elusive Crown Acquisitions, Limited. There was nothing. Whoever they were, they eschewed publicity.

Smith was deep in thought when the phone rang in the

outer reception area. Smith dismissed it as a wrong number, but it kept ringing. He picked up his desk phone and answered, sharp-voiced.

A businesslike woman's voice said, "Mr. Winthrop, of Winthrop and Weymouth, to speak with Mr. Smith."

"It is *Dr*. Smith," Smith said, "and please inform Mr. Winthrop that he should confine his calls to business hours. Good-bye." Smith hung up.

As the news reports scrolled past his eyes, throwing specks of green light onto his rimless eyeglasses, Smith shuffled through his papers for a memo from his secretary regarding Winthrop. He had been so engrossed in CURE matters that he had not glanced at his messages.

Finally he found it. One eye on the computer, he looked it over. The memo was brief: "Mr. Winthrop, of Winthrop and Weymouth, called." No message. It was personal.

Smith couldn't imagine what Winthrop wanted, so he put it out of his mind.

Finally trading began in Asia. The market started down in heavy trading. Then it rose ten points in twenty minutes. Smith's bloodless face suffused with relief—then there came a precipitous twenty-five-point drop.

From there, it was a roller coaster—with Dr. Harold W. Smith following every rise and dip as if his life depended upon it.

It did not, but the future well-being of his country did depend on what was happening in the Far Eastern markets.

In the darkness of his office, a phrase occurred to Harold W. Smith—a line of poetry from his schooldays, which in the heat of the moment were twisted in a rare display of creativity on the part of the unimaginative bureaucrat.

"And ignorant armies trade by night," Smith muttered.

Smith was still at his desk at six A.M. when his secretary came in. The Far Eastern markets had long since closed. The trading had shifted to Europe. It was volatile, there was no doubt about it. Even the blue-chips were softening. The global market was taking a beating, but it was holding together. But anything could happen when the tidal wave of uncertainty hit Wall Street.

During a lull in the trading, Smith went to a closet and took out a gray three-piece suit identical to the one he had worn through the night. He changed in his private rest room, shocked by the emaciated appearance of his limbs as he stood in his underwear before a full length mirror. It still surprised him that he had gotten so old so quickly. The responsibilities he bore on his shoulders as head of CURE were staggering. He had been at them for nearly three decades now. He wondered how much longer he could stay at his post—and what would happen when at last his health failed, as it nearly had only a few months before.

Smith brushed the dark thought from his mind as he shaved with the old-fashioned straight razor that his father had presented to him on his sixteenth birthday. It seemed like a thousand years ago. As he scraped the stubble from his chin, he was reminded again by his reflection how much he was his father's son. The face that stared back at him from the mirror was almost his father's own. Not as full, but the eyes were the same, as was the spare yet crisp white hair.

It was like looking at a family ghost. A ghost whose familiar eyes followed his every move and whose facial expressions mimicked his own. Sometimes Smith hated the taunting familiarity of the face in the mirror. Other times it took him back to childhood, like a long-misplaced photograph.

Smith wiped his face clean of Barbasol and put on a fresh white shirt. He knotted his striped Dartmouth tie expertly in a quick half-Windsor, only because it was faster than the much-preferred full Windsor.

Then, putting on his vest and coat, he returned to his desk, refreshed and ready for the Big Board's opening bell.

The moment he sat down, his knees began to shake. He was prepared to remain at his lonely post long after the closing bell, when the cycle would begin all over again in Tokyo, with no respite until Saturday, a full six days away.

It was going to be a long six days, Harold Smith realized. God had created the earth in six days. He wondered it if would take even that long for modern civilization to unravel.

And then it was ten o'clock. Smith engaged the Quotron window, his heart high and anxious in his throat.

The Master of Sinanju entered the trading room of Nostrum, Ink with a satisfied expression on his wrinkled countenance. All was well with the world once more, now that he had evaded the hostile takeover of Nostrum.

But the very instant he entered the room, his tiny nose wrinkled at a foul but familiar smell. It was fear—the raw mingling of leaking sweat and openmouthed breathing.

"What is wrong, my loyal minions?" he asked in shock.

A trader looked up with the hurt expression of a seal that had been hit by a paddle.

"We're bombed here!" he cried, his voice sick.

"Bombed!" Chiun demanded. "Where? I see no damage."

Remo stuck his head out of Chiun's office.

"It's just an expression," he said.

Another trader clutched his phone and moaned. "It's a massacre!" he wailed.

"Where?" Chiun asked, coming to his side. The trader cradled the receiver between his chin and shoulder. "It's all up and down the street. The blood is flowing."

"This *is* terrible," Chiun squeaked. "Is America at war?"

"It's just an expression, Chiun," Remo called again.

Chiun looked back to Remo. "What are you saying, Remo? My loyal minions would never lie to me. You heard them. People are being bombed. There is blood flowing in the street. It is a calamity. Such things are never good for business."

"This *is* business," Remo said wearily. "The market is crashing. This is how these people talk."

"Is this true?" Chiun demanded.

"The Dow's dropped seventy points in the last half-hour," the trader said in anguish. "It's a rout."

"Never surrender!" Chiun cried. "No matter who the foe, Nostrum will prevail. I promise you that."

"Will you come in here, Chiun?" Remo called sharply.

The Master of Sinanju called out, "Take heart. I am with you now," and floated into his office.

"The market's melting down," Remo told him tightly. "And forget that double-talk. It's just business jargon."

"But it is war talk."

"That's how these people see business," Remo explained. "As war. They call it competition. And listen, this is serious. Nostrum stock is dropping too. Everything's dropping."

"I have no fear," Chiun retorted, "for I have gold."

"Gold is dropping too."

Chiun started. "What is this? Gold is dropping?" He looked around frantically. "Where is Faith? I must have her by my side. She will advise me what to do."

Remo tripped the floor intercom with a toe. He hastily shoved both hands in his pockets when Faith stepped into the room moments later. Her blue eyes sought Remo's half-hidden wrists and expressed heartrending disappointment.

"Gold is dropping," Chiun squeaked. "What do I do?"

"Buy," she said quickly. "Now is the time to pick up bargains."

"But these stocks are becoming more worthless by the hour."

"That's *this* hour. In another hour they could double in price. I would go long."

"Go along with whom?" Chiun asked.

"Not 'along,' " Faith said. "Go long on the stocks. Hold on to your positions in anticipation of long-term growth. And buy more."

"With what?"

"Gold. Gold is dropping. If gold keeps dropping, it'll be worth less than most blue-chip stocks."

Chiun turned to Remo. "Is she mad? Sell gold for paper?"

"Faith's been playing the market for years," he pointed out. "You should see her apartment. I have."

Chiun stuck his head out the office door. "Buy! Buy everything!" he cried. "Nostrum, Ink is paying gold for stock. Let the word go out. Strictly cash-and-carry."

With a wild shout of "Let's go for it!" the traders got on their phones and began trading.

Within ten minutes the messengers began arriving, followed by armored-car drivers and even feverish individual brokers. They crowded the Nostrum trading room and corridors, fighting one another to hand over folded stock certificates in return for gold ingots. They hurried off, carrying them in sacks and stuffed into suit pockets.

As Remo and Faith struggled to keep order, Faith brushed up against Remo. Her tongue tickled his right earlobe.

"Last night was wonderful," she whispered breathily.

"I'm glad it was for someone," Remo complained, shoving a frantic stockbroker so hard his horn-rimmed glasses broke in two.

The phone rang and P. M. Looncraft's secretary informed him that it was the chairman of the New York Stock Exchange.

Looncraft took the call. The market was down another dozen points in the last nineteen seconds. At this rate, the bargains would be enormous, just as he had hoped.

"Yes?" he said.

"We've suspended trading twice today."

"The circuit breakers are working admirably."

"Except every time trading resumes, so does the panic," the chairman said grimly. "I'm polling all NYSE board members. We should consider suspending trading for the remainder of the day. Give the institutions time to regroup."

"I think that would be premature," Looncraft said, smiling tightly to himself. If the chairman was panicked, then it would be a rout. His avid eyes slid to his Telerate screen.

P. M. Looncraft blinked. The market shot up two points. Then ten. Then twenty. It was like a thermometer on an August day in Panama.

"Wait a minute," the chairman said, cupping his hand over the phone.

When his voice returned, it was jubilant. "The market's regrouping. There's a buying frenzy going on."

"Capital," P. M. Looncraft said in a shaky voice. His cheeks squeezed tight. His mouth became a puckered pink rip in his long face.

"Apparently Nostrum, Ink is offering gold for blue-chip stocks," the chairman said excitedly. "Others are upticking."

"Why is that?" Looncraft asked, making no attempt to keep the peevishness from his tone.

"Haven't you heard? Everyone is saying Nostrum is run by a wizard. They're calling him the King of Wall Street."

"*What?*" Looncraft shouted. "But I am the King of Wall Street. *Forbes* says so."

"Don't shout at me, P.M. That's the rumor on the street. Everyone knows that this Chiun person is a financial genius. Right now, where he goes, others follow. It's a herd reaction. And thank God for that. He may have saved the market."

"Excuse me," Looncraft said huffily. "I have trading of my own to attend to."

"Good luck."

"Luck is not a factor." Looncraft stabbed his intercom.

"Send Johnson in," he barked, forgetting not to mention the man by name.

When Ronald Johnson entered, nervously fingering his gold tie, Looncraft looked up at him with a face like a stormcloud.

"I am prepared to go forward with my offer for Nostrum, Ink," he said angrily. "Set it up."

"Yes, sir. And what about the Global acquisition?"

"It goes forward. Full-bore. I will handle the details myself."

In his office at Folcroft Sanitarium, an ashen-faced Harold W. Smith watched the Quotron numbers rise. He brought up a news digest and learned that the market was responding to the confidence shown by the mysterious financial wizard of Nostrum, Ink. Smith blinked. "Inc." was misspelled. He had never seen his computer misspell a word before. But that imponderable was lost in the torrent of buy orders reflected on the electronic ticker tape.

It was 10:45. In London, the Financial Times Stock Exchange was winding down on a modest up note. It was the same in other European markets as they neared the end of their trading day.

Harold Smith removed his glasses. He knew the psychology of the market. There was no guarantee it would hold at these high prices, but a climb of 265 points in an hour was an encouraging sign.

If it continued, perhaps the crisis had passed.

At four o'clock, the closing bell sounded and Wall Street, up a stunning six hundred points, breathed a collective sigh of relief.

"Rich!" Chiun cried, standing among the exhausted heap of floor traders who lay sprawled in their deskless cubicles. "We are all rich beyond our wildest dreams."

"On paper," Remo put in.

Chiun's outspread arms froze. His uptilted head snapped around. He fixed Remo with his steel eyes.

"What do you mean, on paper?" he demanded.

"You're rich only if you sell your stock."

"Then sell!" Chiun cried. "Sell everything!"

"Can't do that," Remo said firmly, shaking his head. "The market's closed." Faith was by his side, her arms wrapped around his bare forearms. She was trying to tug one of his hands out of his pocket, but Remo refused to budge.

Chiun turned on Faith. "What is this?"

"He's right, Chief," Faith said, giving up Remo's hand for the moment. "You have to sell the stock to realize its value. But that would be a mistake. Hold on to it. The price will go up more. The market is bullish."

"Bullish," Chiun mused. "I have heard of this bullishness. Sometimes called B.S."

"That's not the kind of bullish Faith means," Remo said. "And she's right. If the market keeps climbing, the stock value could double or triple."

"Ah. *Then* I should sell, correct?"

"No," Faith said. "Go long. Hold on to it as long as you can. Never liquidate a solid position with growth potential."

"Then how am I to make my profit if I do not sell?" Chiun asked in a puzzled tone.

"Don't think profit," Faith said, "think value. Think equity."

"Right at this moment," Chiun said, an edge creeping into his voice, "I am thinking of the gold I have sold."

"It's not your gold, remember?" Remo pointed out. "It's Nostrum's."

"Why do you think I sold it?" Chiun retorted. "If it were my gold, I would never have sold it."

"Just think of it as money in the bank," Faith said.

Remo uncoupled Faith's reactivated fingers from his wrist. "If the market drops tomorrow," he asked her, "what kind of shape would we be in?"

"Depends. Almost all of our assets are tied up in stock now. We could be wiped out."

"Wiped out?" Chiun squeaked. "By whom?"

"More business talk," Remo said hastily. "It means 'broke.' "

Chiun's eyes slowly widened. "Broke. As in 'impoverished'?"

"As in 'destitute,' " Remo said, nodding.

"Almost impossible," Faith said firmly. "The market is on an upswing."

"Almost?" Chiun squeaked.

"It's a volatile market," Faith admitted. "But this is where the big bucks are. If you want security, you don't invest in stocks."

"What do you invest in?" Chiun wanted to know.

Faith frowned. "Any number of things. Money-market accounts, CD's—"

Chiun's phone rang and Remo went into the office to answer it. He stuck his head out and mouthed the name "Smith" silently. Chiun hurried to the office and closed the door on Faith's annoyed face.

"Smith?" Chiun said urgently. "I need your advice."

"That's quite flattering, coming from the man whom the networks are calling the King of Wall Street."

"I?"

"I am calling to congratulate you," Smith continued. "You did an excellent job."

"Why not?" Chiun said proudly. "I am the King of Wall Street."

"But there is a problem," Smith added cautiously.

"Yes?"

"I have just learned that Looncraft is attempting a series of hostile takeovers. Global is a prime target."

"I am not concerned with that," Chiun retorted.

"Nor am I. One major block of GLB is owned by

DeGoone Slickens. He will never sell to Looncraft. And there are still the mysterious Crown people and the Lippincott holdings. Lippincott is Looncraft's banker and has been chary of takeover moves since last year's junk-bond shakeout. I can't imagine Looncraft could pull off such a risky deal."

"Why tell me?" Chiun said peevishly.

"Because Looncraft has also tendered an offer on Nostrum, Inc."

"That deceiver!" Chiun shrieked. He turned to Remo. "Looncraft is attempting to attack Nostrum, my precious Nostrum, again."

"We can handle him," Remo said confidently.

"Where is the suit?" Chiun hissed.

"Safe."

"Get it."

"I don't think Looncraft's frightened of Bear-Man."

"Then terrify him," Chiun said. Returning to his phone conversation, Chiun asked, "I am told my stock positions are not secure, Smith. I wish to invest in less risky instruments. What do you suggest?"

"CD's are very safe."

"Then I will sell all my stock and invest in CD's," Chiun thundered.

"No, Master of Sinanju," Smith said quickly. "Please make no major moves. All of Wall Street is watching you. If you sell off, others will too. Hold on to your positions."

"But they are risky," Chiun complained. "I could be wiped out at any moment."

"Sell some stock, if you wish," Smith said placatingly. "A little here and there. But for God's sake, do it quietly. Wall Street must not get the idea you are fleeing into cash."

"I am not fleeing into anything," Chiun said indignantly. "But I will do as you say. I will buy CD's. Quietly."

"Thank you, Master Chiun. Now, if you'll excuse me, I must prepare myself. The Asian markets reopen in another few hours. They will tell me if the international situation is stabilizing or not. I will be in touch."

15

The busy hum of Folcroft Sanitarium was winding down as Harold W. Smith watched the first reports come in from the Far East exchanges.

Prices remained firm. The volatility of the American market hadn't spilled east. Slowly, tentatively, the tense-ness in Smith's unhealthy face slackened.

After an hour, Smith felt confident enough to log off the Reuters overseas ticker feeds. He got to his feet and stretched. Every joint felt starch-stiff. For a moment his vision grayed over. It was something that happened to him more and more these days when he got to his feet too suddenly. The blood rushed from his head, starving his brain of nourishment.

Steadying himself with a hand on his silent terminal, Smith waited for his vision to return. When it did, he turned and looked out the one-way picture window be-hind his desk. It framed a view of Long Island Sound, now benighted and dancing with silvery moonglade.

It was a view Smith had seen a thousand times, but it never failed to quiet his restive New England soul. It reminded him of his childhood. The wild forests of his Vermont childhood and the rocky New Hamphire moun-tains of his adolescence.

Harold Smith missed few things of his childhood, but the sense of place was one of them. Rye, New York, was not far removed from Putney, Vermont, but it was not the same. The red leaves of fall were not as scarlet, the golds nowhere near as scintillating. He missed the scent of burning leaves and the sharp bite of frost in the air.

But most of all he missed the stability. In New England, Harold Smith had known from an early age that he would go into law. His ambitions took him from Dartmouth to Harvard Law, and ultimately to a professorship at Yale. It was all he could ever want. But World War II had intervened and Harold Smith had found his sharp mind and steady nerve needed in the European theater of operations, where as a clandestine OSS operative he mastered explosives and fear and, ultimately, victory.

After the war, Yale no longer seemed enough. And as the old OSS gave way to the new CIA, Harold Smith found a place in cold-war counterintelligence. The years had turned him into a bureaucrat, not a warrior. But it was the stability of a desk and an office routine and the absence of sudden death that spoke to Harold Smith. He had gotten his fill of war.

Smith never completely abandoned the dimming hope of one day returning to Yale—until the day in the early 1960's when a young President, in the last months of his tragically brief presidency, offered him the directorship of CURE. Smith had never heard of CURE. In fact, the agency that supposedly didn't exist, really *didn't* exist when it was offered to Smith. Smith would be CURE. Without his sterling qualities, CURE might not be viable, he was told.

With reluctance, Smith accepted the most awesome responsibility in the world outside of the Oval Office.

Only then did Harold Smith finally put away his dream of returning to Yale. There would be no Yale in his future. There was only his duty.

It was that same sense of duty that had infuriated Harold Smith's patrician father, Nathan. Any other man might have been proud of a son who had so distinguished himself in law and service to his nation.

Not Nathan Smith.

Even after all these years, Harold Smith could still hear his father's cold voice rising in indignation.

"What about the family business, Harold?"

"I have no aptitude for publishing, Father," Smith had said with the simple, unchallengeable logic that dominated his thinking.

"You can learn, boy. The Smiths have been in publishing for over a hundred years."

"My mind is made up," Smith said stiffly. He did not want to remind his father that the family firm of Smith & Smith had gotten its start publishing dime novels during the Civil War and graduated to cheap fiction magazines at the turn of the century. Nathan Smith never allowed one of his firm's magazines into the house. He didn't object to publishing them, but he felt it beneath the dignity of a true Smith to be caught reading one.

"Take the summer off. Come work for the firm." For the first time, Nathan Smith's voice lifted. It was almost wheedling.

"I am sorry, Father," Harold Smith said, and he meant it. It was the first time Harold had ever stood up to his father, and it was painful beyond endurance. He had received a full scholarship to Dartmouth. The matter was out of crotchety Nathan Smith's hands. To a man used to being obeyed without question, it was an unforgivable slight.

Smith's unwarm relationship with his father cooled completely after that day. He continued to pay the usual respects during family holidays, but as the years passed and his responsibilities increased, it became less and less possible to visit the family compound in New Hampshire.

His mother had passed away first, in her sleep. Harold and Nathan Smith, although over twenty years apart in age, were by then two aging men. At the funeral they spoke barely a word to one another. Harold had tried, but was curtly rebuffed. Nathan Smith's bitter disappointment in his son was expressed in his too-loud complaints to other mourners that Harold's lazy cousins were mismanaging the family firm, preventing Nathan Smith from entering honored retirement.

The next time Harold saw his father, six years later, he was in a wheelchair and his wheezing breath fogged the clear plastic oxygen mask affixed to his mouth. The eyes were unchanged, pale, disappointed, and cold as glacial ice.

Harold hadn't known what to say to his father. He never had. By that time, Smith had assumed his responsibilities as director of CURE.

"Father, I think we should put aside our differences," Smith had suggested in a quiet voice.

Old Nathan Smith looked daggers at his grown son. He spoke three words, the last words he would ever speak to his only son, who had always been dutiful except for that one matter.

"You disappoint me," Nathan Smith had croaked.

And as Harold Smith left his father in the Gilmore County Retirement Home—the same brick building he used to walk by every day on the way to high school—he felt an aching void in the pit of his stomach. By then the family firm was only a publisher of movie fan magazines and crossword-puzzle books, but CURE was the fire wall that stood between American democracy and anarchy.

Smith had fulfilled his resolute sense of duty to a degree his narrow-minded father could never have imagined, and never learned. He died a week later.

But the sense of guilt Harold Smith had felt after their final meeting never went away. It was like a cold pill forever caught in his throat.

As Smith came out of his reverie, the shadowy reflection of his face in the Folcroft picture window shocked him. It was his father's face. Harold Smith's eyes darted to the wheelchair standing alone in the corner like a stainless-steel ghost. It might have been the very chair his father had ended up in. The thought that Smith had, for a few months, been consigned to one just like it chilled him anew.

Returning to his desk, Smith wondered what had made him reflect on his troubled family past. He decided it was just that he was overworked.

He logged onto the Far Eastern stock reports. From Sydney to Singapore, the markets remained stable. Smith wondered if the world's economy was out of the woods yet. He hoped so. He itched to isolate the forces that had triggered a global near-meltdown.

For he wanted to punish them. He wanted to punish them more than he had wanted to punish anyone who had ever come into the CURE operational orbit.

Above all, Harold W. Smith treasured the stability of modern civilization. It was what he had fought to hold together all his adult life, from Yale to CURE.

16

Remo Williams tooled his Buick Regal around the area of Wall Street, looking for a parking space. He found one an instant before a Federal Express truck could slide into it.

He reached back into the back seat for a paper-wrapped package. It was under his arm when he left his car and strolled into the lobby of the gleaming Looncraft Tower.

Remo waited patiently for an elevator. The lobby was filled with well-dressed men and women, each carrying a briefcase in one hand, a neatly folded copy of *The Wall Street Journal* in the other. They looked like they had all been outfitted by the same maiden aunt, who, instead of combing their hair, baked it.

When a car arrived, Remo jumped in ahead of the pack.

"Sorry, private car," he said, pushing a man into the others. He hit the "Close" button.

The elevator shot up. Quickly Remo stripped the paper wrapping off his Bear-Man suit. The car abruptly stopped and the doors started to separate. Remo hastily donned his bear-mask helmet.

"Next car," he told a pair of secretaries, hitting the "Close" button.

"Did you see that?" one squealed. "It's the Wall Street Bear!"

When the door opened again, Remo was completely enveloped in his Bear-Man suit. He stepped out onto the thirty-fourth floor, causing an instant commotion on the Looncraft, Dymstar & Buttonwood trading floor.

"It's back," a man cried. Several security guards ran in Remo's direction. He set himself. He needn't have bothered. They ran past him and escaped into the waiting elevator.

"That's right," Remo rumbled, taking up the cue. "I'm back. And I'm here to tell you that greed is bad. Never mind what you've heard elsewhere."

An eager young trader leapt from his desk and approached Remo with expectant eyes. He was dressed in a striped shirt and red suspenders and was almost identical to the others—except for his bright gold tie.

"Tell me, sir," he asked, "are you really a harbinger of a coming bear market?"

"Think again, pal," Remo told him gravely. "I'm here to prevent a bear market. You listen to Bear-Man, and the bulls will run forever."

A cheer went up from the floor.

"Tell us," the traders cried. "Tell us what we should do."

"Go long. Long and strong. Save your money. Brush your teeth regularly."

"Teeth?"

"Brushing your teeth leads to good working habits."

"Should we invest in pharmaceutical companies?" Gold Tie asked sincerely. "Do you have inside information?"

"Bear-Man knows all. Just remember, the market is fundamentally sound. It was only a correction."

A trader raised his hand eagerly. "Mr. Bear-Man, do you expect corporate profits to—"

"Sorry. Can't chat now. Got to see your boss."

Remo sauntered up to P. M. Looncraft's office. His secretary recoiled as if from a viper. She ducked behind her desk.

"Mr. Looncraft is not in," she said in a quivering voice. "He's in a meeting. In another building."

"I've heard that one before," Remo said, brushing past her.

He pushed open the door. P. M. Looncraft's office was unoccupied, unless one counted the array of ancestral Looncrafts on the walls.

"I told you so," the secretary's voice said. "Now, will you go away? Please?"

"I'll wait," Remo said, closing the door. He lumbered

over to the desk and plunked his hairy butt down. It was hot in the suit, and the smell was heavy in his nostrils, like used cotton. He hoped Looncraft would not be long.

While he waited, Remo drummed his claws on the desk. He noticed the Telerate machine at his elbow. He found the "On" switch and finally hit it with a claw after stabbing at in several times.

Remo got a listing of ten active stocks, some with arrows pointing up, others pointing down. He looked for Nostrum, Ink but remembered that it traded over the counter, on NASDAQ, not NYSE.

When boredom set in, he rummaged through the desk. There were no papers. The desk reminded Remo of Smith's desk. Very Spartan, almost paperless, with everything in its place.

Remo went back to drumming his bear claws on the leather blotter.

When he exhausted the entertainment possibilities of that, he noticed the computer beside his chair. He turned to it, and brushed the "On" switch. The computer blipped into life.

Behind his bear mask, Remo's brown eyes blinked.

The heading read: "MAYFLOWER DESCENDANTS." Below that was a single line: "QUEEN'S ROOK TO KNIGHT THREE."

Remo's eyes narrowed. He started hitting buttons, until he had written "Rook's Queen to King None," give or take a typo.

He looked for a "Send" button, knowing they made things happen.

When he found it, he tapped it with a claw.

The screen blipped. There was a pause. Then the screen went crazy. Lines of amber exclamation points appeared, and replicated themselves until they filled the screen. A concealed amplifier began beeping, annoying Remo. He tried to shut it off by pressing several buttons at random.

Instead of shutting down, a remote printer in a corner of the room rattled to life. The print head began racing and buzzing. Paper started to spew out.

Remo pressed more buttons. The printer kept printing, so he looked for a power plug. When he found it, he yanked hard. The computer and the printer both shut down.

Remo examined the printer and ripped away several sheets of paper. He looked at the top sheet. Deep within his bear mask, he made a puzzled sound.

Rolling it up, Remo went back to the desk and started to scratch a message onto the polished mahogany desktop. The claw barely cut the finish, so Remo shucked off one bear-paw glove and used his natural nail, which had been hardened to glass-cutting precision through diet and exercise.

When he was done, the mahogany desktop bore the words: "LEAVE NOSTRUM ALONE OR I'LL COME BACK OUT OF MY BEAR CAVE AND EAT YOU ALIVE.—BEAR-MAN."

Remo left the LD&B trading floor with a hearty, "Carry on, yuppies. And don't forget to brush your teeth."

He smiled under his bear mask at the chorused, "Yes, sir!" that followed him to the elevator. Chiun wasn't the only one who knew how to motivate workers.

17

P. M. Looncraft saw the shocked look on his secretary's face, which rather reminded him of a frightened lighthouse, all the way across the bustling Looncraft, Dymstar & Buttonwood trading floor.

"I'm terribly sorry, Mr. Looncraft," she stammered as he stormed past her and into his office. His normally neat desk was in disarray, the morocco-leather blotter shoved aside. The message carved into the fine wood was like a long crazy wound.

Looncraft whirled, fixing his secretary with a cold, imperious glare.

"How could you let this happen?" he demanded.

"I didn't know how to stop him, Mr. Looncraft. He was a bear."

"He was no more a bear than I," Looncraft said acidly. "And you are fired, Miss McLean!"

"Yes, Mr. Looncraft," Miss McLean said timidly, backing out of the room. In her heart, she felt a curious elation. Mr. Looncraft had actually called her by name. She had waited years for him to do that. It made being fired almost worthwhile.

Looncraft brushed bear hairs from his executive's chair before taking it. He spent several minutes rearranging his desk, and his thoughts. When both were satisfactorily tidy, he engaged his Telerate machine. Its glowing green three-letter stock symbols and decimal-point quotations helped restore his sense of well-being. A pinch of snuff also helped. Then, turning in his chair, he brought up his personal computer and the Mayflower Descendants bulletin board.

The message on the screen said: "ROOK'S QUEEN TO KING NONE?"

Looncraft frowned. The message made no sense. There was no such chess move.

He typed the same message and added two question marks at the end. He pressed "Send."

The silent reply Looncraft got back had nothing to do with the game of chess. It read: "IDENTIFY."

Looncraft typed his name.

"HAVE YOU BEEN COMPROMISED?" was the response.

Looncraft typed: "UNKNOWN. WILL CHECK."

He called up a readout of all his files. Next to each was the date and exact time of the last update. He saw with a start that made his long face even longer that a key file had been accessed only this morning. Looncraft had not looked at that file in weeks.

He returned to the bulletin board, and typed: "ANSWER AFFIRMATIVE. HOSTILE PARTY IDENTIFIED. PERMISSION TO ACTIVATE CORNWALLIS GUARD AND MAKE REBEL PARTY REDUNDANT."

Looncraft pressed "Send." The answer bipped back instantly, despite thousands of miles of distance: "GRANTED."

Looncraft pecked at the keys with two long fingers, switching to another program.

He wrote: "ACTIVATE. TARGET: NOSTRUM, INK. ASSEMBLE

AT 1700 HOURS GREENWICH MEAN TIME. ERADICATE ALL RE-SISTANCE AND MAKE CEO REDUNDANT."

Then he pressed "Send" and leaned back, a bitter smile creeping into his grim expression.

All over greater New York and New Jersey, and in parts of lower Connecticut, personal computers and office mainframes repeated the message on silent screens. Men excused themselves from work, from family obligations, and took cars or boarded commuter trains, clutching bundles tied with string under their arms.

They were all headed for Manhattan.

William Bragg of the Connecticut Braggs received his activation orders while at his desk in his New Canaan real-estate office.

"Right, then," he said, going to the office safe. He pulled from a double-locked drawer a neatly folded white wool garment and a scarlet coat. In the privacy of his office he carefully changed his clothes. The white breeches fitted as snugly as his wife's panty hose. The matching waistcoat was also a perfect fit. He attached the black horsehair neck stock around his collar before donning a long red coat that almost touched the floor with its viper's-tongue tails. After he finished buttoning the front, he anchored the tails to his back with silver hooks so they wouldn't trail, and pulled on the white shoulder belts. They formed an X over the coat after he attached the regimental buckle stamped with the letters CG. Finally he stepped into his black half-gaiters, enjoying the feel of real footwear for the first time in what he mentally called "a dog's age."

William Bragg pulled loose-fitting trousers over his leggings and, flattening his heavy turnback lapels, drew on a rumpled raincoat, buttoning it to the top so no hint of scarlet peeped out. He carried an oilskin-wrapped package to his waiting car.

On his way to New York City, William Bragg hummed the familiar melody every American schoolboy learned as "America" under his breath. Occasionally he broke out into song. But the words were not the words of the national anthem. Instead of "My Country 'Tis of Thee," he sang "God Save the Queen."

Bragg parked in a lot near Wall Street and carried the oilskin package from the car.

He walked briskly to the Nostrum Building, the morning sun glinting off the cloisonné flag button on his lapel. He didn't notice—or perhaps care—that the American flag was upside down.

As he climbed the short broad steps to the Nostrum entrance, a taxi pulled up and a man in a business suit alighted, clutching a paper-wrapped package similar to Bragg's. He, too, wore an American flag on his lapel. It, too, was upside down.

Bragg waited for the man to approach the lobby.

"Bragg," he said, low-voiced. "Commanding."

"Braintree, sir. I hope I'm not late."

"Let us see for ourselves, shall we?"

In the Nostrum lobby, six others stood about, looking at watches, all dressed in business clothes and all clutching packages of various sorts close to their upside-down U.S.-flag buttons.

Bragg strode up to the knot of expectant-faced men. They were a tall lot, sound of limb, he saw. Well-bred, and fighters to a man—if William Bragg was any judge of men.

"Colonel William Talbot Bragg here," he said, executing a sharp salute. When his right hand snapped to his forehead, it showed palm-out.

The others returned identical awkward salutes.

"All ready, then?" Bragg asked.

"Right, sir," they whispered.

"Follow me, and step smartly," Bragg said, leading them to the elevators. The next available cage was empty. They stepped aboard, and as it ascended, the men hastily removed their outer clothing to reveal cotton waistcoats and white breeches. The package wrapping tore under busy fingers and dropped to the floor like paper scabs. Those who came in business suits donned red coats with royal-blue regimental facings. White-powdered wigs and black cocked hats went on their heads.

When the overhead indicator flashed that they had reached the eighth floor, they were grimly checking their Sterling machine pistols.

The steel doors rolled apart and Bragg exited first.

"Look smart now, lads," he barked.

The others jumped out and formed a line on either side of him. Their gun muzzles rose. Fingers caressed triggers.

Then, like a sinuous red centipede, the line of men advanced down the corridor to the Nostrum trading room.

The Master of Sinanju heard the sounds of automatic weapons as they penetrated the soundproofed sanctity of his office. He came to his feet as if sprung from a box. Glass shattered. A hole punched in the door, exploding the insulated window behind his aged head.

His hand reached for the doorknob. But the door flew inward. A red-suspendered trader flung himself in.

"What is wrong?" Chiun demanded, trying to see past him.

"It's a massacre!"

"What kind?"

"A real one. They're slaughtering the floor."

The Master of Sinanju flew past the man and took in the awful sight of his trading room as glass partitions shivered and sprayed shards under punishing bursts of automatic-weapons fire.

The firing was coming from a handful of red-costumed gunmen who stood ruler-straight, like a firing squad, inside the door.

"Take that, you traitors!" one shouted. He wore the gold-fringed epaulets of an officer. The stringy fringe shivered in sympathy to his firing.

Huddling traders crawled for safety before the Master of Sinanju's outraged eyes. Faith Davenport squeezed herself into a corner, crying, "I'm not a trader! I'm a secretary! Please don't shoot me."

A palm-size shard of glass flicked toward Chiun. He caught it, redirecting its flight with a casual continuous gesture. The shard ended up in the face of one of the red-coated assailants, bisecting it with mathematical precision.

He dropped his weapon and eased himself onto the rug to die, shivering from polished toe to powdered wig.

"I am Chiun!" the Master of Sinanju cried above the

carnage. "Perhaps it is me you seek with your cowardly bullets."

"That's the one," the officer said, pointing. "Take him, lads."

The firing stopped, the smoking muzzles focusing on Chiun, who took a single step forward.

Remo Williams finished hiding his bear suit under the passenger seat of his car and got out. He walked toward the Nostrum Building, a mass of computer printouts clutched in his hand.

The lobby was calm when he entered. But when an elevator opened, it spilled terrified Nostrum workers, who fought and clawed at one another to escape the cage.

Remo grabbed one by the suspenders and demanded, "What the hell is going on?"

"We're getting murdered!" he said, tearing free.

Remo dropped the suspenders and called after him, "Maybe it's only a correction."

He shrugged, and took the elevator. He was anxious to show Chiun what he had found at Looncraft's office.

Two floors below the Nostrum office suite, the tang of gunsmoke infiltrated the elevator. Remo dropped to one knee and got ready, in case the doors opened on an ambush.

He was unprepared for being knocked off his feet by a torrent of stampeding Nostrum workers.

"What's going on?" he shouted as the doors closed and the cage sank.

"Massacre!" several voices wailed at once. One of them he recognized. Pushing his way toward it, he took Faith Davenport by the arm.

"What's happened?" Then Remo noticed the blood on his clutching hand. It was coming from Faith's torn sleeve.

"Machine guns," Faith gulped between breaths. "It was horrible. They're killing traders for no reason."

"What about Chiun?" Remo asked urgently as the car opened on the lobby.

"He's fighting them. Oh, poor chief!"

Just then a shattering of glass came from outside the building.

A scarlet figure struck the sidewalk with bone-pulverizing force. For a heartbeat of fear, Remo thought it was Chiun dressed in a scarlet kimono. But then he remembered that Chiun had worn emerald this morning.

Remo rushed out to the sidewalk, stopped, and turned the body over so he could see its face. There was no face to speak of—just a red ruin. It almost matched the long red coat with its regimental facings and large silver buttons.

Then a white-powdered wig plopped on the face, covering it.

"That's one of them," Faith said, cupping her mouth in her hands.

"One of what? He looks like an extra in a historical movie."

"One of the killers. They kept calling us 'traders' like it was a dirty word."

Remo reacted to the first concussion before the sound of the exploding window glass warned that another costumed killer was on his way down. He hustled Faith back into the lobby. The second body landed beside the first, but Remo didn't wait to see it hit. He flashed inside an elevator, stabbing the eighth-floor button impatiently and saying, "Come on! Come on!"

This time he heard gunfire on the way up. It was sporadic.

Remo charged out of the elevator without regard for his own safety. His eyes were wide, taking in everything. Time seemed to slow down, but he was moving like a flash of light up the corridor, every sense attuned to his surroundings.

Two red-coated gunmen suddenly came in his direction. They were marching backward, shoulder to shoulder, their pistols making short spiteful sounds at whatever they were in retreat from.

Remo skidded to a stop and let them come to him.

"Curse you, ye heathen wog!" one of them spat. He wore gold epaulets on his shoulders.

Remo waited until he was almost on him before he tapped him on the epaulet. The man whirled as if electrified, his lips peeled back to expose snarling teeth.

Remo broke every tooth in his mouth with a quick

upward stroke of his hand. The officer dropped his machine pistol and grabbed his throat. He began vomiting teeth. Remo left him to that and shattered the other man's kneecaps with two rapid-fire kicks.

He swept past them and into the trading room.

There the Master of Sinanju had another gunman by the throat. The man was on his knees, so he and Chiun were eye-to-eye. Chiun was leaning into his stranglehold and the man's face was purpling like an animated bruise.

"I got two," Remo called, looking around the room. He saw bodies. More red coats. But several bloody Nostrum employees too.

Chiun looked up from his work. "Do any of them live?"

"Who?"

"The vicious ones."

"Yeah, I didn't waste them."

"Then we do not need this dog," Chiun said, snapping the struggling man's neck with a quick sideways motion. Chiun kicked the twitching corpse away.

Remo went among the wounded, feeling for pulses. He found few. From outside came the whine of approaching sirens.

"That's probably the police," Remo said quickly. "I can't stick around. My face would end up on every newscast from here to Alaska."

"There is time yet," Chiun returned. "We must learn who these savages are."

Remo followed Chiun out to the corridor, where the officer had finished emptying the contents of his stomach onto the rug. He whimpered as he tried to pick his teeth out from a sour puddle of cream-of-asparagus soup.

The other man was moaning as he clutched his shattered knees. Chiun stepped on his throat on his way to the other one. His windpipe collapsed without a sound. So did he.

Remo pulled the red-coated officer to his knees.

"Unless you want your brains to join your lunch," Remo said fiercely, "you're going to tell us who sent you and why."

"Damn you, you traitor," the man said mushily through bleeding gums.

"I'm not a trader," Remo said. "And what have you got against traders?"

"He not say 'trader,' " Chiun intoned. "He is calling you a traitor."

"How can you tell? Without teeth, he sounds like Grandma Moses."

"Because he also shouted 'traitor' when he had his teeth," Chiun added. "Your name, dog."

"Bragg, William. Colonel."

"And who is your master?"

"I am pleased to serve on Her Majesty's Cornwallis Guard, wog."

Chiun slapped the bloody sneer from Bragg's face.

"Call me not a wog, murderer."

Bragg fell silent. His eyes were sullen.

"I asked you to name your master," Chiun repeated sternly.

"I owe my allegiance to the queen," Bragg said sullenly.

Remo looked to Chiun. "I just came from Looncraft's office. He wasn't there. So I left a message. I think this is his answer."

"There is one way to find out," Chiun said, girding his emerald skirts.

He made a pass at Bragg's face with one long-nailed hand, his hazel eyes hard and glittering.

"Know, murderer," he intoned, "that any one of these nails can inflict exquisite pain. But for you, I shall employ them all."

"Do your worst," Bragg spat.

And Chiun's hand clutched the man's face. His nails dug in at brow, cheeks, and jaw. Bragg threw his head back in anguish. His howl actually caused hanging glass in the next room to fall to the floor.

"Speak!" Chiun demanded. "Who sent you?"

"I . . . don't know . . . name," Bragg screeched. "I am a soldier!"

Chiun's nails dug in more deeply. Bragg threshed and fought, but the old Oriental's grasp was unshakable.

"Damn you!" he cried. "Curse your black heathen soul!"

"I don't think he knows," Remo said unfeelingly.

"Then he will suffer," spat Chiun.

But Bragg did not suffer. He suddenly clutched up and his bloodshot eyes began to jerk about in his head. His arms flapped like a wounded bird trying to fly. His kneeling legs went slack.

Then all movement ceased, and the Master of Sinanju realized he was holding up inert flesh.

"Dead?" Remo asked.

Chiun nodded. "His wicked heart could not stand the strain, he has dropped his body."

Chiun released Colonel William Bragg's head. It swayed forward with sickening slowness. Bragg hit the rug with his face. His body curled like a hunched red question mark.

Down the corridor, the humming elevator doors released a cacophony of shouting voices.

"The cops," Remo said. "I gotta go."

"I am going with you," Chiun said.

"No, you gotta keep Nostrum going. Just leave me out of it. I'll be at the hotel. Check with me after this is over."

And Remo drifted back into the trading room. He stepped out through a shattered window and used the molding between windows to get him to the roof. There he walked to the back of the building, where the alley below was empty of official vehicles.

Remo began his spiderlike descent to the ground, his face hard.

18

Dr. Harold W. Smith was monitoring the stock market when three things happened simultaneously.

His secretary buzzed him.

The first bulletin telling of the massacres at Nostrum, Ink, flashed on his computer.

And the news of P. M. Looncraft's successful takeover of the Global Communications Conglomerate appeared beside the first bulletin.

For a rare moment, Smith sat paralyzed, uncertain what to deal with first.

His eyes on the screen, he fumbled for his intercom.

"Yes?" he snapped harshly.

"Mr. Winthrop calling. Again."

"I've no time right now. Tell him I'll call him back."

"Yes, sir."

Smith's widening eyes followed the twin bulletins. As an electronic facsimile of the New York Stock Exchange broadtape marched across the top of the screen, two text windows below it scrolled out news digests.

Smith tried to read them both simultaneously. As a consequence, he had the momentary impression that P.M. Looncraft had massacred the stockholders of Global Communications Conglomerate.

Smith squeezed his eyes tightly, striking a key that froze the Looncraft bulletin. He recalled the Nostrum digest from the top, and started over.

According to the bulletin, there had been a massacre on the trading floor of Nostrum, Ink, resulting in casualties. The assailants had all been killed during the attack, which the New York police were blaming on disgruntled investors wiped out by Dark Friday. The CEO of Nostrum was answering questions, but was unable to shed any more light on the attack.

Smith exhaled a sigh of relief. That meant Chiun had not been harmed. There was no mention of Remo. Another relief. No mention meant that Remo was neither dead nor being questioned. That was all Smith needed. He had long ago programmed his computers to flag any news reports of anyone named Remo, regardless of last name. Five minutes per day were spent scanning news reports of newsworthy Remos from coast to coast, but it was worth it.

At the end of the digest, there was a curious addendum. It was a single sentence: "Police could not explain why the assailants were dressed in pre-Revolutionary military uniforms."

Smith blinked. "Pre-Revolutionary?" he muttered to himself. "Which revolution? Russian? Chinese? Filipino?"

That was one of the problems of relying on news digests. Important details were often squeezed out by the automatic digest program.

The report on the Global acquisition was even more astonishing. According to it, P. M. Looncraft had announced an eighty-dollar-per-share buy-out offer for Global Communications Conglomerate. He had obtained financing from the Lippincott Mercantile Bank. And within an hour of the public announcement, arrangements had been made to obtain large blocks of GLB owned by Crown Acquisitions, Limited, and the infamous DeGoone Slickens. The financial world was abuzz, the report concluded, with the speed with which Looncraft had obtained Slickens' holdings, because it gave him the edge he needed to absorb Global.

"This is very odd," Harold Smith told himself.

The intercom buzzed again.

"Yes?" Smith said distractedly.

"It's Mr. Winthrop again. He says it's urgent."

"Urgent? Ask him his business."

Smith recalled the Looncraft bulletin once again and went through it. His secretary's voice interrupted once more.

"He says it's personal and private, but won't say any more."

"Take his number," Smith snapped. "I'll get back to him."

"Yes, Dr. Smith."

By the time Dr. Smith finished rereading the Looncraft bulletin, he had already forgotten about Winthrop's call.

Hours later, he still had not returned it, as other bulletins came to his attention. P. M. Looncraft had moved quickly to take control of GLB, promising that new programming would begin at once, and would consist of significant blocks of foreign programming designed to broaden America's cultural horizons. Existing news programs would continue as before, Looncraft had assured Global News Network subscribers.

On the Nostrum massacre, the first identifications were

coming in on the dead. The assailants who had been positively identified included a Connecticut real-estate broker named William Bragg, a Princeton classics professor named Milton Everett, and other people of middle- and upper-middle-class backgrounds. They appear unconnected except that they all fitted the typical stock-market-investor profile.

There were no further reports about their odd costuming, and Smith decided it was probably one of the wild details that often find their way into early news accounts, and usually prove erroneous.

Smith put in a call to the President of the United States after five o'clock.

"Mr. President," he began, "I am updating you on the Nostrum operation. As you know, the market has stabilized."

"What's this massacre thing about, Smith?" the President asked in his twangy voice.

"I am unsure. My reports indicate the assailants were disgruntled investors. This often happens in the wake of drastic market upheavals. My operatives are safe and I expect Nostrum to continue to act as a moderating influence on the market."

"Good. As soon as this thing settles down, start selling off its holdings. We can't have all this government money tied up in private enterprise."

"I understand, Mr. President. Expect another update within the next forty-eight hours, regardless of events."

Smith had no sooner hung up the dialless red telephone than his intercom buzzed like an angry hornet.

"Yes, Mrs. Mikulka?" Smith said in a much calmer voice than before.

"The downstairs guard wants you to know that they are on their way up."

"I understand," Smith replied. Remo and Chiun.

"And Mr. Winthrop is on line two. Do you want to take it?"

Smith hesitated. He had meant to deal with that annoying intrusion, but not with Remo and Chiun on their way to see him.

"Give him my apologies. I'll try later."

Smith quickly got out of his chair and pushed it aside.

He pulled the wheelchair behind his desk so hastily he cracked his shin. When he sat down, he really needed its support.

Remo and Chiun entered his office, grim-faced.

"I have heard the reports," Smith told them without preamble.

"Barbarians!" Chiun said angrily. "They have always been barbarians!"

"Who have?" Smith asked.

"Let me tell it," Remo said quickly. "Here's the scoop, Smith. I went over to Looncraft's to put a scare into him, but he wasn't in."

"I know. He was putting together a deal to take over GLB. He succeeded."

"The fiend!" Chiun said.

"I left Looncraft a message," Remo continued. "He must have got it, because before I got back to Nostrum, they'd been hit. It had to be Looncraft. Who else has a motive?"

"No, it was not Looncraft, despicable as he is," Chiun said. "His soldiers would have spoken his name rather than die in the agony I visited upon him."

"I still say it was Looncraft. Who else is there?"

"There are the British," Chiun spat. "Rome should have slain them all when they ruled that miserable island."

"The British?" Smith said in a dubious voice.

"They wore British army uniforms."

"The new reports said nothing about that," Smith blurted. "Were they Royal Army? Or SAS?"

"Not modern military uniforms," Remo explained. "Revolutionary uniforms. You know, the kind the British wore when they fought Washington, when they were called lobsterbacks."

"That makes absolutely no sense," Smith said. "Those uniforms are two centuries out of date."

"Don't ask me to explain it, but there it is," Remo added. "I saw them with my own eyes."

"The police theorize that they were crazed investors bankrupted by the market meltdown," Smith said.

"Makes perfect sense to me," Remo said. "One kept shouting at us, calling us 'traders.' "

"No, 'traitors,' " Chiun snapped. "I heard them clearly. They accused my minions of being traitors."

Smith's frown furrowed like cloth. "Traitors? To what?"

"They didn't say," Chiun admitted.

"Maybe they were on some kind of patriotic kick."

"I have a report that the police found discarded clothing in the Nostrum lobby," Smith said slowly. "The jackets all had U.S.-flag pins on the lapels."

"They were British," Chiun insisted.

"They had American accents," Remo said. "Will you get off this kick of yours?"

"This is not a kick. My workers have been killed, my business is in ruins, and those responsible will have to account to me."

"Please, please, both of you," Smith said, lifting placating hands. "Let us stay on the subject."

"Fine," Remo said, throwing a flapping length of computer printout onto Smith's desk, "Check this out. I got it off Looncraft's computer."

Smith took up the sheets. He carefully pulled away the perforated carrier strips and dropped them in a wastebasket before looking at them, causing Remo to roll his eyes in impatience.

Smith lifted the continuous form to his eyes. It was filled with a double-column list of names and numbers. One column was headed "LOYALISTS." The other said "CONSCRIPTS."

Smith scanned the list. The names meant nothing to him. The numbers might have been social-security numbers. Then he realized that could not be. They were one digit too long. They might be long-distance phone numbers, he realized.

Smith looked up and adjusted his glasses. "These names mean nothing to me," he admitted.

"Keep looking. Your name is on the list."

Startled, Smith returned to the list. He found his name on the third sheet, under "CONSCRIPTS": Harold W. Smith.

"Not me," Smith said. "The world is full of Harold Smiths."

"But not Harold W. Smiths."

"It does not say Dr. Harold W. Smith," Smith said

reasonably. "And there is no reason I would be on a Looncraft, Dymstar & Buttonwood client list. I do not invest in the stock market."

"Well, there's more," Remo said. "The computer I got that off had a chess move displayed on the screen."

"Yes?" Smith said doubtfully.

"That Reuters guy." Remo snapped his fingers impatiently. "What's his name?"

"Plum, O brilliant one," Chiun sniffed.

"Right, him. When I cornered Plum in his office, he was on the phone. He said 'Knight to Queen's Bishop Three' before he hung up. Said he played phone chess—if there is such a thing."

"And Looncraft plays computer chess?" Smith asked.

"That's right. Get it? There's a connection."

Smith shook his head. "Coincidence. Many people play chess by long distance. Playing through the mail, for example, is quite common."

Remo's face fell. "I'm telling you, there's more to this. And it connects Looncraft with the Reuters guys."

"Do not listen to him," Chiun said firmly. "When was the last time Remo was correct in anything?"

Remo opened his mouth to retort. He blinked. Nothing came to mind, so he shut it unhappily. He fell onto the couch and folded his arms under his glowering face.

Smith addressed the Master of Sinanju.

"Master Chiun," he said. "The stock-market situation is stabilizing. With the killings at Nostrum, I suggest you begin selling off your stock holdings carefully over the next several weeks. If there is no more volatility, then we will close down Nostrum."

"I will not close down Nostrum until my employees have been avenged," Chiun said harshly.

"If the police reports are correct—"

"And they are not!" Chiun snapped.

"—then the massacre was an unfortunate aftermath of the market meltdown," Smith finished stubbornly.

"If you will not listen to reason," Chiun said huffily, "then I will prove it to you." Chiun turned. "Come, Remo."

Remo paused by the door on his way out.

"If you take another look at that list," he said evenly, "you'll see that the President of the United States is on the list, too."

Smith looked. He found the President's name under "CONSCRIPTS."

"What of it?" he asked Remo blankly.

"And the Vice-President's name."

Smith looked again. He found the Vice-President listed under "LOYALISTS."

"Looncraft, Dymstar & Buttonwood is very prestigious," Smith said calmly. "It does not surprise me to find their names on a list of the firm's clients. I see other prominent names here. Businessmen. Educators. Here is a senator from Illinois. And a Maine congressman."

"Well, it means something," Remo said.

"Yes," Smith returned coolly. "It means they are LD&B clients."

"Fine," Remo said. "Be that way. Just remember what I told you."

"I will," Harold W. Smith promised.

Remo slammed the door after him. It sounded like an anvil falling.

19

"It's Looncraft. It was Looncraft all along."

"And I say it is the British."

"That's crapola. Whoever's causing this, they almost dragged down the British economy along with our own."

Remo folded his arms angrily and looked out the circular porthole at the clouds sliding below the Nostrum corporate jet's silvery wing.

The Master of Sinanju sat on a mat in the middle of the cabin, disdaining the leather chairs. One yellow hand rested on a plastic-wrapped package beside him.

"You yourself once said that Looncraft was British," he pointed out.

Remo frowned. "No, I said he *sounded* British."

"Ah-hah!" Chiun cried triumphantly.

"That didn't come out right," Remo admitted. "He talked British. He used British expressions. But so does Smith from time to time. I don't know. It's probably New England talk."

"I have sojourned in America nearly two decades," Chiun said quietly. "Yet I am still Korean, not American. No one would dispute that."

"Least of all me," Remo said, looking toward Chiun. "What's in the plastic bag, anyway?"

"That is not your concern," Chiun sniffed, pushing the package behind him.

"I wondered what you were doing in that record store, back in Rye. I never figured you for a music fan. Are you back in love with Barbra Streisand?"

"Cheeta Ching is my one true love."

"Well, you acted pretty mysterious, having me wait outside while you shopped."

"I did not shop," Chiun spat. "Americans shop. I purchase. Do not try to make of me an American. I am not. I am Korean."

"No argument. You are definitely Korean."

"The British were bad enough in their day, but Americans are the lowest."

"Where do you get that crap?" Remo wanted to know.

"When the British had an empire, they tried to force their will on the rest of the world. Spreading their poison."

"I think the opium trade is a thing of the past, Little Father," Remo pointed out. "Lyndon LaRouche to the contrary notwithstanding."

"That was the least of their poisons. I am referring to their ruinous philosophy."

"Give me a clue. Grade school was a long time ago."

"Liberty." Chiun spat the word as if it seared his tongue.

"And what is so bad about liberty?"

"It weakens the social structure and leads to the anarchy of choice."

"Some people like choice."

"The worst thing about British liberty was that it was limited to the British," Chiun said bitterly. "They ruined India—not that the Indians had not already begun the task. They enslaved China with their opium—not that the Chinese weren't addled to begin with. They looted Egypt of their most magnificent treasures—what little the Egyptians had bothered to preserve. They called this wholesale theft their white man's burden. The only thing burdensome about it was the carrying away of their pelf—which they usually forced natives to do for them."

"Do I have to listen to you rant? So you don't like the British. It doesn't make them the bad guys."

"But their worst crime is that they created the Americans, who have replaced the British as the supposed masters of the world. Liberty. I spit upon it." Chiun expectorated on the rug, forcing Remo to turn away.

"It's your corporate jet," he said wearily. He wondered how much longer this would go on.

"That is all right," Chiun replied. "I have lackeys to clean it up. White lackeys. Heh heh heh. White lackeys."

Chiun cackled to himself for a moment, then went on.

"Do not think that I consider the British completely without redeeming qualities. Once they were an acceptable client. Henry the Eighth. Now, *there* was a monarch. Rude of speech and forever belching from every orifice, true. But he knew how to rule. No, the royal family have become so much popular entertainment, accepting unearned money from the royal treasury like an American ghetto family on welfare. This is one reason why the House of Sinanju has had so little truck with the House of Windsor."

Remo threw up his hands. "Another country heard from," he said. "Why don't we simply pack it in for the rest of the flight? Is there a TV in this thing?"

"Somewhere," Chiun said, waving one long-nailed hand vaguely.

Remo went in search of a television. He opened up a row of maplewood cupboards, finding drinking glasses in one, bottles of purified water in another. The third opened on a small TV screen. Remo hit the "On" button and changed channels impatiently.

"Why do you bother?" Chiun said querulously. "There is never anything good on anymore. Not since your daytime dramas began wallowing in sex."

"Wait, here's the Global News Network," Remo said. "Let's see how they report the news of their own takeover." Remo settled back in his seat to watch.

The Global News Network call sign showed for a moment and an impeccable voice sounding very much like Alaistair Cooke said, "Next, a retrospective on British-American relations entitled *The Mother Country*."

"Auugh!" Chiun said, clapping his hands over his seashell ears. "I cannot bear to watch."

"So don't," Remo said, popping the top off a bottle of mineral water and drinking without benefit of a glass.

The narrator's mellow voice launched into a history of early British-American relations, the founding of the early American colonies, and what the narrator referred to in a deepening and doleful voice as "the unfortunate rebellion."

"Does he mean the American Revolution?" Remo wondered aloud.

Chiun's hands pressed against his ears even more tightly. His annoyed eyes closed.

The narrator's voice lifted while describing the eventual forgiveness the crown showed to the wayward American colonies, despite their ungratefulness and the particular provocations that led to the War of 1812, during which the good English refrained from making war on the childlike Americans.

"Am I missing something here?" Remo growled, sitting up. "What happened to burning Washington, D.C., to the ground? And the impressment of Americans into the British navy?"

"I am not listening to this," Chiun said.

"You'd better. Check this out. It's bullshit."

Curious, Chiun uncovered his ears.

"Too late," Remo said. "Now he's talking about the British-American alliance during World War I."

"Paugh," Chiun spat, re-covering his ears. "This is all King John's fault. Had he been a true monarch, he would have run those upstart lords through the heart and buried them with the ashes of their Magna Carta."

"You know, Chiun—"

"I cannot hear you," Chiun said.

"You may have something, after all."

"What?" Chiun said, his hands dropping.

"Global never showed this kind of stuff before. And didn't Smith say that Looncraft was importing foreign broadcasts for the network?"

"Yes. And nothing is more foreign than a British program."

"Maybe to you, but not to me."

The program ended on a wistful note, lamenting the separation of the poor colonies from Mother England. The narrator sniffed and reached for a handkerchief, which he used to dab at his eyes.

"I can't believe what I'm seeing," Remo said.

A news break followed. It led off with a soundbite from Britain's House of Commons, shown over a still photograph of Parliament's richly appointed chambers. The prime minister was addressing the lower house to a chorus of boos and hoots of derision coming from what the newscaster described as the Labour back bench, mixed with cheers of "Hear, hear!" from the Tories.

"Tories," Remo said. "I thought they died out after 1776."

"The Black Death still thrives in certain backwaters too," Chiun noted curtly.

Then there was a clip of the chancellor of the exchequer's soothing voice pronouncing the latest economic earthquake as passed.

When the news ended, Remo asked, "What happened to America? Global is supposed to be an American station. Didn't we make any news today?"

The next program was called *Canada, Gentle Northern Giant*. Remo got up and turned off the set with an angry punch that cracked the screen.

"I think we should call Smith on this," he said firmly.

"I leave that to you, my secretary."

"I'm not that kind of secretary," Remo snapped, grabbing a phone off the cabin wall.

"Then why are you making the call?" Chiun said, smiling broadly.

Dr. Harold W. Smith entered his modest Tudor-style home in Rye, New York, his eyes bleary from a full day before a computer screen. He clutched his ever-present worn briefcase in one hand.

"Maude?" he called.

"In the den, Harold," Mrs. Harold W. Smith's frumpy voice returned. It was clogged with emotion and Smith moved quickly into the den.

There Mrs. Smith was dabbing her eyes with paper tissue. She was seated before the television set in an overstuffed chair. The set was black and white. Harold Smith did not believe that color was worth the extra money. Black and white was just as watchable.

"I just watched the most interesting program," Mrs. Smith sniffled.

Harold Smith watched the news break, which began with the Parliament report and concluded with the chancellor of the exchequer.

"Must be sunspots," he remarked. "This is BBC programming."

"It's that Global network," Maude Smith told him. "They have the most wonderful new programs."

"Global?" Harold Smith said. His eyes grew intent as *Canada, Gentle Northern Giant* began with an upper-class British voice-over against a map of Canada, which extended deep into the Ohio Valley.

"Once this gentle giant of a nation stretched from the Arctic Circle down to include present-day Ohio, but rather than enter into conflict with its beloved southern neighbor, the formerly rambunctious colonies, Canada in its infinite wisdom ceded all that valuable land rather than shed blood."

"I didn't know that," Mrs. Smith gasped.

"You didn't know it," Harold Smith snapped, "because it's not true. We fought a war more than a century ago over that border."

"Do you mind if I watch the rest of this before I put on supper?" Mrs. Smith said, as if she hadn't heard.

"I won't be eating supper home tonight," Harold Smith said, turning on his heel.

"Thank you, Harold," Mrs. Smith said absently, her

voice lost in the impeccable consonants of the narrator's voice.

On his way back to Folcroft Sanitarium, Smith heard the cellular telephone in his briefcase buzz.

Smith answered it with crisp authority.

It was Remo.

"Smith," Remo said. "I was just watching Global, and you'll never guess what."

"I know what. I saw it too."

"Which program?"

"*Canada, Gentle Northern Giant.*"

"I bailed out when that one came on. This is crazy."

"No, it's propaganda. Looncraft is up to something."

"You think Chiun's wild British plot is our answer?"

"It makes no sense. I see no point to it, but I'm on my way back to Folcroft to dig further."

"Want me to lean on Looncraft?" Remo asked.

"Yes," Smith said, tight-lipped. "Don't forget the suit."

"How could I?" Remo said acidly. "I scratch myself every time I think of it."

Smith hung up the phone and pressed the accelerator. He went right to the edge of the speed limit, which for Harold W. Smith was tantamount to speeding.

Simultaneously, miles away in Manhattan, P. M. Looncraft picked up the telephone in his rapidly darkening office. It was after-hours, but Looncraft had been too busy to leave early. He pointed a remote control at a corner TV set and turned off *Canada, Gentle Northern Giant.* He had already seen it. In fact, he had supervised its filming, as he had other documentaries that would soon air nationwide over the Global News Network.

"Ah, quality programming," he muttered to himself as he punched out a number. "It's a breath of fresh air."

"Pugh here," a young man's voice said.

"Pugh, this is Looncraft. I have been watching tonight's lineup. Quite good."

"Thank you, Mr. Looncraft. I'm pleased you like it."

"Like it? I love it. This dreary land has been culturally starved far too long, don't you agree?"

"Absolutely," Pugh said nervously. "When are you going to come down to meet with the staff?"

"Not soon, Pugh. Things are hectic right now. I just wanted you to know that you have my full confidence as director of programming."

"Thank you, Mr. Looncraft," Pugh said quickly. "I'm very relieved. Some of us had expected you to install your own people."

"If something's not broken, I don't fix it. And I would never replace good Anglo-Saxon stock with some foreign-born person."

Pugh's nervous laughter returned. "As a matter of fact, I *am* of British extraction. But my family's been in America for over a hundred years."

"It's the blood, man. The blood always tells. Princeton?"

"Yale, actually."

"Good school. It's not Princeton, but then, what is? Carry on, Pugh."

"I will."

"And, Pugh?"

"Yes?"

"If any of your staff complain about the format change, fire them instantly."

"I won't hesitate, Mr. Looncraft."

Smiling bloodlessly, P. M. Looncraft went to his deskside computer and logged onto the Mayflower Descendants bulletin board.

He pecked out rapid words: "SUCCESS. READY FOR NEXT PHASE."

The reply was almost instantaneous: "PROCEED."

Looncraft logged off and went to his desk Rolodex. He picked through the cards until he came to the home number of the chairman of the New York Stock Exchange.

"P. M. Looncraft here," he said crisply. "Paul, I have just received the most disturbing news. It seems there is a rumor about of a problem with tomorrow's auction of treasury bonds. A scarcity of buyers."

"My God," the chairman sputtered. "That's never happened before!"

"It may mean that the investors who fled the market are

worried about the government's solvency. The deficit, the
trade imbalance, and things of that sort."

"I'll look into it. But if no one shows, and the word gets
out . . ."

"It would represent the ultimate failure of faith," Looncraft
put in solemnly. "The market will crash. And we can't
have that."

"Thank you for alerting me, P.M."

"Think nothing of it. Cheerio."

P. M. Looncraft hung up, rubbing his lantern jaw
thoughtfully. The chairman would check with his usual
sources, who in turn would go to theirs. Soon it would be
all over the street. The media would seize upon it like a
pit bull. No amount of denial would kill the story once
that happened.

Then, like a house of cards, the American economy
would begin to totter.

P. M. Looncraft left his office feeling quite chipper,
unaware that he had forgotten to remove his powdered
wig.

He missed the bear by only six minutes.

20

Remo Williams stood in P. M. Looncraft's empty office,
redolent of formaldehyde, trying to figure out how to
scratch a sudden itch behind his left knee without bending
over and popping the seams in his bear suit. He focused
his breathing, and the nerves behind his knee went
quiescent.

Then he got an itch under his right armpit. That itch,
he simply scratched.

The office suite of Looncraft, Dymstar & Buttonwood
was completely unoccupied. Remo clawed through Loon-

craft's Rolodex until he found the man's home phone number.

The butler answered. "I am sorry, but Mr. Looncraft is not in."

"Are you sure about that?" Remo asked.

"I beg your pardon?" the butler said unhappily. "Who is calling?"

"How's your back?" Remo asked coolly.

The butler's tone of voice lost its aplomb. "Oh! It's you. Mr. Looncraft is not in. Really, really not in. Please believe me, sir, when I say that I do not know when to expect him."

"I believe you," Remo said unhappily. He hung up.

Disgusted, Remo left the Looncraft Tower and joined Chiun, who sat quietly in the passenger seat of Remo's Buick. It was parked on a side street.

Remo got behind the wheel. He had to slouch to avoid crushing the ornamental bear's head mounted on his hairy head.

"Looncraft's gone. The whole place is deserted."

"Let us go, then, to his home."

"I got a better idea," Remo said, starting the car. "Let's see Faith."

"That is a better idea?" Chiun asked as Remo pulled away from the curb.

"I called his house. He's not home either."

The blue-blazered security guard at Faith's apartment-house lobby looked up at Remo and Chiun as they entered and assumed a smirking demeanor.

"Back again, I see," he chirped. "And who is this?" He pointed to Chiun. Remo had left his bear suit in the car. He dug into the small of his back with a thumb, pulling out a stiff hair.

"My chaperon," Remo told him.

"Well, I'm afraid you brought him out of the rest home for nothing," the guard said. "Miss Davenport left strict instructions not to be disturbed. She was caught up in that Nostrum massacre, you know."

"She'll see us," Remo said firmly.

"Sorry," the guard said.

Chiun lifted on tiptoe so he could see over the top of the high circular security desk.

"I demand you announce us, hireling, for I am Chiun, chief of Nostrum."

"No can do."

"Sure, you can," Remo said brightly as he vaulted the horseshoe-shaped desk.

The guard reached for a buzzer as Remo joined him. Remo hit the buzzer first. It sprang from its mounting like a jack-in-the-box.

"Broke," Remo said. "Now, announce us."

"No, I will not," the guard said shortly.

"Then I'll do it," Remo said. He went to the fax machine, found Faith's name beside a speed-dial button, and pressed it.

"That won't do any good," the guard sneered. "You have to put something in the fax."

"I was coming to that," Remo said, taking the guard by the scruff of his blazer. Remo mashed the protesting guard's face into the fax window and held it there.

"Anytime you feel like pressing the appropriate button," Remo sang out, "feel free."

The guard stabbed the "Send" button.

Remo held him there until the phone rang. He scooped it up.

"This is Miss Davenport in Twenty-one-C. I just received this weird fax. Is anything wrong?"

"This is Remo. I guess the guard pressed the wrong button or something. I'm down in the lobby. Can I come up?"

"Up?" Faith said pleasurably. "You can come up, down, or anywhere you want."

"I'm on my way," Remo said, wondering if he had made a mistake.

Faith met them at the door, wearing only a smile and holding up two bottles of mineral water.

Remo took in the sight of her nakedness without surprise and with both hands stuffed into his chino pockets.

"Thank goodness you're safe," she cooed.

"*Chiun* and I are safe," Remo corrected, pulling the Master of Sinanju into view by his sleeve.

Faith's eyes went to Chiun. Chiun's hands went over his eyes in mortification. He gasped.

The stars went out of Faith's eyes and she made an eek of a surprise noise like a cartoon mouse. She hopped back behind the door.

"Why don't I handle this alone?" Remo suggested.

"I did not know she was like that," Chiun said, taking his hands from his shocked eyes.

"Must be the stress of high finance."

"I will wait here," Chiun said. "Do it quickly."

"It may take a while to pump her."

"That was not what I meant," Chiun said disgustedly, turning his back.

Remo closed the door behind him. "Hello?" he called.

Faith came out of the bathroom holding a towel around her shapely body.

"Where's the chief?" she asked.

"There are some things that upset him. He decided to wait in the hall."

The smile returned to Faith's face. She dropped the towel, revealing, among other things, possible evidence that she was a natural blond.

"Let's not keep him waiting," she said, reaching for Remo's hand, the better to guide him into the bedroom. Remo kept his hand in his pocket.

"Actually, I came to ask you about Looncraft. I think he was behind the shooting today."

Faith stopped. "Looncraft? Why?"

"We don't know why. But it was something to do with the British. Do you remember anything that would connect Looncraft to the British government or any British agent or interest?"

"I doubt it. He was always humming patriotic songs under his breath. You know, 'My Country, 'Tis of Thee,' 'The Star-Spangled Banner.' Stuff like that."

"Doesn't add up," Remo muttered. "Are you sure about that?"

"I think better when I'm lying down," Faith suggested, arching a provocative eyebrow.

Remo sighed. "Okay, whatever works."

Faith jumped onto the bed so hard she bounced. Remo

sat on the edge. He was forced to take his hands out of his pockets. The sight of Remo's fingers sent Faith digging into the drawer of a side table.

"I know that Looncraft had a bug in his ear about people's ancestry," Faith said as she searched. "He asked me once if I had any English forebears."

"Do you?"

"Search me. I guess so. And German and Dutch and maybe a little French. Ah, here it is."

Faith took what Remo at first mistook for an individually wrapped Alka-Seltzer tablet in her mouth and tore the blue foil packet apart with perfect white teeth.

"What's that?" Remo asked.

Faith smiled. She dangled a yellowish rubbery ring under his nose.

Remo made a face. "I hate condoms."

"I believe in practicing safe sex," Faith told him, grabbing Remo by one thick wrist. "Now, put it on. It won't bite you. But I might," she added deliciously.

"First answer a few more questions. Think. Anything British about Looncraft?"

"Well," Faith said slowly, "I do remember one time I brought some reports into his office. He was at his computer."

"The one on his desk?" Remo asked.

"No. Not the Telerate machine. The other one. He was glaring at something on the screen like he was angry at it. He muttered something about the London relay being down."

"The London relay? Do you remember what was on the screen?"

"Something about a king or queen, or both."

"Could it have been a chess move, like Bishop's King Twelve?"

"That's no chess move."

"Just answer the question."

"Yeah, I think it was a chess move. Satisfied? Can we play now?"

"A deal's a deal," Remo said without joy.

"Oh, goody," Faith cooed, grabbing his wrist again. "Close your eyes and I'll put it on for you."

"Shouldn't I undress first?" Remo wanted to know.

"No. This is my party. We play my way."

Remo closed his eyes. Faith took hold of his wrist. He heard the condom creak at it was unrolled. He frowned. He didn't feel his zipper slide down. But his forefinger felt suddenly tight.

"Open your eyes," Faith called musically.

Remo opened his eyes. He saw Faith sitting there, her eyes closed, her left wrist held out as an offering.

And Remo's right index finger was sheathed in pale yellowish lambskin.

Sighing, Remo began tapping Faith's wrist with it.

"I hate using these things," he groused.

Five boring minutes later, Remo left the apartment, his face at half-mast.

"I got something," he told Chiun.

"No doubt she did too," Chiun sniffed.

"Hey, I kept my pants on. Honest."

"Do not lie to me, Remo," Chiun scolded. "I heard her disgusting cries of ecstasy."

"Have it your way," Remo said. "Looncraft's getting his computer chess moves from London, or near London. Faith remembered him complaining about the London relay, whatever that is."

"Smith should know," Chiun said.

"We can call him from the Nostrum office," Remo suggested.

Harold W. Smith took the call in the near-darkness of the Folcroft office. The glowing green screen illuminated his pinched, unhealthy face.

"Smith? Remo. I got a lead. Those chess moves are coming from London."

Smith listened to Remo's story. "Take the next flight to London."

"Then what?"

"Contact me when you get there," Smith said in a distant voice. "I have penetrated Looncraft's computer and believe I can break down his passwords."

"Shouldn't be too hard," Remo said airily. "I got a

bunch of files to print out just by pounding a mess of keys all at once."

"I will await your call," Smith said, hanging up. He returned to his task and watched as the screen displayed single words in high-speed sequence. The Folcroft mainframe was attempting to feed the Looncraft, Dymstar & Buttonwood system every possible single-word password in the English language. It was just a matter of time.

The computer beeped and locked on the word "CROWN."

Smith tapped the 'Enter' key.

Columns of file names presented themselves to Harold Smith. He chose one at random. It was labeled "MAP." Smith accessed it with a keystroke.

The sight that greeted Harold Smith's eyes at first appeared commonplace. It was a greenish wire-frame map of the continental United States, divided by states.

Smith was about to abandon the file when he realized there was something odd about the state divisions. He tapped a key which magnified the map. He lost most of the West as it expanded, but the Eastern Seaboard showed quite clearly.

"What on earth?" Smith said to himself as he read the state names. At first he thought he was looking at a foreign-language map of America. On closer inspection he realized "Bofton" was the city of Boston. The name was written with the Old English long 's', which resembled an 'f'.

There were other differences. The border with Canada was hundreds of miles lower, cutting deep into Maine and the Great Lakes region. Vermont and New Hampshire were combined under the name New-Hampshire Grants. Massachusetts was bisected vertically. The western half was called Springfield and the eastern portion labeled New-Ireland Protectorate. Rhode Island's capital was Providence-Plantations. Further south, there were other changes. Pennsylvania was Cornwallis. Virginia was Victoria. Washington, D.C., had been renamed Wellington. Miami was Kingsport.

"This is insane," Smith muttered, bringing the rest of the map into view again. He put his nose to the screen. Further west, the familiar squarish state lines had been redrawn into arbitrary zones bearing names such as King

John's Land, the Princess Diana Grants, New Wales, and, most bizarrely, the Benedict Arnold Mountains were where the Rocky Mountains should have been. Great Churchill Lake occupied the former site of Great Salt Lake.

California and Washington state did not exist under any name. Instead, British Columbia's southern border had been lowered all the way to Baja California. The entire territory was labeled "Dominion of Canada."

And across the entire length of the map, in Old English lettering, was the legend "UNITED COLONIES (CIRCA 1992)."

In one corner, a tiny notation mocked him: *P. M. Looncraft, cart.*

"My God!" Smith gasped. "How does that lunatic intend to make this happen?"

Smith abandoned the file and scanned the other file names. He called up the one called "CROWN," intrigued because it was also the password.

Smith got a table of organization for Crown Acquisitions, Limited. P. M. Looncraft was listed as president. There were two other names listed on its board of directors. Douglas Lippincott, whom Smith knew to be Looncraft's business banker, and, astonishingly, DeGoone Slickens.

"They're all in it together," Smith said. Then, in response to his own outburst, he asked the darkness. "But *what* are they in?"

Smith tried another file, this one called "GUARD."

This time, he got a roster, complete with military rankings, of something called the Cornwallis Guard.

"Cornwallis," Smith muttered. "He was the general who surrendered at Yorktown at the end of the American Revolution."

Most of the roster names meant nothing to Smith. Except for seven of them. They were the killers from the Nostrum massacre. Smith saw that William Bragg was listed as a colonel.

Frowning, Smith abandoned the file and dug out the printout Remo had given him.

"Loyalists and conscripts," he muttered. He picked up the red telephone.

"What is it, Smith?" the President asked, out of breath. Obviously he had run into the Lincoln Bedroom to answer.

"Mr. President, I have nothing new to report," Smith told him. "But I do have a question."

"Shoot."

"Are you a client of the investment brokerage of Looncraft, Dymstar & Buttonwood?"

"No. Why?"

"I can't tell you that," Smith said quickly. "Would you know if the Vice-President is one of their clients?"

"No idea. Want me to ask?"

"No," Smith said. "Do not even mention the name to him."

"Can I ask what this is all about?"

"No."

"Well, is something wrong? You haven't lost the Social Security Trust Fund, have you?"

"No. It remains safe. For now. I must return to my work, Mr. President. I'll update you when I have something solid."

"But, Smith—"

Smith hung up, confident that the President, no matter how agitated, would not call back. He knew the ground rules. CURE was autonomous—a safeguard built in to protect the agency from being abused by a politically ruthless President.

Smith leaned back in his chair. A picture was beginning to form. No wonder Looncraft had acquired Slickens' interest in GLB so readily. They were in cahoots. Infamous business enemies on the surface, they were actually allies. As was Lippincott. Smith shuddered. The Lippincott family went back to the American Revolution, as did Looncraft's family. Slickens was another matter. He was from Texas. He didn't fit the profile.

Smith addressed his computer again. The night was young. He had much to do. But now he had the pieces. It was just a matter of fitting and refitting them until he had a coherent picture.

21

"They are a gray people living in a gray land," Chiun was saying. The lights were low in the British Airways cabin. The window shades were lowered against the mid-Atlantic moonlight. The sound of the 747's engines had settled to a monotonous drone. "Gray and rude." Chiun's voice rose at that last, waking several dozing passengers.

A British Airways hostess came up the isle and bestowed upon Chiun an "I'm-embarrassed-to-bring-this-up, *but*" smile.

"Excuse me, luv," she said in an undertone, "but would you be a dear and lower your voice? Some of the others are trying to catch a bit of sleep."

"Be gone, daughter of Gaul."

"I'll talk to him," Remo said, smiling back with equal politeness.

"That's a dear. If you'd like more tea, let me know."

After the hostess had left, Chiun complained to Remo.

"Can you imagine the rudeness of that one?" he squeaked. "Interrupting our private conversation."

"You were disturbing the other passengers," Remo whispered back. "And I for one am getting tired of your carping."

"I do not carp," Chiun said evenly. "I instruct. If we are to root out this foul plot, you must know the kind of people we are dealing with."

"I know what I'm dealing with," Remo said sourly. "I've been to England a couple of times. Without you. And I got along fine."

"How did you survive? The British know nothing of rice. They eat potatoes." Chiun spat the word like an epithet.

"I used to like potatoes when I was a kid," Remo said in a reasonable voice.

"What do children know? The English are the only people who consider the potato a delicacy. That is why their skins are so unhealthy. They eat too many potatoes, which they dig from the dirt."

"I thought it was the cloudy weather that made them pale."

"A curse from the gods to punish them for excessive potato eating," Chiun sniffed.

Remo rolled his eyes. He noticed an empty seat across the aisle and decided to take it. Left alone, Chiun began to talk in a louder voice.

Remo tried to ignore Chiun's rantings. It was something about the First Great Idiocy of the Barbarians—which Remo knew to be Chiun's code phrase for the First World War—being a squabble between Queen Victoria's grand-children, who had gotten out of hand and effectively closed down the West as a Sinanju client because all the killing was being done by mere soldiers and farmers, not profes-sionals.

Muttering to himself, Remo returned to his original seat. Chiun resumed speaking in quieter tones so that only Remo had to endure them.

"Name one good thing about the British," Chiun said at one point.

"They drink tea, just like you."

Chiun snorted derisively. "They drink black tea. Not green. Black tea and dirty potatoes."

"I give up."

"Good."

The 747 landed at Heathrow just as the sun was coming up. Remo had not slept a wink, but because night had lasted only four hours, his brain was tricked into thinking otherwise.

In the busy terminal, Remo exchanged his money for British pounds. He was about to phone Smith, when he heard the name Remo Stallone paged. He realized that was him.

Smith's voice came through the airport courtesy phone.

"Nice timing," Remo told Smith. "We're at Heathrow."

"Obviously," Smith said without sarcasm. "I've confirmed the worst. This entire plot does have British origins. And somehow the Vice-President is part of it."

"No kidding," Remo said.

"Remo, things are happening here. I'm picking up rumors about the instability of the U.S. treasury-bond market. I know they're false, but these rumors are spreading like wildfire. Once this hits the media, it may start something irreversible."

"Not my problem. What have you got for me and Chiun?"

Smith hesitated. "Nothing but a map of the United States as it will be if the plot succeeds. I pulled it off Looncraft's computer. I'm waiting for morning. Until Looncraft contacts his British superior through his office terminal, I have no way to trace these chess-code messages to their source."

"Source . . ." Remo said thoughtfully.

"Beg pardon?"

"You just gave me a first place to go. The Source. It's that British supersecret counterintelligence agency. I've dealt with them before. Let's see what Chiun and I can shake out of them."

"Do it."

Remo hung up and turned to Chiun.

"Smith says we shake up the place. We'll start with the dippy Source."

"Dippy?" Chiun asked as they entered the underground station.

"They're sort of the British version of CURE. Except everyone knows their address. When I'm in town and I need information, I always go there first. They know everything—except how to keep secrets."

Standing on the platform, oblivious of the occasional arched English eyebrow, Remo and Chiun waited for the next train.

"We're going to Trafalgar Square," he told Chiun. "Any idea if we're on the right line?"

Before Chiun could answer, a man in a bowler and wearing a red carnation in his lapel piped up, "Trafalgar Square, Yank? Be delighted to direct you. You have the right line. Take the Cockfosters train to Piccadilly Circus. It's a short hop, skip, and jump from there."

"Thanks, pal," Remo told him.

"Enjoy your stay, Yank. Cheerio."

A gunmetal train rumbled into the station and they boarded, ducking first to avoid bumping their heads on the low doorframe.

"See?" Remo said. "The British are very friendly."

"Perhaps he was Irish," Chiun snapped, looking around at the passengers' faces. There were as many Indians and blacks as English.

As the train rattled from station to station, Remo remarked, "I'll say one thing. Hearing an authentic English accent is a relief after listening to Looncraft and his pseudo-British crap. At least these people sound the way they should."

Checking the car's railway map, he remarked, "We just left Gloucester Road Station. It's only five more stops."

"It is pronounced 'Gloster,' " Chiun sniffed. "They only spell it that ridiculous way to confuse the unwary."

Minutes later they emerged at Piccadilly Circus. It was a busy six-way intersection of stores and restaurants.

"Which way?" Remo wondered.

"You are asking me?" Chiun said, annoyed.

A turbaned East Indian happened to pass by and Remo grabbed him by the sleeve.

"Excuse me, pal, but we're looking for Trafalgar Square."

"Trafalgar, gov?" the man asked in a thick cockney accent. "Hit's just down 'Aymarket. You can't miss hit, eh?"

"Yeah, thanks," Remo said in a vague voice. He saw the street sign that read "HAYMARKET." He figured that was what the man meant. Maybe.

"You were saying?" Chiun asked.

"Nothing," Remo said. "This place takes some getting used to."

As they walked through the bright English morning, a red double decker bus trundled by.

Chiun, looking at a billboard on its side, let out a shriek of disbelief.

'The barbarians!" he cried.

Remo followed his shaking finger. The billboard showed a lady's hand dangling a piece of string over a cup rim. It said: "Do the Jiggle Dip Dunk." Remo couldn't imagine what was being advertised, and said so.

"Tea bags!" Chiun spat. "The British never stooped this low before."

"Tea bags?"

"It is barbarism at its worst."

As they walked along, they passed a McDonald's a Kentucky Fried Chicken, and a British fast-food establishment called Wimpy.

"This is unbelievable," Chiun said shrilly. "They are sinking into . . . into . . ."

"Americanism," Remo suggested.

"Exactly! Americanism. It is beyond understanding. A century ago the world suffered under what they called Pax Britannica. Now it is Shop American that rules."

"I don't see why you're getting so worked up about a people you don't like in the first place," Remo said reasonably. "Besides, I hear they even have Kentucky Fried Chicken in China now."

"The British used to have standards, miserable as they were," Chiun complained. "But this is a new low even for them."

Chiun didn't stop complaining until they came to Trafalgar Square and its four proud lions guarding Nelson's Column. Remo looked around for the apothecary shop that occupied the ground floor of Source headquarters.

"There it is," Remo said. He led Chiun to a door that connected to the second floor. The door was locked. Remo popped it with the heel of his hand. They walked through cobwebs and up the steps to the musty second floor. It was unlocked. The suite of offices on the other side was empty.

"I don't get it," Remo said wonderingly.

"What is there to get? They moved."

"Hold on," Remo said, heading back down the stairs.

At the apothecary shop Remo put a question to the chemist.

"I'm looking for Guy Phillistone."

"Would you mean Sir Guy?"

"That's the one. Know where he lives?"

"That I do. He has a flat at Number One Buckingham Place."

"How long ago? He might have fixed it by now."

The chemist looked doubtful. "I was referring to his digs."

"You mean his apartment."

"I imagine that I do."

"That near Buckingham Palace?" Remo asked.

"Righteo."

"Much obliged."

Remo joined Chiun outside, where a brief morning sprinkle was just beginning.

"Want to take a bus?" Remo suggested.

"No," Chiun retorted. "When one comes to London, one must expect to get wet."

"Suit yourself."

They strolled under the massive Admiralty Arch and down the tree-lined Mall, past the Queen Victoria Monument, which faced Buckingham Palace's huge forecourt.

"It's gotta be around here somewhere," Remo said outside the Buckingham Palace gates. The sidewalk was thick with tourists.

"I will ask that one," Chiun said, slipping between bars that a child could not squeeze through. He strode up to a red-uniformed guard whose tall bearskin hat resembled a black licorice cotton-candy cone.

"Forget it," Remo called after him. "Those guys never talk."

"You, potato eater!" Chiun accused. "Direct us to Buckingham Place."

The guard stood stolidly, looking neither right nor left.

"I told you so," Remo said.

"You are well-trained," Chiun told the man in a quiet voice. Then, his tone darkening, "But I am in a hurry." And he took the guard's rifle from his rigid two-handed grasp.

The guard looked to either side frantically. The nearest guard looked stolidly ahead, pretending to be unaware of his comrade's predicament. The first guard took a crouching step toward the Master of Sinanju. Chiun swatted him on the head with the butt of his own rifle. The hat swallowed his head. The guard reached up with both hands to remove it.

Chiun took that opportunity to trip him. He stepped onto the guard's squirming stomach.

"Buckingham Place!" Chiun repeated. "Where is it?"

"Go left. Off Buckingham Gate!" his muffled voice said.

"Thank you," the Master of Sinanju said, dropping the rifle on the guard's black-furred head. He stepped off his scarlet stomach and joined Remo outside the gate.

As they walked off, Remo said, "That wasn't necessary."

"That man was rude. The economy of the world is hanging in the balance and he is playing soldier."

Number One Buckingham Place was a Georgian brick town house at the end of a row of town houses. Remo knocked on the door and waited politely.

The man who answered was tall and had sandy hair and eyebrows. A meershaum pipe whose bowl was carved to represent Anne Boleyn's decapitated head smoldered before his sharp nose.

He took one look at Remo and dropped his pipe. He couldn't get the door closed fast enough.

Unfortunately for Sir Guy Phillistone, head of Britain's supersecret Source, he couldn't get it closed ahead of Remo's strong arms. Remo pushed his way in, Chiun trailing.

"Remember me?" Remo asked brightly.

"Rather. You are that American lunatic."

"That's not polite. And here I've been telling my friend how nice you British are."

"How did you find me? What do you want of me?"

"In answer to number one, I asked at the apothecary shop."

"Drat!" said Sir Guy Phillistone.

"That's not the word I would have used," Remo said. "But to answer number two, I want everything you know about the plot to wreck the world's stock exchanges."

"What plot is that?"

"Wrong answer," Remo said, taking Sir Guy Phillistone—

who knew exactly what Remo Williams could do with those terrible thick-wristed hands of his—by the throat.

"What is the correct answer?" Sir Guy choked out. "Tell me and I shall tell you."

Remo turned to Chiun. "Did that make any sense to you?"

"No. But he is telling the truth."

"Look, Guy. It's a British plot. I know it, even if you don't. Someone in your government is trying to create economic panic. Whom should we be looking for?"

Sir Guy hesitated. Remo squeezed.

"The queen!" Sir Guy bleated. "The prime minister! Perhaps the foreign secretary! The chancellor of the exchequer has always struck me as a right berk. Anyone but myself. I know nothing of this. I really do not."

"I believe you, Sir Guy," Remo said. "Be a good chap and don't warn anyone."

"I was just on my way to the pub around the corner. I feel the urge for a pint of stout."

"Don't let us keep you," Remo said.

Sir Guy left hurriedly, not stopping to pick up his cracked pipe. He left the door open for Remo's convenience.

"Trusting sort," Remo said, picking up the phone and asking for the overseas operator.

When he heard Smith's cracked voice, he explained that every lead had evaporated.

"Sir Guy suggested we shake up the local government," Remo concluded. "What do you think?"

"Do it," Smith said. "Things are heating up here. The treasury-bond rumors have reached the Far Eastern markets. The dollar is going south."

"We're on it." He hung up.

To Chiun, Remo said. "We've got his blessing. We can do this faster if we split up."

"You may treat with the House of Windsor," Chiun said, "I will have none of them."

"Parliament's yours."

"We will meet afterward beneath that ugly clock."

"Big Ben?"

"That is what they call its bell," Chiun sniffed. "I do not care to know what they call the clock."

They walked together as far as Birdcage Walk, which Chiun took. Remo continued on and mingled with the knots of tourists outside the palace gates.

He considered going over the wall, when suddenly the gates were thrown open. Remo turned to see a tiny coach pulled by two white horses rounding the circle dominated by the Victoria Monument and realized he had found the perfect way in.

John Brackenberry huddled in his bright red coat as the light rain pattered the top of his high black stovepipe hat, his coach whip rigid in his right hand.

He was proud to drive the wooden-wheeled clarence which carried state papers from Whitehall to Buckingham Palace, where they would be affixed with the royal assent. Driving a clarence, which seldom carried passengers, and never a member of the royal family, was not as prestigious as driving a state coach, but it was honorable work, and suited his traditional sensibilities.

As the clarence passed through the gates, Brackenberry never heard the coach door open. The springs never shifted despite the 155-pound weight that settled into the velvet cushions, brushing aside the box containing state documents fresh from Whitehall.

Thus, when John Brackenberry dismounted to open the coach, the last thing he expected was to find a passenger within.

"I say," he demanded, "who the bloody hell are you?"

"Don't mind me," the man said in a crude American accent.

"Tourists are not allowed in the royal clarence," he sputtered. He was nearly apoplectic. Nothing like that had ever happened before. He had heard of Yank tourists urinating in the parks and neglecting to pay their bus fare, but this was the limit.

"I'm just here to see Mrs. Windsor," the man said, stepping out. "Know where I can find her?"

"I do not know whom you could mean."

"The queen."

Brackenberry drew himself up in indignation. "One does not address the queen as Mrs. Windsor, my good fellow."

"I love the way you people are so polite even when you're upset. Restores my faith in humanity. I thought Windsor was her last name."

"It is not! That is, it *is* Windsor, but Her Highness is not permitted to use it."

"Heavy hangs the head, huh? Look, this is fascinating, but just point me to the royal chambers and I'll take it from there."

That was too much even for John Brackenberry. "Guards!" he shouted.

"Damn!" Remo said. "I hoped you were going to be British about this."

"I *am* being British about this, you sluggard!"

A trio of Household Guards appeared as if out of nowhere. One of them happened to be the one Chiun had roughed up earlier. Remo gave him a little wave. The man stopped dead in his tracks, then beat a hasty retreat.

The other two were only too happy to escort Remo into Buckingham Palace after he relieved them of their rifles and dismembered the unloaded weapons before their eyes. For good measure, he took one of their high hats and, rolling it between his hands at high speed, set it afire by friction. He replaced it on the guard's head.

"The queen is not in," the guard with the flaming hat said.

"Prove it," Remo countered.

"Happy to."

Remo was escorted through the palace. The Household Guards even showed him the queen's private chambers and offered him the souvenir of his choice. Remo politely declined. Instead, he asked after the queen's current whereabouts.

There was some dissension on that score. One guard thought the queen was sojourning at Windsor Castle, the other thought she was somewhere in Wales. Perhaps on holiday at Portmeirion.

Outside the palace, the guards escorted Remo to the big gate and opened it for him. They wished him well as he sauntered up Birdcage Walk, his eyes on Big Ben.

The Master of Sinanju regarded the garishly carven Houses of Parliament from the foot of Westminster Bridge, on the north side of the Thames River. His hands, behind his back, were tucked into his kimono sleeves, and he was heedless of the light rain, which evaporated almost as soon as it touched his aged head.

He examined the moat below street level, covered by immaculate greensward. His nose wrinkled at the high green fence whose top almost paralleled the sidewalk. It might possibly be electrified, but that did not matter. He could achieve it with one leap, and the grass in two.

He wondered who would be so foolish as not to fill the serviceable moat with water.

Chiun strolled up Westminster Bridge to gain a view of the southern face of Parliament. He spied a patio filled with awninged tables—no doubt for the pleasure of the lords of Parliament. But those tables were empty now.

Chiun paused on the bridge. He looked down. The water was unspeakably discolored. Its smell offended his sensitive nostrils. But for that he would have gone all the way to the end of the bridge and, from its other bank, raced across the water to that most vulnerable point of attack.

It was a sound plan, except the Master of Sinanju would never have been able to get the stench from his sandals, no matter how lightly he raced across the thick waters.

Chiun returned the way he came. There would be a way. There always was.

On Millbank, he paced before the grimy facade of Parliament, cleaned for half of its length by sandblasting. It only made the sootier section all the more ugly.

He crossed Millbank to get a better view. Standing in the smallish Old Palace Yard behind Westminster Abbey, Chiun considered that no fortress was ever built that did not have a secret escape tunnel, which to the professional assassin could serve as an entrance. He went in search of one.

Chiun found what he sought tucked away at one end of the yard—a concrete ramp that led to an underground parking garage.

Smiling to himself, Chiun realized he had found the entrance he required. He floated down the concrete ramp, past the guard box and yellow-and-black-striped dropgate.

The guard in the box noticed him coming down, happened to look away, and when he looked back, there was no sign of the approaching Asian.

The underground garage covered several acres, and was lit by overhead fluorescent lights. The Master of Sinanju floated through it in the general direction of Parliament until he found what he wanted.

It was an elevator, marked by steel doors and guarded by two stone-faced bobbies. They would not be a problem, Chiun knew. Bobbies never carried firearms.

In the lower house, the Prime Minister of England listened to the inane prattle of the Labour representative with a polite expression on her strong motherly face, knowing that if she gave him enough rope, he would say something astonishingly stupid.

"And I submit, Mr. Speaker, that it is Madam Prime Minister's wretched policies that have contributed to the state of near-chaos that the City is currently in."

That did it. The woman known, loved, and feared throughout the British Isles as the Iron Lady leapt to her feet. Her voice reverberated through the ancient halls of Parliament.

"I beg your pardon," she said coldly, "but the honorable gentleman's remarks are further proof, if any is needed, of Labour's utter and callous irresponsibility. The City is suffering from the identical ailment that inflicts the markets from Hong Kong to New York. It has nothing to do with England, never mind the Tory government. Perhaps the gentleman should excuse himself now and read the last weeks' papers. Starting with his own *Guardian*."

The chambers broke into howling laughter. From Labour and a few Tory back-benchers came dark mutterings. The prime minister sat down, having scored a major point.

She was satisfied. But in her heart, she would have liked nothing better than to have caned the Labour representative.

Labour stood up to rebut, but his first words froze in his mouth. From somewhere in the great halls of Parliament came a ruckus.

"What the devil is that?" the prime minister said. "See to it, one of you."

Bobbies hurried in the direction of the commotion. They came running back just as rapidly. One whispered in the speaker's ear.

The speaker stood up. "Madam Prime Minister," he announced, "I must ask that you and the gentlemen present vacate Parliament."

"Leave?" the prime minister shouted. "But we are in session."

"Parliament is also under attack."

Labour was out the door like a flood of lemmings. Several Tories formed a protective cordon around the prime minister.

"Do not fear, Madam Prime Minister," one said bravely. "They will have to strike us all down to get to you."

"Let us hope it does not come to that," the prime minister said worriedly. "Has anyone any idea what is the problem?"

Before anyone could answer, the problem burst into the richly carved chambers, hurling bobbies before it like an emerald tornado.

The problem was a small man of Asiatic extraction, who deftly evaded the down-swinging clubs in the bobbies' hands. Guns were held high in their hands.

"Do not shoot!" the prime minister called out. "This is Parliament."

"How many of them?" a Tory asked, craning to see beyond his fellows.

"Just the one," he was told.

The Tories exchanged glances.

"What does he want?" the prime minister called from the knot of protective men.

The Asian answered.

"I am Chiun, Reigning Master of Sinanju!" His voice, coming from such a frail figure, was awesome in its volume.

"Never heard of you," the prime minister called back, intending to humor the man.

"What! Never heard of the House of Sinanju? Barbarians! We were the greatest assassins known to history while your ancestors were fending off the Danes."

"Did he say assassin?" the prime minister asked.

"That he did," a stuffy voice said. "You men. Shoot! Shoot the bugger down!"

The guns came down. And for the first time since the days of Guy Fawkes, violence was threatened against the Houses of Parliament. And as before, it was about to be perpetrated by Englishmen.

The prime minister stared as three bobbies dropped their Webley revolvers to sight on the old Oriental's bald head. She was too strong, despite her grandmotherly features, to look away from violence.

Three revolvers thundered at once. Everyone in the room blinked. And in that blink, something inexplicable happened.

Everyone from the prime minister on down expected to witness the eruption of the aged Oriental's head as three bullets tore it asunder like a pumpkin.

Instead, the shots buried themselves in a richly carven wall.

The old Oriental was no longer there.

Everyone gasped at once.

"Where could he have gone?" the prime minister demanded.

No one knew. And as they pondered the inexplicable, Chiun, Master of Sinanju, reached the apex of his somersault. He had gone high, the better to confuse his foemen. Parliament's vaulted ceiling allowed a high graceful leap and time to pause at the apogee, while the Englishmen below looked everywhere but where the Master of Sinanju was. The bobbies, convinced he had fled, ran out into the corridor, shouting and waving their pistols. Chiun wondered what the world was coming to, when even bobbies carried pistols, like American cowboys.

"Could it have been a ghost?" someone wondered aloud.

"Boo!" a squeaky voice said. The Tories jumped. For the sound came from within their very midst.

"That was not amusing," the prime minister said sternly.

"It was not meant to be," said the author of the boo, none other than the Master of Sinanju. He was standing beside the prime minister, having landed with no more sound than a pillow falling onto a comforter.

The Tory guard were looking out from their circle. At the sound of Chiun's voice, they looked inward. They saw him. They gasped. And they reacted. The circle broke apart and dashed for the exits.

In a moment that seemed even less that a millisecond, the prime minister found herself alone and exposed in the center of Parliament, facing her apparent assassin.

"I am not afraid of you," she said stiffly, clutching her purse tightly.

The old Asian looked up, his mouth compressed.

"You are either very brave or very foolish," he said.

"Thank you, but I reject the former and firmly deny the latter accusation."

"Spoken like a true Englishman."

"Woman. And thank you."

"It was not intended as a compliment," Chiun said. "I will be brief. Your government is in some way responsible for the vicious attack on the world's economy. It will stop. Today. Or all of the remnants of your pitiful crumbling empire will suffer horrendously."

"My dear man," the prime minister said, fixing the Master of Sinanju with her metallic glare, "would you by any chance belong to the Loyal Opposition?"

"I owe no allegiance to England. I am Korean, working for the American emperor, whose name I am forbidden to speak, for he rules secretly."

The prime minister's mouth froze in the open position. Was this man mad? She rejected asking the question point-blank.

"Do I understand you to say that the Americans sent you to ask me this preposterous question?"

"Unofficially," Chiun said flatly.

"Unofficially or officially, your suggestion is absurd, and you may tell whomever you wish that you have this on the most direct authority. Our own financial district, the City, is suffering under calamitous pressure, as is the rest of the civilized world. Surely you understand that."

"Lying will not deter me from my quest," Chiun warned, his face puckered into a web of dry wrinkles.

"Not believing the truth will not achieve your ends any more quickly," the prime minister countered.

"You are telling the truth," the old Oriental said at last.

"I thank you for your faith," the prime minister said stiffly.

"Pah, I do not trust you. But I hear your heartbeat. It tells me you are not lying. I will have to look elsewhere for the answers I seek."

"Nevertheless, that is very good of you."

"I am not merely good," said the person called Chiun. "I am great." He left the empty room as if he were free to stroll out to the street with impunity after turning Parliament topsy-turvy.

The prime minister wondered how far he would get.

22

Remo Williams wondered how Chiun was doing as he walked along the park side of Birdcage Walk in the direction of Parliament.

The string of police cars and ambulances that roared by, their discordant sirens in full cry, gave him his first clue.

Remo started to run. He had been walking on the St. James's Park side, and cut across the traffic. A bobby tried to give him a ticket for reckless walking. Remo recklessly walked over him and picked up speed.

Parliament Square, when he came to it, was milling with indignant faces. The ambulances and police cars disgorged bobbies, who converged on Parliament like blue ants.

Remo slowed down and mingled with the crowd.

He found Chiun standing at the foot of Parliament's Clock Tower, his hands modestly tucked into his sleeves, his face registering quizzical interest in the confusion swirling around him.

"Any luck?" Remo whispered.

"The plot does not come from Parliament. And you?"

"The queen's out having tea and crumpets or something."

"I do not think it is her anyway. Modern English queens are good only for collecting their pensions."

"That leaves . . . what, the chancellor of the exchequer?"

"There are also the home secretary, the foreign secretary, and other functionaries." Chiun frowned. "That is the problem when there is no proper emperor," he lamented. "Too many lackeys and no center of power. Would that a strong king still ruled this miserable isle. We would not be leaping about like confused grasshoppers."

"Spare me the if-onlys. Which one should we tackle first?"

"None. Let us walk."

Chiun led Remo across the street and down a flight of steps marked "SUBWAY."

"We taking a train somewhere?" Remo asked. Chiun said nothing. They emerged on the other side, by the River Thames. Remo had seen no sign of the subway system in the long tunnel, and remarked on that.

Chiun shrugged. Wordlessly they strolled down Victoria Embankment, past a pier where sightseeing boats were moored and cockney voices hawked excursions along the river.

"They all used to talk that way," Chiun remarked. "Before they took on airs."

"Do tell." The walk was pleasant, and Remo noted the cast-iron dolphin light standards that studded the concrete embankment every few feet. Strings of light bulbs hung between them like Puritan Christmas ornaments.

They passed under the ornate monstrosity that is Hungerford Bridge, which rattled with trains from nearby Charing Cross Station, following the curve of the Thames.

Police cars rushed by them often, caterwauling rudely.

Remo was content to walk by Chiun's side in silence. No conversation meant no carping. Remo was in a no-carping mood. The wind was blowing from the Victoria Embankment gardens on the other side of the avenue, bringing the smell of wet grass—a distinct improvement over the dank odor coming from the Thames.

After a while Remo ventured a question.

"Why do they pronounce it 'Tems' and not 'Thames'?"

"Because they have forgotten how to pronounce 'Tame-sis,' " Chiun told him, "which is what the Romans called it—just as in their laziness they no longer bother with this city's true name, which is Londinium."

"It's their city," Remo said nonchalantly.

"It was the Romans who made it great. The British are merely squatters."

"They squat pretty well," Remo said, looking about with a hint of admiration at the variety of architecture.

Chiun stopped in his tracks suddenly. "No!" he squeaked, leaping ahead.

"What is it?" Remo asked, racing to catch up to him.

The Master of Sinanju came to a halt before a pock-marked granite obelisk covered with Egyptian hieroglyphics set on the embankment.

"The idiots!" Chiun cried. "The base cretins!"

Recognizing the beginning of one of Chiun's tantrums, Remo folded his arms. The Master of Sinanju stamped his sandaled feet. He accosted a British businessman in a mackintosh.

"Do you know nothing?" he raged. "Are you people that ignorant?

"Release me, you yobbo!" the man demanded.

"Pah, you are not worth speaking to," Chiun said, sending the man spinning away with a casual flick of his wrist. "You people are uneducable." His voice rose with righteous indignation as the man rushed off. "Do you hear? Uneducable!"

"So what's the problem?" Remo asked after Chiun had settled down to merely tearing at the puffs of hair over his tiny ears.

"Not you too!" Chiun screeched.

"Okay, okay. Give me a second to figure it out."

Remo approached the monument, which was flanked by two basalt sphinxes, which, like sentinels, faced the obelisk in feline repose. They reminded Remo of the lions at Trafalgar Square.

There were plaques on all four sides of the obelisk, which Remo quickly learned was called Cleopatra's Needle. It was an authentic Egyptian monument, discovered buried in the ruins of Alexandria, Egypt, and shipped to London by boat in 1878. En route, it was lost in a gale, and later salvaged. One plaque explained that the needle was struck by bomb fragments during the first air raid on London during World War I, resulting in the many pits in the stone. Remo found the story fascinating. He hadn't known London had been bombed during the First World War.

"Okay, I give up," he told Chiun. "What's the problem?"

"I do not know which is the most insulting," Chiun said, his hands on his hips. "That they had the temerity to appropriate this magnificent monument or that they put it up wrong."

Remo looked back. "Don't tell me it's upside down."

"No."

"The sides are facing the wrong way, right?"

Chiun stamped one foot impatiently. "No!"

"I give up," Remo admitted.

"The sphinxes!" Chiun cried shaking a finger at them. "Look at them."

"Yeah . . ." Remo said slowly.

"They are facing inward! Everyone knows that sphinxes face outward, to protect their charge."

"Oh, is that all?"

"All! You would not say that if you knew the Egyptians as I do. They would laugh at this foolishness—those who did not cry at the desecration."

"Well," Remo said casually, "nothing we can do about it now. It's been like that for over a hundred years."

"A hundred years," Chiun grumbled. "A mere instant in time." He regarded the sphinxes at length. One was scarred along its black flank from the same attack that had injured the granite spire.

"I said," Remo repeated, "nothing we can do about it now."

Chiun considered. Then he said, "You are right, Remo. There is nothing we can do about it now."

Chiun started off again, Remo at his side.

"For a minute there," Remo said in a relieved voice, "I

thought you were going to have me turn the sphinxes around."

"We have no time."

"Good."

"Perhaps on the way back," Chiun added.

"Not on your life." And because he wanted to change the subject as quickly as possible, Remo added, "Where are we headed, if it's not too much to ask?"

"The Tower of Londinium.

Remo made a face. "I've been there. And I have no desire to repeat the experience—and shouldn't we be doing something more constructive than taking in the tourist sights?"

"Bear with me."

Remo winced. "Speaking of which, that's another good thing about London."

Chiun cocked his head inquisitively. "Yes?"

"They don't get the *National Enquirer* here. And I don't have to wear the bear suit."

Chiun frowned. "I wonder how Faith is doing?"

"Search me. Why?"

"I put her in charge of Bear-Man marketing."

"You what?" Remo burst out.

"I would not be surprised if by now every person in America is wearing a Bear-Man hat or T-shirt."

"Just as long as my name isn't connected to any of this."

Chiun looked up. "Do I take it to mean you waive all rights to Bear-Man royalties?"

"Now and forever," Remo said solemnly. Chiun beamed.

"And no personal appearances either," Remo added.

Chiun's face fell. "We will discuss this another time," he sniffed.

Victoria Embankment came to a stop at Blackfriars Bridge, so they crossed the busy street, wending their way to the Tower of London. Remo recognized it from afar, thanks to the nearby castlelike blue Tower Bridge, which reminded him of a Coney Island ride.

They came to the Tower of London, which is not a single tower but a grouping of crumbling battlements enclosed by the ancient walls of a keep originally built on the Thames by William the Conqueror. Chiun led Remo around its age-discolored stone walls to the long line that whip-sawed from the streets down to a walkway beside a dry moat containing a tennis court.

Chiun stopped at the end of the line.

"You've gotta be kidding," Remo said. "You're actually going to wait in line with the peasants?"

"Shh," Chiun admonished. "We do not want to attract undue attention."

"A little late now. Half the constabulary must be memorizing our descriptions right now."

"All the more reason to blend in with the other tourists."

"Suit yourself," Remo said, leaning against the fence. The line moved slowly. It took twenty minutes to reach the walkway below. By the time they got to the ticket offices, in a stone courtyard patrolled by outlandishly garbed Yeoman Warders—popularly known as Beefeaters—Remo was thoroughly bored and had said so several times, without drawing a response from the Master of Sinanju.

They walked through the Tower green. The Tower ravens were, if anything, bigger and more menacing than Remo had remembered. They seemed as large as vultures.

Chiun led Remo on a quick tour of the various towers, taking delight in pointing out the Bloody Tower and the cruelties it concealed. At one point he stopped beside a Roman wall that had been worn down to the ground like old teeth, and proclaimed, "This is the true Londinium!"

By the Waterloo Barracks, Chiun pulled him into the Torture Chamber exhibit, which displayed medieval devices like thumbscrews, the rack, and the iron maiden.

"Grisly stuff," Remo said, examining a recreation of the gibbet—an iron birdcage in which the bodies of executed criminals were suspended at crossroads as a warning to potential lawbreakers. "I had no idea the English were once so barbaric."

"It was only after they became powerful enough to vent their baser passions against other peoples that they ceased to inflict cruelties on their own," Chiun told him.

"Tell that to the Irish," Remo grunted.

As they left the hole-in-the wall exhibit room, Remo remarked, "You know, I was always taught that the English were the fountainhead of civilization and democracy."

"Whoever taught you obviously never heard of the Greeks or the Romans," Chiun retorted. "Or the Persians, for that matter."

"Where are we going now?" Remo wanted to know.

Chiun drifted up to the end of a line of tourists next to a low building.

"Here," Chiun said.

"Not another line."

"This is the last line we will stand in, I promise you."

The line folded in on itself several times between low uprights. Overhead signs warned in several languages that taking pictures of the Crown Jewels was expressly prohibited.

"Why are we bothering with the Crown Jewels?" Remo wanted to know as the line moved along with sluggish irregularity.

"Because the English value them," Chiun said flatly.

Remo folded his arms. It seemed to take forever, but eventually they came to the entrance.

"Step lively," a Yeoman Warder called out in a boisterous voice. "Step right in. Keep it moving, now."

"Great," Remo said, noticing several rolls of confiscated film suspended in tiny plastic net bags. "*Now* they want us to rush."

"What happened to your admiration of the fine British people?" Chiun inquired pointedly.

"I left it back with the thumbscrews," Remo snapped. "And it's been a long day, so don't rag me, okay?"

They followed the line as it moved between museum-style display cases. Remo absorbed the displays of royal gilt salt cellars and historical costumes without interest.

Finally they descended a flight of steps into a cool basement area and into a literal vault. The open door was a massive thing of stainless steel. It looked exactly like a bank-vault door.

The Crown Jewels were arranged in a huge circular display. A curved, railed walkway ran around its circumference, and below it an area where one could step up to the glass case fronts as long as one did not hold up the line.

"Keep moving," the guards said. These were ordinary blue-uniformed bobbies. "Don't dawdle, now."

"I don't feel like I'm getting my money's worth," Remo grumbled as they were jostled along by other tourists.

"Do not worry," Chiun whispered ominously. "You will."

"I don't like the way you said that," Remo whispered back.

Chiun stopped before the case that held the jewel-encrusted Royal Sceptre. A plate informed Remo that the large faceted jewel held in a heart-shaped mounting was the world's largest diamond, known as the Star of Africa.

"Distract the guard," Chiun said quietly.

"What?" Remo said.

"Do as I bid," Chiun hissed. "And do not ask questions."

Remo glanced around, fixing the three guards, each equally spaced around the circular walkway, in his mind. He wandered back so he was near two of them, with the third in his field of vision.

He decided the best way to capture their interest was to strip off his T-shirt.

He was right. No sooner had he exposed his bare chest than outraged expressions appeared on the bobbies' faces.

"Here, now," one called to him. "You can't disrobe in the presence of the Crown Jewels." He bore down on Remo like a blue tornado.

"Relax," Remo said unconcernedly. "I'm hot. And it's stuffy down here."

"It is delightfully cool, and I am afraid I shall have to escort you from these premises."

Remo smiled broadly. "It's going to take two of you," he taunted.

"Right," the bobby said, signaling to his nearer colleague.

Actually, it took three constables. The first two took Remo by the biceps. Remo let them do that much. But that was all. They pushed. Remo did not budge. They stepped around and tried pulling. Remo folded his arms, and no matter what limbs the bobbies took hold of, Remo stayed in place, as if he had taken root.

The third bobby strode up at that point, his hands on his hips like a flustered schoolmaster.

"Here, now," he said. "Take hold of him properly, chaps."

"The bounder won't budge, sir."

After some low-voiced conversation, they decided to lift Remo bodily. One took him around the waist and the others grabbed his forearms.

"Right we go now, lads," the head bobby said. The sound of three men grunting in exertion came at once. Remo stayed in place.

"His feet appear to be stuck," one ventured, wiping his brow of sweat.

"Perhaps he has glued himself to the floor," one offered.

"No, I haven't," Remo said politely, lifting first one foot, then the other as proof.

The bobbies grabbed at his ankles and tried to repeat the maneuver. But Remo's feet stayed where they were.

By now a crowd had gathered, more interested in the hapless bobbies and the half-naked Yank than in the Crown Jewels.

Remo looked around. There was no sign of Chiun. He took that as a sign that it was time to wrap this up.

"Tell you what," Remo suggested. "How about I just put on my shirt and walk out under my own steam?"

The bobbies consulted among themselves.

"So long as you do it now," the head bobby said with face-saving authority.

Obligingly Remo donned his T-shirt and started for the half-open vault door.

A high squeaky voice brought him whirling around.

"Remo! Catch!"

Instinctively Remo's hands came up. The Royal Sceptre plopped into them. Remo looked at it uncomprehendingly.

"Do not just stand there, run!" Chiun called.

Remo hesitated. He looked to the bobbies, their attention shifting back and forth between Chiun and himself, as if uncertain whom they were more angry with. One bobby ran toward Chiun. The other two came after Remo.

Remo jumped into the corridor, clearing the vault door. He gave the massive door a tap with one toe. The vault rolled shut. Remo grabbed at the control wheels and tried dogging them. There were too many of them, so he gave it up. The size of the vault was enough to hold the bobbies back, he figured.

Rushing up the stairs, Remo looked for an exit. He spotted a sign that said "Way Out."

"Close enough," Remo muttered, ducking through it.

Out in the cobbled walk, Remo wrapped his T-shirt around the Royal Sceptre. He attracted disapproving stares from about three-quarters of the passersby. It was an instant litmus test of who was British and who was not.

Remo hugged the inner walls until he came to a break near the so-called Bloody Tower. He slipped through it, finding himself on the cobbled walk in front of the Traitor's Gate. He ducked down into the cool overhang of St. Thomas' Tower, where tourists were not allowed. The wooden gate was in three sections—an arched top and a double lower section. To Remo's surprise, the lower gates opened outward at a touch. Traitor's Gate gave way. And Remo went out.

He found himself on a stone wharf overlooking the Thames.

The unsavory color of the river was enough to discourage Remo from swimming, so he ran, hugging the tower walls.

He stopped when he came upon a sign that said "SUBWAY."

"Great," Remo said, ducking down the steps. He ran along the foot tunnel and up a set of steps at the opposite end.

Remo's I-did-it expression evaporated when he found himself on the other side of a busy street, standing beside another sign that said "SUBWAY."

"Must have missed it," he muttered, running back down the stone steps.

But the only other set of steps he found was the first one. Remo paused uncertainly. A young man came along and Remo accosted him.

"Excuse me, pal, but I'm looking for the subway."

"In that case," the man said, "I fancy you should be jolly well pleased. For you are standing in it."

"I am? Where are the trains?"

"Trains?" The Londoner's eyes went to Remo's upraised hand. His T-shirt had slid from the Royal Sceptre, exposing an ornamental golden cross.

"I say, that rather resembles the—"

"It's okay," Remo said. "I have permission to carry it. I'm in training for the next Olympics. I'm entered in the scepter toss."

"Never heard of the ripping thing."

"Just point me to the trains."

"You mean the underground."

"In America it's called the subway."

"And in England it is the underground. Pop back the way I came and look for the sign. You can't miss it."

"Thanks," Remo said, sprinting away.

"Luck with the Olympics, Yank," the Englishman called after him.

Remo found the Tower Hill underground station on the other side of the street, recognizing it from afar by the red-and-white sign that looked like a No Smoking sign with the red slash tipped to the horizontal.

Remo caught the first train, having no idea where it was going, and for the moment, caring not at all. He took the train as far as Barking, getting off for no other reason than that Remo almost burst out laughing at the name.

He looked around for a pay phone. He found one near an old church.

It was a red wood-and-glass kiosk.

Remo started feeding coins into the slot, having no idea if it was enough. He got an overseas operator and gave her Smith's code phone number.

"I can scarcely believe that there is such a number as 111-111-1111," the operator said reprovingly.

"Look," Remo said, "it's a special number. Okay?"

"There is no such American area code as 111. Without a correct area code, I cannot put through the call."

"It's a special number," Remo repeated. "Just do it."

"There's no need for rudeness, luv," the operator said. "I will attempt to ring."

"Thank you," Remo said. He got the sound of a ringing phone, then Smith's voice saying hello.

Then the line disconnected.

"Dammit!" Remo said, putting in more coins. He got the same operator again. He recognized her voice.

"I got disconnected," he complained.

"You failed to insert the proper payment."

"So you disconnect me!"

"That is how the system operates," the operator said. "It is automated. We will require twenty pence inserted at thirty-second intervals."

"Okay, okay, I'm putting in coins. Is that enough?"

"I will attempt the call again. Was the number 111-111-1111?"

"Yeah," Remo said in exasperation. "Just lean on the one button until you hear the line ring. That's how I do it."

When Smith's voice came on again, Remo said breathlessly, "Remo here. Gotta talk fast. These screwy British phones shut you off when they get hungry."

"Just keep feeding coins," Smith said.

Remo put in more coins as he talked. "I lost Chiun."

"He just called. He told me everything. You have the . . . er . . . item?"

"In my hot little hands," Remo said.

"Chiun believes he can blackmail the British government into talking. I have my doubts about that, but it is all we have. Chiun is on his way to the Morton Court Hotel, near the Earl's Court tube station. I suggest you join him there. We'll see what develops. It's all we can do until Looncraft's computer comes on-line. Please hurry, Remo. The Far Eastern markets are restive."

"On my way, Smith." There was a click on the line. "Smith? Smith?" The line was dead.

Remo hung up and went down the underground stairs. A wall map showing the vast maze of the London underground system baffled him.

"This is worse than New York," he muttered.

Finally he found Earl's Court. It was on the same line. Remo boarded a Richmond train, holding the Royal Sceptre tightly in his T-shirt.

He got a number of stares from staid Britishers, which he pointedly ignored.

Earl's Court was a huge sand-colored fortress of a station. Remo rode the escalator to a busy street, which was lined with food shops and ethnic restaurants. The neighborhood smelled of curry.

The Morton Court Hotel was a modest establishment on a residential side street which seemed to be given over to small hotels. There was one on every block. Sometimes two.

The reception desk was manned by a thirtyish Indian woman with a coffee complexion and a sugar smile.

Remo turned on the charm.

"Friend of mine is registered here," he said. "Chiun. Where can I find him?"

The woman smiled back. "Take the lift," she said in a crisp Oxford accent that made her sound like a puppet controlled by an invisible British ventriloquist. "Around the corner. Third floor. Room twenty-eight. He's expecting you."

"Thanks," Remo said.

Remo took a rickety elevator to the third floor. He knocked on the door.

"Who is it?" Chiun demanded querulously.

"Me. Remo."

"It is open."

Remo entered. "You should have locked the door," he pointed out, closing it after him.

"It is broken. Everything in this room is broken."

"Except the TV, I see," Remo said.

Chiun sat on the bare floor, his neck craned back to watch the TV, which sat on a high shelf in the corner of the room beside a tall walnut wardrobe.

The room was long and narrow. The two side-by-side beds dominating the room almost touched. A small writing desk half-blocked the bathroom door.

"Where's the rest of the room?" Remo wanted to know, tossing the Royal Sceptre onto one bed.

"Ask Smith."

"Smith recommended this place, I take it," Remo said, throwing himself onto the bed beside the Sceptre.

"Hush, Remo," Chiun admonished, his eyes transfixed by the TV screen.

"What are you watching? It sounds like a beer commercial."

"Do not be ridiculous. And I am beginning to change my mind about the British."

"So am I."

"Like the Americans, they do produce one thing that is good. And it is their British daytime dramas."

"This is a soap opera?" Remo cocked an ear. "Sounds more Australian than English."

Chiun shrugged. "What is the difference?"

"You tell me. Anything on the news about our little escapade?"

"I do not know. I have been watching this program."

"How are we going to know if we're getting results?"

"We will know. Now, be quiet. I am enjoying this."

"You are? I thought you got tired of American soap operas years ago."

"These are different. They do not corrupt the stories with sex."

"Wonderful," Remo said, leaning back. "Wake me up when it's over."

"It is over now," Chiun said, standing.

Remo looked around for the remote control. But all he found were a broken radio and a digital clock that displayed military time.

Giving up, he got up to change the channel by hand. He flipped by a high-school quiz show, a documentary entitled *The History of Bamboo*, and an *Untouchables* rerun.

"If this is typical British TV fare," Remo said, "I'm not very impressed by it. Half of it's American reruns and the rest is like our public TV."

Chiun said nothing. He was examining the Royal Sceptre.

"You think they'll actually expose themselves just to get that thing back?" Remo asked, settling back onto the bed.

"Perhaps. In any event, I expect to hear from them soon."

"How's that?"

"I left a ransom note with the guard at Whitehall."

Remo shot up again. "What!"

"They should be arriving soon."

"Who exactly are 'they'?" Remo asked worriedly.

"I do not know. Perhaps boobies. Possibly soldiers."

Remo sat bolt upright. "Coming here?"

"Oh, do not worry, Remo. They do not know the room number. Just the hotel name."

Remo rushed to the door, saying, "I'd better lock it."

"The lock is broken," Chiun said casually.

"Damn. That's right. So we just sit here—is that it?"

"You have a better plan?"

"I don't have any plan at all."

"Then sit quietly. I wish to meditate."

Remo returned to the bed. "I don't know why I let you get me into these situations."

"It is because you trust me implicitly."

"Really? I always thought it was because I'm gullible."

Chiun beamed. "That too."

23

In the predawn darkness of his Folcroft office, Dr. Harold W. Smith felt his gorge begin to rise.

The glowing terminal was nauseatingly green. But its unpleasant color was not what made his stomach bubble and roil like a chemical experiment gone awry.

With one hand Smith reached into his right-hand desk drawer. He fumbled his fingers around the necks of several bottles.

With nervous hands he opened one and popped two pills into his mouth, dry. He coughed them down, his eyes never wavering from the screen. They tasted bitter going down. Aspirin. Smith had wanted Alka-Seltzer. He found the other bottle by feel and shook out a tablet, with the consequence that a dozen tablets rattled over the desktop and onto the floor.

Smith brought one to his mouth and began chewing it like a candy wafer. It was only six steps to his water dispenser, but Smith refused to leave his seat.

As he chewed the tablet to bits, swallowing the bland chemical grit, Smith began to admit to himself that he might have committed a tactical error.

He should have sent Remo and Chiun after P. M. Looncraft.

Smith's reasoning was that Looncraft was an agent of the British government—or possibly one of its ministries or departments. A rogue operation, perhaps. As Smith saw it, getting to the top was more important than getting Looncraft.

A mistake. Events were moving more swiftly than Smith had suspected.

The Global News Network was carrying stories of the softness in the treasury-bond market. P. M. Looncraft's own reporters were quoting his cautious but leading statement that Looncraft had heard of the rumors, but could not say any more except that if true, it was a troubling development, not only for Wall Street but also for the U.S. economy.

It was the dead of night in Rye, New York. But in Tokyo, Singapore, and Hong Kong, trading was heavy. Key stocks were being dumped across the board as investor uncertainty over the future of the American economy fueled a skittishness that had not completely abated since Dark Friday. What had begun as a nervous profit-taking exercise was fast becoming a panic sell-off.

The dollar was down against the yen. Even Nostrum—currently the darling of investors—was taking a beating. And if Nostrum fell, like Global Communications before it, it would take the rest of the market with it.

As the latest Reuters stock quotations marched across the top of Harold Smith's screen, he pounded the desk with an angry fist.

"I should have sent them after Looncraft," he said again, his voice bitter.

Now it was too late. Looncraft was fueling the panic. It was deliberate. There could be no doubt about it. His acquisition of Global Communications had been the key to it all. It had kicked off the first panic, weakening the market. But it had obviously been a goal unto itself. First, as a propaganda organ, and now, like the use of plants in Reuters, a way of fanning the flames further.

As the Far East traded at a frantic pace, Smith desperately worked to figure out where this was going, all thoughts of attempting a computer trace of Looncraft's superior gone from his mind. Looncraft, Dymstar & Buttonwood was hours from opening, its computer inoperative.

Smith went back to the files he'd siphoned from it and tried to make the pieces come together into a plausible scheme.

Somehow, some way, Looncraft's superiors intended to gain control of the United States and remake it into a bizarre extrapolation of what it might have become had there never been an American Revolution.

But how? Smith wondered. The Cornwallis Guard numbered fewer than three thousand men nationwide. The Scientologists had more manpower than that. It obviously had been set up as a death squad or enforcement arm, but its numbers were pitifully small for an occupying army.

There were U.S. military officers in the Loyalist group, including three generals. But three generals weren't enough to take over all four branches of the military.

Smith had to assume the Vice-President was part of the plot. There could be no doubt what was meant by the term "loyalists."

But who were these conscripts? The President was one of them. Was it possible that somehow the Vice-President, working through the President, was going to hand over the country?

Smith shook his head even as the thought occurred. No, that could not be. The checks and balances built into the American democratic system made that impossible. There were not enough members of Congress on either list. Congress would revolt, and the military would stand by the Constitution. Of that, Smith had no doubt.

No, it was not a coup. Or at least a coup was not going to trigger the master plan.

Smith went to the Crown file. There was no record of Crown Acquisitions, Limited, ever having acquired any U.S. firm. Technically Crown was a separate entity from Looncraft, Dymstar & Buttonwood. Looncraft's apparent control of it had less to do with LD&B than with this plot.

Perhaps Crown was the key to it all.

But what were they planning to acquire?

Tokyo was down another hundred points, Smith saw as he turned the problem over in his mind.

"I should have had Remo and Chiun take out Looncraft," he said ruefully. "Anything to slow this down."

It had not been easy to accept Looncraft as part of the plot, Smith reflected. His family had come from the same social set and good Yankee roots as had Smith's. It was a personal blind spot, he saw now. He had seen Looncraft as being of such wealth, position, and breeding that crime on this scale should have been beneath him.

A mistake. It was all a tremendous miscalculation.

The red telephone interrupted Smith's self-recriminations.

"Smith?" The voice was sleepy.

"Yes, Mr. President," Harold Smith said, his throat rumbling from disuse.

"We're getting frantic cables from the British government, accusing us of attacking their most sacred institutions. What do you know about this?"

"Everything," Harold Smith said without hesitation. "I have sent my people over there. Mr. President, I can no longer withhold this from you. I have uncovered a scheme of incredible magnitude, designed to take over our country. It's of British origin, apparently."

Smith paused. If there was any chance that the President was involved in this scheme, he had to know now.

"British! Smith, they are our staunchest allies."

"Currently."

"For as long as I can remember."

You obviously do not remember the War of 1812, when they burned down the White House, as well as the Capitol Building."

"The British did that?"

"Surely you know your history."

"It's been a few years, Smith," the President said ruefully.

"If you'd prefer that I withdraw my people from Great Britain, I will agree to that. But I cannot take responsibility for the consequences."

Smith held his breath while he waited for the answer. This was the moment of truth.

"No," the President said firmly. "Do what you think is best. But tell me, what do I say to the prime minister?"

Smith cupped his hand over the red receiver to mask his audible sigh of relief. The President had not been compromised.

"Tell her . . ." Smith hesitated. An idea struck him.

"Ask her to invite P. M. Looncraft of Looncraft, Dymstar & Buttonwood for a state visit. Tell her to give no reason. Just invite him. Get him out of this country. Inform her that Looncraft is suspected of complicity in the market upheavals plaguing the world. By the time he arrives in London, my people might have some answers."

"The British are complaining that someone stole the Royal Sceptre. Would that be your people?"

Smith cleared his throat in discomfort. "Assure them it will be returned unharmed. Now if you will excuse me, Mr. President, I have a great deal to do."

Harold Smith hung up. Suddenly a thought had occurred to him. Looncraft's computers had given up the secret of Crown's board of directors. But who were the stockholders, if any?

Smith thought he knew. He began paging through the Crown file, hoping to learn the answer.

As he pecked at his keyboard, Smith gave thanks that Looncraft had been so confident in the security of his system that his files had not been encrypted. Not that any code the human mind could devise would have long defeated the CURE mainframe. But the Nikkei Dow had lost another twenty-five points, and at his back, the sun lurked beyond the glittering expanse of Long Island Sound. Dawn was coming to America. Dawn and the early editions of *The Wall Street Journal*, carrying news of the new tidal wave of panic about to sweep the globe like an invisible steamroller, were hitting doorsteps and corporate mail slots all over the nation.

The list of stockholders was in a separate file. It matched, exactly, the list of Loyalists.

"Yes," Smith told himself as the waning moon silvered his back. "Crown is the key."

But what was the lock it was intended to open?

24

P.M. Looncraft enjoyed the uplifting sensation of the Looncraft Tower elevator against his shoes. It was like a bracing tonic, pushing him to higher and higher plateaus of power.

On the thirty-fourth floor he stepped off, nodded to the doubled security guard, and paused inside the trading floor of Looncraft, Dymstar & Buttonwood.

He spoke a single word: "Sell."

Every trader looked up from his work. The stock exchange was not due to open for an hour, but its computerized Designed Order Turnaround system, or DOT, would accept any sell orders that LD&B put into it, holding them for execution at the opening bell.

"Sir?" The dumbfounded bleat came from Ronald Johnson.

"I said sell," Looncraft repeated urgently. "Sell everything!"

And like well-trained soldiers, they took to their phones and made frantic calls.

"Liquidate every position," Looncraft shouted like a general commanding his troops. "Divest fully. I want Looncraft, Dymstar & Buttonwood to be completely liquid by the time the Dow opens. And damn the man who trades in his own portfolio before he has liquidated the firm's!"

With that, Looncraft marched into his office.

The office copy of *The Wall Street Journal* lay open to the front page. Looncraft absorbed it at a glance: "NIKKEI DOW IN MASSIVE SELL-OFF."

"I knew those damned Japanese would be good for something other than cameras someday," Looncraft snorted, doffing his chesterfield coat and taking his chair.

He logged onto the Mayflower Descendants bulletin board and typed out a question:

"PERMISSION TO CONTACT OTHERS DIRECTLY."

"GRANTED," came the reply.

The message had obviously been monitored at other terminals, because before Looncraft could tap a single key, other messages began flashing.

"LIPPINCOTT HERE. WHAT IS THE WORD?"

Looncraft typed: "SELL!"

And all over America, the selling began. Sell orders rushed into the DOT system so rapidly, the computers balked at the volume. Orders backed up. Wall Street had never seen anything like it. It was an hour before opening, and nervous floor specialists at the New York Stock Exchange were going white.

The chairman of the New York Stock Exchange heard the reports coming up from the pit. He went out to the observation balcony. The floor was already littered with paper scraps. But more important, he could feel the rising body heat, smell the sweat. The broadtape ticker was blank. Suddenly the chairman felt a wave of sick anticipation of the numbers that would soon appear on it.

He consulted with the DOT-system computer people, nodded grimly at their projections, and returned to his office, where he began working the phone.

P. M. Looncraft typed merrily. He hummed an old English drinking song, "To Anacreon in Heaven," which Francis Scott Key had pillaged for the familiar "Star-Spangled Banner" melody.

"NOTHING LIKE GOOD OLD ANGLO-SAXON INGENUITY," he typed.

Another line appeared under his:

"THE REBELS WILL NEVER KNOW WHAT HIT THEM."

"WHAT GETS UP MY NOSE IS THAT IT TOOK SO BLOODY LONG," another typed.

Looncraft typed in his reply: "BE GRATEFUL YOU LIVED TO SEE THE GLORIOUS DAY, AND THAT YOU WERE A PART OF THE UNWRITING OF THE BLACKEST PAGE IN BRITISH HISTORY SINCE CROMWELL."

"HOWDY, BOYS! YOU AIN'T STARTING WITHOUT ME?"

Looncraft frowned. It was that infernal Texan, Slickens.

The man was an embarrassment, British roots or not. When the new order was in place, Looncraft intended to shunt Slickens into some barely visible position. Perhaps governor-general of Boston, or something equally unsavory. Let him deal with the bloody Irish-Americans.

Looncraft forced himself to be polite. He typed: "HAVE YOU BEGUN DIVESTING?"

"WHAT'S THE BLAMED RUSH? THE PIT DON'T OPEN FOR ANOTHER HOUR."

"YOU WILL NOT GET THE BEST PRICE IF YOU DAWDLE," Looncraft typed.

"PRICE, SMICE," DeGoone Slickens typed back. 'WE'RE GONNA END UP OWNING THE WHOLE SHOOTING MATCH BY THE TIME IT'S OVER. WHY SWEAT A FEW NICKELS HERE AND THERE?"

It sickened Looncraft's proud British soul to think that a man who came from such a fine family as Slickens could have, in little more than a hundred years, become so degradingly Americanized.

"AS YOU WISH," Looncraft typed. "MUST TODDLE." He left the computer on and turned his attention to the glass office wall, beyond which his traders were shouting into their phones.

Their panic appealed to him. For it presaged the absolute anarchy which would soon reign when the opening gong sounded.

Looncraft got up and stuck his head out the door.

"Are we liquid yet?" he called.

"No, sir, the DOT is backing up. It isn't taking our orders."

"Then get over to the Exchange!" Looncraft shouted. "Deal directly with the floor specialists. We must be liquid. The entire economy is about to collapse. I hear it on the street, and I hear perfectly!"

Traders stumbling and struggling against one another, the trading floor emptied into the elevators.

The phone on the secretary's desk rang. Looncraft strode toward her as she was telling the caller, "Let me check."

Looncraft's secretary put her hand over the receiver. "It's the chairman of the Exchange."

"I'll take it."

In his office, P. M. Looncraft took up the phone without
bothering to sit down. "Yes, Paul?"

"We're on the brink," the chairman said hoarsely. "The
DOT's in trouble. My God, if there's that much dumping
going on now, you know what will happen when the
Exchange opens."

"Perhaps you are panicking prematurely," P. M. Looncraft
suggested, his tone soothing. "After all, we came through
the recent market upheavals without difficulty. This too
may pass."

"My information is that when we open, there will be
more sellers than buyers. You know what that means."

Looncraft knew. The knowledge brought a tight smile to
his long cadaverous face. It meant that the entire fabric of
Wall Street was close to unraveling. No buyers meant the
sellers could not unload their stocks—not even at fire-sale
prices. No buyers also meant that the consentual understanding that ran the stock market—the one that said no
matter how much prices fluctuated, stocks would always
have some irreducible value—was disintegrating. And when
that went, perhaps the monetary basis for currency would
begin to unravel. If the Japanese hadn't already driven the
dollar down to near-worthlessness.

"We have less than an hour to act," the chairman urged.

"Perhaps we should convene a meeting," P. M. Looncraft
said soothingly.

"I'll call the others."

Less than fifteen minutes later, the board of directors of
the New York Stock Exchange met around a long mahogany table which resembled an aircraft-carrier deck.

The chairman of the Exchange stood up, his face haggard.

"You all know the situation," he said. "The Far Eastern
markets are in an uproar. The DOT is buried. When the
gong sounds, I anticipate a fifteen-hundred-point instant
drop. It would be more if the DOT was able to accept the
load of sell orders that continues to pour into the system.
In short, there is no question that we stand on the brink of
a cataclysmic crash. Perhaps even a bottoming out of the
market's total value."

"What do you propose?" P. M. Looncraft asked smoothly.

"I propose we not open today."

"Not open? Wouldn't that exacerbate the panic?"

"It doesn't matter," the chairman retorted. "It's so bad it simply cannot get any worse. I move the Exchange not open until we sort this out. We can blame it on the computers overloading. Your votes, gentlemen."

"I vote against," said Percival Marylebone Looncraft, turning to the others arrayed around the table.

"Against," voted Douglas Trevor Lippincott.

"Against," voted Henry Cecil Hyde.

"For," voted Aristotle Metaxas.

"Against," said Lowell Cabot.

"Against," said Alf Wenham.

"For," said Sol Sugarman.

In the end, the Brahmins had won, as P. M. Looncraft knew they would. Anglo-Saxon blood never betrayed its heritage.

"If that is all," Looncraft said to a stunned chairman, getting to his feet, "I am needed back at the office."

The others filed out of the meeting room, leaving the three dissenters, a Jew, an Italian, and a Greek. They looked at one another with sick, incredulous eyes, never realizing that they had been sandbagged by a two-hundred-year-old conspiracy.

The Dow did not drop fifteen hundred points at the opening bell, as predicted. It dropped seventeen hundred. The DOT system had processed more sell orders than anyone had expected. In fact, it was working marvelously— all things considered.

Trading was halted for an hour, in accordance with NYSE rules regarding two-hundred-point drops. But when it resumed, so did the collapse.

There was panic in the pits. Several traders sold their expensive seats on the Exchange before trading had progressed five minutes. More than one trader sold off his Rolex—worn as a hedge against calamity—to cover option puts.

Men who had made fortunes speculating, not on the value of the firms they invested in, but on the projected prices of stocks, were bankrupted in seconds. Windows all over Wall Street were shattered by chairs, and men jumped

to their death rather than face the financial ruin they had
brought upon themselves. It was 1929 all over again.
Except that now the repercussions were not limited to
Wall Street and its satellites—brokerage houses and mutual-
fund groups around the country. It was a global panic.

In London the Financial Times Stock Exchange was still
trading. As word of the Dow's nearly two-thousand-point
plunge hit the City, prices dropped faster than some of
the bodies striking Manhattan pavements thousands of
miles west. The pound sterling lost value against everything except the U.S. dollar.

Dr. Harold W. Smith saw it all happen on his computer
screen. The declining broadtape numbers marched by his
eyes with sickening speed. Then certain stocks dropped
off the tape. That meant they were no longer being traded,
having dropped below their yield value. Despite their
being worth the return their yearly dividends realized, no
one was buying them.

No one, that is, until precisely 11:02, when with the
Dow fluctuating between 766 and 967 points, one investor
began to buy, and buy heavily.

The numbers fluctuated so slightly, in comparison to
the drop, that at first Harold Smith didn't perceive the
new factor for what it was.

When he realized there was a buying splurge going on,
he logged onto the Looncraft, Dymstar & Buttonwood
mainframe, assuming that was where the activity originated.

But Looncraft, Dymstar & Buttonwood computers were
simply standing by. They were not buying, they were not
selling.

Smith accessed Looncraft's personal computer. It was
buzzing with strange cross-talk, but no selling activity.

Smith went around the chain of conspirators. None of
them was buying. They were too busy communicating
with Looncraft on the Mayflower Descendants' net.

Smith checked with Nostrum. Nostrum was not buying.
Of course, with Chiun in London, there was no one there
to orchestrate a response to the increased selling pressure.

Frustrated, Smith logged onto the DOT computers at
the New York Stock Exchange. He saw the stream of buy

orders. They were starting to back up. Every buy order bore the same origin.

"Oh, my God," Harold W. Smith said hoarsely.

It was Crown Acquisitions, Limited. It was buying up everything in sight, obtaining significant interest in major banks, insurances companies, newspapers, radio and television stations, and major industries. Key stocks and blue-chips were being gobbled up by its voracious maw.

Crown was buying America's economic and industrial underpinnings.

Only then did Harold W. Smith understand what the whole mad scheme was all about.

It was a hostile takeover—on a scale never before imagined.

25

In Oxford, England, Sir Quincy Chiswick sat in the dimness of the far corner table in the Wheatsheaf pub, away from the common herd. The pub buzzed with low voices. Occasionally a student would enter his field of vision to take away tea or a shepherd's pie from the worn wooden kitchen counter.

They never looked his way, even those who were his students. Sir Quincy preferred it that way. It was the reason he wore his raven-black professorial gown in the pub.

It was bad enough that he had to earn his bread teaching the spotted bastards, but to socialize with them was more than a body could bear.

Every year it became more of a chore.

Sir Quincy drained the last of his shandy, tossed a pound coin on the table, and rose to leave.

He overheard several people speaking about the stock market's travails, but paid them no mind.

"Oh, Professor," one of them called out.

Sir Quincy was so flummoxed by the lad's temerity that he forgot himself and turned.

Three young students were hunkered over their ale. One had his hand up, as if in a lecture hall. He looked like a right prat.

"Yes, what is it?" Sir Quincy deigned to say.

"You've doubtless heard of the economic chaos brewing in the States, Professor. Our own markets are coming a cropper. What do you suppose this augurs for the U.K. economy?"

"I have not heard of the economic chaos, as you so quaintly put it," Sir Quincy retorted. "And I pay no attention to the dreary modern world. My field is history. Now, if you will excuse me, unlike yourselves, I must prepare for tomorrow's classes."

And with that, Sir Quincy Chiswick, Regius Professor of History at Oxford's Nuffing College, turned about and fled the Wheatsheaf like a fugitive from an abbey.

He stepped out into the early dusk already blanketing Oxford's multitudinous spires.

His haggard fortyish visage was glum as he trudged along like an ebony-winged crow. He took no comfort from the sight of the witchlike spire of his own Nuffing College on his left.

He walked up High Street, past the Covered Market, and turned up Cornmarket Street. From Magdalen Street he took the Friar's Entry shortcut to Gloucester Street. Its blue lights were sepulchral tonight.

At the end of Gloucester, he crossed Beaumont to come, at last, to St. John's Street and its modest row houses.

Sir Quincy entered number fifty by a blue door in the scabrous white stucco facade, locked the door behind him, and glanced at the row of antique grandfather clocks at the foot of the stairs. The last one was a minute slow. He made a note to have it adjusted as he trooped up the stairs, one hand on the banister, the other lifting his black gown so as not to snag a step.

"Is that you, sir?" a middle-aged woman's voice called from the downstairs flat.

"Yes, Mrs. Burgoyne," he called down. "Has there been any mail today?"

"No, sir. I set tea and scones for you, as always."

"Odd," Sir Quincy muttered. In a normal voice, he said, "Thank you, Mrs. Burgoyne. You are very kind."

"Good night, Professor."

"Good night, Mrs. Burgoyne."

Sir Quincy unlocked the door to his shabbily genteel room. It was high-ceilinged, its eastern wall dominated by two beds, set like bookends, each covered by a yellowing bedspread.

In the center of the room stood a small writing desk burdened by a tea-cozy-covered object, a tarnished pewter tray heaped with scones, and two varieties of jam in serving compotes set beside the lion-patterned tea cozy.

Sir Quincy sat down. From a drawer he took a coil-shaped heating element, plugged it into a floor socket, and dropped the reddening element into the china teakettle.

While he waited for the water to come to a boil, Sir Quincy plucked the oversize tea cozy from a tiny computer terminal. He hated to use the bloody device, but the mails to America were dreadful these days. He wondered what J.R.R. Tolkien, who had once occupied this very flat, would have thought of the infernal thing.

The water began bubbling as Sir Quincy turned on the computer. He logged on. The legend "MAYFLOWER DE-SCENDANTS" appeared at the top of the screen.

The board was busy with scrolling paragraphs. The Loyalists had become a chatty lot since he had given them permission to communicate amongst themselves. It worried Sir Quincy. He was a bit foggy on the security of these computer devices. Perhaps it was safe enough, but he would have thought that his principals would know enough to keep shtum until the matter was concluded.

When Sir Quincy felt the steam coming from the kettle warming his face, he knew that it was ready. As he poured, he watched the ever-changing cross-talk.

"DO YOU SUPPOSE BEAR-MAN WILL SHOW HIS FURRY FACE AGAIN?"

"DID YOU ALSO RECEIVE A WARNING TOOTH FROM THE BLIGHTER?"

"I SHOULD SAY SO. BUT I AM READY FOR HIM THIS TIME."

"YOU BOYS HAD BETTER CIRCLE YOUR WAGONS. I TANGLED WITH THE VARMINT. HE DON'T TAKE NO CRAP FROM ANYBODY."

Sir Quincy frowned. What manner of English was that one communicating in? Must be some vulgar American slang. Well, that, too, would soon become a thing of the past.

He used a dull butter knife to separate a fresh hard scone into equal halves. The computer talk was focusing on the crisis in the New York stock market. Sir Quincy looked away, frowning. Economics was not his forte. And at the moment he faced a pressing problem. Mrs. Burgoyne had set out for him both of his favorite jams.

Which did he most fancy—greengage or plum?

26

At five P.M. London time, crack British SAS counterterrorist commandos surrounded the Morton Court Hotel in London's busy Earl's Court district. They took up sniper positions on the rooftops of neighboring apartment buildings, behind shrubbery, and in the hotel's modest lobby.

Remo Williams peered over the sill of the third-floor room's single window. It looked down over the leaf-strewn yard of an apartment building.

"We're surrounded," he told Chiun, who sat cross-legged on the floor, the Royal Sceptre on his lap. The Master of Sinanju's shiny bald head was tipped back to see the high-shelved TV set.

"Shh," Chiun said.

"Will you shut that off?" Remo snapped. "These guys are heavily armed. I think they're getting ready to storm the place."

Chiun touched his wispy beard. "They will not invade the hotel without first asking our demands."

"What makes you think they give a flying jump about our demands?"

The phone rang before Chiun could reply.

Remo scooped up the receiver and barked out a rude hello. He listened. Then, turning to Chiun, he said, "They want to know our demands."

"Tell them that as a gesture of good faith, the sphinxes guarding the so-called Cleopatra's Needle will be set correctly."

"You're joking."

"And they will broadcast the fact," Chiun went on firmly, "or the Sceptre will be pulverized down to its smallest ruby and emerald."

Sighing, Remo relayed the message. Then he hung up. "They said they'll get back to us. They're not going to do it, you know."

"They will, for they know that they are dealing with the House of Sinanju."

"What makes you think they'll care?"

"We performed a minor service for one of their recent queens."

At Buckingham Palace, Her Britannic Majesty, the Queen of England, received the news with indignation.

"We will do nothing of the sort!" she said furiously.

She quieted down when the queen mother entered the sumptuous throne room, clearing her throat.

"Yes, Mum?" the queen said in a timid voice.

"This letter left at Whitehall bears the insignia of the House of Sinanju. They did a job of work for us during Victoria's reign. The Ripper matter."

"Ah," said the Queen of England, understanding perfectly. No wonder the rotter had never been captured. He had been assassinated.

"We will comply with these demands instantly," the queen mother directed. "Broadcast the work as requested."

"At once, Mum," the Queen of England said meekly.

*   *   *

BBC 1 and BBC 2 broke in on regular programming with simultaneous bulletins. A stuffy red-faced newscaster read from a trembling sheet of paper as a graphic of Cleopatra's Needle floated beside his ear. A barge-borne crane was lowering the second basalt sphinx into place, facing outward to guard the granite monument. The other sphinx had already been set to rights.

"They did it!" Remo exploded in an unbelieving voice. "They actually did it."

"They still remember," said Chiun in a tight, pleased tone.

"Remember what?"

"The royal house had a minor problem at the end of your last century. An embarrassment they called John the Cutter."

"Not Jack the Ripper?" Remo said. "We took care of him?"

"*We* did not," Chiun said haughtily. "My grandfather attended to that one. You were not even born then."

"I was using the collective 'we,' " Remo said defensively.

Wordlessly, Chiun stood up, the Royal Sceptre gripped in both hands.

When the phone rang, the Master of Sinanju took it.

"Do not speak," he said. "Listen. The problem that is plaguing the world's economy comes from somewhere in your government. This person will be brought to my quarters by dawn." Chiun paused. "I tell you it is true, and I will have him."

Chiun hung up. He returned to his spot on the floor.

Outside the window, SAS snipers were repositioning themselves.

"Don't look now," Remo said. "But I don't think they like your latest demand."

"They do not have to like it," Chiun said distantly. "They merely have to execute it."

"I think execution is exactly what they have in mind," Remo said glumly.

Down in the lobby, Colonel Neville Upton-Downs listened to the voice of the prime minister as it came through the desk telephone.

"At once, ma'am," he said.

Hanging up, he nodded to a trio of soldiers crouched in the corridor, facing the elevator and stairs, their telescopic rifles at the ready.

"We're going in, lads," he told them. "Half of you hold the lift. The others go up the staircase. Third floor. End of hall. Look sharp."

The men deployed. Three guarded the elevator while the others went up the steps, their boots making a frightful racket.

Colonel Upton-Downs was so confident in his men, noisy feet aside, that he did not feel compelled to lead them into battle. By all accounts, the two terrorists were unarmed. One was an ancient Chinese or some foreign sort. As he waited, he wondered why it had taken so long for the prime minister to give the green light.

Going outside, Colonel Upton-Downs signaled his men that the matter was about to be brought to a successful conclusion. They visibly relaxed at their posts. He strode around to the rear of the hotel and into the yard beneath the window they had pinpointed as belonging to the terrorists.

He borrowed a pair of field glasses from a spotter and trained them on the target window.

"Be over soon, chaps," he muttered.

It was. The window glass abruptly shattered under the force of an SAS soldier in full flight. He struck the concrete like a sack of potatoes. After a short time, he was joined by a second man and then a third. They made a neat pile on the pavement.

A man's face poked out of the broken window.

"Don't make that mistake again," an American voice shouted from the wrecked window.

"The ruddy bastard!" Colonel Upton-Downs shouted. "Take him out! Take the bounder out *now!*"

Rifle muzzles jumped to the ready. Fingers caressed triggers.

"Uh-uh," the American said. "Naughty, naughty."

Colonel Upton-Downs abruptly changed his mind. "Hold fire! Drat it! Hold your damned fire!"

For the American was holding the Royal Sceptre in

front of his face. He shook one finger at them as if at pranking children.

"Let's not make any messy mistakes," he said, withdrawing from the window.

Dejectedly the colonel trudged back to the hotel lobby. The prime minister was not going to take this in good humor.

The prime minister accepted the news with a flinty "Thank you, Colonel. Stand by." She laid the phone down without hanging up and faced her cabinet, who were arrayed around a conference table at Number Ten Downing Street.

"The assault has failed," she told them. "We must now consider other options."

"Such as?" the home secretary inquired.

"Such as, my dear man, that these terrorists are sincere in their belief. You all know the American situation. Our exchange has just closed after taking a tremendous beating. It can only get worse. The Far Eastern markets are bound to react badly to what is happening in Europe and America. And we will feel the brunt of the next wave of selling panic. It may never end."

"I fear if the American situation is as bad as they say," the minister of finance pointed out, "it will not matter. They are practically bankrupting their exchange in their frenzy to sell."

"*Could* someone be causing this?"

"Balderdash." The murmur of assent that followed the foreign minister's remark reminded the prime minister of Parliament during her heyday, when she used to ride roughshod over the simpering cowards.

"What manner of bloody fool would attempt such a thing, knowing it would ruin our own economy?" the finance minister remarked pointedly.

"Communist plant, possibly?" Sir Guy Phillistone blandly suggested between sucks on his broken pipe.

"It's a thought," the home secretary muttered. "Lord knows we've had enough of them."

No one joined in the home secretary's uncertain laughter.

The prime minister shook her head. "The Communist

world looks to the West for economic salvation," she said. "This is not one of their operations. If we sink, they follow us to the bottom." She spanked the table with a palm. "Think, gentlemen. Think. If you have the knack for it."

Stung, the cabinet looked to one another in embarrassment. But the cutting remark cleared the air. They stopped talking and began thinking.

"You know," the chancellor of the exchequer began slowly, "I have been receiving these wildly incoherent letters of late. About one every fortnight, informing me that the signal has been received and something called the Grand Plan has commenced."

"And what do you do with these letters?" the prime minister inquired.

"Why, I dispose of them, of course. They are obviously the scrawling of a crackpot."

"And does this crackpot have a name?"

"Yes, a Sir Quincy, I believe."

"And have you none of these letters at all?"

"I fear the most recent of them has gone into the rubbish," the chancellor of the exchequer admitted.

The prime minister rose quickly. "Find that letter. Get down on your hands and knees in the rubbish, if you must. It is all we have. Gentlemen, let's get on this, shall we?"

As they filed from the room, the prime minister picked up the still-open telephone line and began issuing new instructions to a very surprised Colonel Upton-Downs.

The letter, smelling of old cigarette butts and loose tea, was on the prime minister's Downing Street desk within the hour.

She picked it up with sure fingers and an offended expression on her face. The letter was still in its crumpled envelope. The return address was smudged, but the bottom line was still legible, reading "Oxford, Oxfordshire, OX1 2LJ.

"This narrows it down,' she murmured, extracting the letter. It did indeed read as if written by a crackpot. It rambled, dwelling on the fading glory of the British Empire, soon to flower again like a phoenix. A colorful if illiterate metaphor, the prime minister thought.

The final paragraph said, "Vide Royal Reclamation Charter." It was signed: "Faithfully yours, Sir Quincy Chiswick."

The prime minister looked up Sir Quincy Chiswick in her office copy of *Burke's Peerage*. She learned that he was Regius Professor of History at Nuffing College. A call to the college brought the news that the staff had all left for the day. There was no one competent to retrieve his address or telephone number.

The prime minister called for directory information and asked if there was a telephone subscriber known as Sir Quincy Chiswick in Oxford or Oxfordshire. The prime minister was assured, after a ten-minute delay, that there was none.

She thanked the operator and hung up. Ringing her secretary, she told him, "Have them go through Public Records for a document called the Royal Reclamation Charter."

"That could take a bit of doing."

"Then I would begin now," the prime minister said sharply, giving her secretary the benefit of her piranha smile.

The man went away. The prime minister personally put her own call through to the Morton Court Hotel.

"Hello, desk? Could you kindly put me through to the terrorists in Room Twenty-eight? Thank you."

Remo Williams picked up the phone. The woman's voice sounded familiar, so when she identified herself as the prime minister of England, he didn't give her an argument.

"Pssst! Chiun, I got the prime minister on the line."

"I only speak with royalty," Chiun curtly replied.

"Sorry," Remo told the prime minister. "He's indisposed. Your sexless soap operas have him enthralled." Remo listened for five minutes without getting in a word edgewise. Then he turned to the Master of Sinanju.

"She says they have the guy's name," he said. "They can't find him, but they think he lives in Oxford. Isn't that a shoe?"

"Inform the prime minister that I will allow you to search for this person in the town of Oxford."

"You? Allow me?"

"Tell her," Chiun commanded.

Remo returned to the phone. "Here's the deal," he said. "I get safe conduct to Oxford, free rein to search for this guy, and the Sceptre and my friend stay here, unmolested. Got that?"

The prime minister did. Remo hung up.

"Okay, it's a done deal," he told Chiun. "Are you sure this is the best way to go about this?"

"No," Chiun said flatly. "But if I go, I will miss the end of this story." He did not look away from the screen when he said it.

"Good thinking," Remo said airily. "I'll be in touch."

Remo strolled through the lobby, passing the sullen-faced SAS soldiers.

"Keep a stiff upper lip," he called as he went down the steps.

At the curb, a car waited for him, along with an unarmed SAS colonel holding a set of keys up for Remo's inspection.

"Here you go, Yank," the colonel said in a civil if testy voice. "We've got you a Vauxhall Cavalier. Nice machine. British-made, you know."

"Thanks," Remo said, taking the keys. He opened the left-hand door.

"The wheel is on the other side," the colonel said, smirking.

"I knew that," Remo lied, sliding all the way in. He put the key in the ignition and started the engine.

The colonel leaned into the window. "Take the roundabout at Regent's Park. There you can pick up the A-Forty north to Oxfordshire. That will get you to Oxford in jig time."

"How many kilometers?"

"Haven't the foggiest. But it's about fifty miles as the crow flies, if that means anything to you."

"It does," Remo growled.

"There's a map in the glove box. There's extra petrol in the boot, and the motor's under the bonnet, just as in the States."

"I sure wish we both spoke the same language," Remo remarked dryly.

"As I do, chap. Toodles."

Remo pulled away. He found the road. But as he drove along, the green-and-white signs that he assumed marked the A40 became the A35 and then the A40 again. None of them actually had an A before the numbers. Remo began wondering if maybe he was mistaking the speed-limit signs for highway markers. Occasionally he passed blue signs that also said 40.

After he got out of the city, Remo found a blue sign that said 404. He knew he had it figured out then. It must be the A404. Nobody, not even the British, drove 404 miles an hour.

Remo settled down for the long ride.

27

The New York Stock Exchange bottomed out at high noon, after only two and a half hours of stop-and-start trading.

The Dow stood at 1188.7 like a rock poised at the edge of a precipice, buoyed by Crown Acquisition's insatiable appetite for undervalued stocks—which was virtually everything that traded over the New York and American stock exchanges, as well as NASDAQ.

Then others jumped in. Still monitoring the DOT system, Smith saw that the first wave consisted of frantic buying by Looncraft, Dymstar & Buttonwood. The Lippincott Mercantile Bank also leapt in with slavering jowls, buying up airline and electronic stocks. DeGoone Slickens went for the oil companies. And others came in—all prestigious centuried firms with good sound Anglo-Saxon names.

And Smith began to see it for what it truly was. An

old-fashioned investor pool—the kind stock speculators used to employ to corner the market before SEC regulations put a stop to it. It was the original hostile-takeover scheme. The so-called Loyalists were working in concert, and no one could stop them.

For they represented the nation's oldest business concerns, its most affluent families. A hundred years ago, they would have controlled ninety-five percent of American commerce, education, and politics. But this was the late twentieth century, when even the Boston Brahmins no longer lorded it over Boston.

But soon all that could change. They were buying up the country, literally cornering the market in American business. Ten years ago this scheme could never have worked. But a decade of mergers and leveraged buy-outs had consolidated the national economy into a tight circle—most of whom were either Loyalists or so-called Conscripts.

Smith had seen the bulletin announcing that the New York Stock Exchange board had voted to keep trading no matter what. Their voting was a matter of public record. No wonder the chairman's warning had been overridden. They were the New York Stock Exchange too. They were also the Securities and Exchange Commission. Although what was transpiring before his eyes was flagrantly illegal, there might be no way to enforce those laws without crushing the nation's economic center of power. They *were* the economy.

More chillingly, they were America.

Smith sank back in his leather chair, his face haggard. The stock market was coming back, slowly, haltingly. But there was momentum. The bulls were running again. The market might even come roaring back. The Global News Network was already predicting it through its spokesman and owner, P. M. Looncraft.

But when it was all over, the economy of the strongest democracy on earth would have changed hands like a rumpled dollar bill.

Smith leaned into his computer like a fighter pilot about to trip his machine guns. It was time to play his trump card. He brought up the Mayflower Descendants bulletin board and engaged a program labeled "TRACEWORM."

When it was up and running, he pressed the "Send" key. He grabbed the red telephone next.

"Mr. President," he rapped out. "Do not ask questions. Just listen to me. This is merely a precaution. I want you to purge your Secret Service protective detail of all agents bearing Anglo-Saxon surnames. Just do it. Please . . . Yes, Italians are fine. It doesn't matter, just avoid persons of British ancestry." Smith paused. "Yes, it would be a good idea to cancel your meeting with the Vice-President. One final matter: were you successful in arranging Looncraft's summons to London? Excellent. I will explain everything later. Good-bye, Mr. President."

After he hung up, Smith wiped away the steam a sudden flash of nervous perspiration had caused to condense on his eyeglasses.

His intercom buzzed.

"Mr. Smith. Mr. Winthrop is here to see you."

Smith started. "Here?"

"He's very insistent."

"Tell him to go away," Smith snapped.

"I've tried to, but— Wait! You can't go in there."

Smith hit the concealed stud that sent the CURE terminal dropping into his desk interior. The desktop panel clicked into place just in time. The office door flew open.

Smith rose from his seat angrily.

"What do you mean by barging in like this?" he demanded.

The man who paused at the open door was well over six feet tall and built along the lines of Ichabod Crane. His face was red with indignation.

"I am Nigel Winthrop, Dr. Smith," he said testily. "And I will be put off no longer. This matter is urgent."

Smith hesitated. "Urgent?"

"If you will give me but a moment of your time . . ."

"Make it quick," Smith snapped. "I'm extremely busy. It's all right, Mrs. Mikulka," he added, nodding to his secretary, who hovered behind Winthrop like a nervous hen.

The door closed and Nigel Winthrop pulled a chair up to Smith's desk.

"I don't know if you remember me, Dr. Smith . . ." Winthrop began.

"Your name *is* familiar," Smith admitted.

"I managed your father's estate."

Smith blinked. Yes, it came back to him now. Winthrop and Weymouth. His father's law firm. He could remember seeing the letterhead on his father's desk many times as a boy.

"My father's estate was settled years ago," Smith said, stiff-voiced.

"And you were cut off."

"Ancient history," Smith snapped. He didn't like to be reminded that his own father had disinherited him.

Winthrop opened a leather briefcase and took out a sealed letter. He handed it to Smith.

"This letter was entrusted to me by your father, Dr. Smith. It was to be given to you, or to your eldest son in the event of your decease."

"I have no sons, only a daughter," Smith said.

"Open it, please."

Smith opened the letter with a red plastic letter opener and extracted a thick sheaf of folded papers. He read the salutation. It was addressed to him.

Smith read along, his eyes widening.

To my son, Harold:

I write this to you in life, but I will be dead when and if you read it. We have had our differences, Harold. You have failed me as a son. I know you bear me ill will because I could not accept your refusal to take over the family firm. I could not tell you otherwise while I lived, but this letter will help you understand that my hopes and dreams for you had nothing to do with publishing those cheap, shoddy magazines, but with something immensely greater.

If there is any family loyalty left in you, Harold, if any particle of red Anglo-Saxon blood flows through your veins, heed it now. Put aside your differences with me, for queen and empire are calling to you with clarion voice to rewrite a terrible wrong that a band of ragtag lawless rabble perpetrated on this

proud colony many years ago. I refer to the shameful
severing of this country from Mother England.

"Good God," Smith choked. He looked up at Winthrop.
"Do you have any idea what this says?"

"I do. Please finish the letter, Dr. Smith."

Smith read on. It was all there, in his own father's
handwriting. How after the signing of the Treaty of
Yorktown, ending the American Revolution, a cell of Tory
sleeper agents had been created on order of King George
III. They were to await the proper time, and a signal from
the crown, to activate. And by whatever means possible,
to bring America to financial ruin.

"My own father . . ." Smith said under his breath. The
papers in his hands shook. He shook. His weak gray eyes
seemed to recede into his gaunt patrician face.

"Your father is offering you a second chance," Nigel
Winthrop was saying quietly. "Here is an opportunity to
redeem yourself in his eyes, Smith. You loved your father.
Like these colonies, you were strong-willed, stiff-necked,
and stubborn. All that is past. I must have your decision
now, for my inability to contact you has kept you from
entering the fray like the true Englishman that you are by
birthright."

Smith looked up from the letter. There were tears in his
eyes.

"But . . . I love my country," he said in a quavering
voice.

"Surely you must love your father more," Winthrop said
firmly. "And do not fear for America." Winthrop smiled,
exposing tea-stained teeth. "It is our country too. We are
merely returning it to its proper place in the grand scheme
of things. Now, I must have your answer."

28

Remo Williams got lost on the A40 and ended up in a pastoral hamlet called Aylesbury.

He had to ask directions of three different people—not because the natives weren't forthcoming with directions, but because he had to hear the same directions three times before the thick local accent was comprehensible to him.

As he got back on the A40, he understood what was meant by whoever had said that Americans and British were a people separated by a common language.

Oxford resembled a crumbling fairyland from a distance, but when he found his way onto its narrow ancient streets, he was surprised to see a Kwik Kopy photocopy outlet and the usual fast-food restaurants. There was even a store that dealt exclusively in comic books, called Comic Showcase.

Remo looked around for a place to park. He caught sight of a space in a long row of undersize European cars on High Street, and he pulled into it—only then noticing the bright red cast-iron device set in the sidewalk. It looked like an overgrown fireplug, and Remo wondered if he'd be towed for parking there.

He decided the economy of the world mattered more than being ticketed.

When he got out, Remo saw that the supposed fireplug was actually a postal drop box. It made him wonder what a British fireplug looked like—a litter basket?

The street was busy with passersby, many of them students carrying books. Remo decided to start with them.

"Excuse me, pal," he asked one. "I'm looking for a Sir Quincy."

"Sorry. Never heard of the chap. And it is pronounced Quinsee, not Quin-zee, you know."

"Thanks a heap," Remo said, next approaching a middle-aged woman, on the theory that no one knew a neighborhood better than a native housewife.

"Sir Quincy, you say, Yank?" she replied. "I don't believe there's ever been a Sir Quincy in these parts. Not as long as I've been here. Are you lost?"

"No," Remo muttered, "but Sir Quincy is. Any suggestions what I could do?"

"Yes. What you should do is have a good sit-down with a nice strong cuppa tea, while you get your bearings. You look positively knackered."

"Actually, I'm just wet," Remo said, wondering what "knackered" meant.

"Good luck to you, then," the woman said, walking away.

"I'll need it," Remo said glumly. "I'm wet, lost, and I barely speak the language."

It started to rain again, and Remo ducked into the nearest store. It was the comic-book shop.

Remo pretended to browse, wondering why there were no copies of *Captain Marvel* on the shelves. Maybe Billy Batson had finally grown up.

The bell over the door rang, and a pair of book-laden students came in, talking among themselves. One of them spoke American English in a distinctly Oklahoma accent, and to Remo it was as if he'd heard a foghorn in a sea mist.

"Hey, pal. Maybe you can help me," Remo began.

"Sure."

"Ever hear of a Sir Quincy? He's supposed to live around here."

"Sir Quincy Chiswick?" He pronounced it "Chizick."

"That's it," Remo said.

"I know him. He's a don."

"He's Mafia?" Remo said in surprise.

"No. He's a professor. Teaches history. They call them

dons. Walk to the end of High Street and turn right. He's on St. John's Street."

"Thanks," Remo said, leaving the store. He ran through the rain, one hand over his eyes. He got lost immediately.

Remo stopped an elderly man in a tweed cap, who seemed completely oblivious of the downpour.

"Can you point me in the general direction of St. John's Street?" Remo pronounced it "Sinjin's Street," because, unlike the American student, he knew that the Brits pronounced "Saint John" as "Sinjin."

"Sorry," the elderly man clipped out. "No Sinjin Street in Oxford."

Remo watched him go, muttering, "I must have accidentally blundered into the Twilight Zone or something."

Deciding the old man might possibly have misheard him, Remo entered a dark musty pub.

"Sinjin's Street," he called out. "Anybody ever hear of it?"

"It's pronounced 'St. John's Street,' Yank," a gruff voice called back.

"I thought you Brits pronounced 'St. John' as 'Sinjin,' " Remo complained.

"That we do. But 'St. John's' we pronounce 'St. John's.' "

"Do you people have a rulebook for this stuff, or do you just make it up as you go along?"

"Do you want directions or do you want to hang about complaining?" he was asked.

"I'll take directions. I can always complain later."

"Up the street, walk east and it's at the crosswalk."

Remo found St. John's Street just as the rain began to slacken off. He was soaked to the skin and cold. He willed his blood to move faster through his system to generate heat. Steam actually began to rise from his shoulders and back.

Instead of cold and wet, he felt hot and wet. It was not much of an improvement, and Remo started to look forward to leaving Great Britain.

At Number Fifty St. John's Street, Remo found several nameplates. One said "Chiswick." That couldn't be it. The student had said the last name was "Chizick."

Remo canvassed the street in both directions twice before he realized that finding Sir Quincy Chizick wasn't
going to be easy.

It was all he had, and so reluctantly he pressed the bell
under the Chiswick nameplate at number fifty.

A mousy-haired woman with long yellow teeth and a
faded housedress answered, her face peering around the
door as if she'd been expecting the Grim Reaper. "Yes,
what is it?"

"I'm looking for Sir Chizick."

"No Sir Chizicks hereabouts."

"Are you sure? I was told that Sir Quincy Chizick lived
on this street.

Her face brightened. "Oh, Sir *Chiswick*. Yes, yes,
come in. You have the right place."

The inner hall was dank with old wood and several
hundred years of accumulated food odors. Remo noticed
the phalanx of grandfather clocks as the woman called up
the stairs, "Professor, you have a caller."

"He'll be just a mo," the woman assured Remo.

"You say 'Chizick' and the nameplate says 'Chiswick.'
Which is it?"

"How does that little ditty go? 'You say "potato" and I
say "potato." You say "tomato," and I say—' "

"Never mind," Remo said sourly. "I get it."

A querulous voice called down from the landing at the
top of the stairs.

"Yes, what is it, Mrs. Burgoyne?"

"An American to see you, Lord Chiswick."

A head popped out of the doorway. "An American, you
say? What about?"

"Why don't you ask me that?" Remo asked, mounting
the stairs.

"And who are you?" demanded Sir Quincy Chiswick.
He was a bookish man of indeterminate age, with his
haired combed back like a 1930's movie star's. His fune-
real black gown made Remo wonder if the clock had
stopped for him the day he graduated from college.

"Call me Remo. I'm here about the letters you've been
sending to the British government."

Sir Quincy Chiswick perked up. "You have?" he said in delight. "At last! I had been wondering if the postal department had mislaid them. Come in, come in," he added, waving Remo in.

The room was what Remo imagined his grandmother's place might have looked like—had he ever known his grandmother. It was neatly shabby, if vaguely effeminate. There was an electric heater in the much-painted-over fireplace, and one wall was all bookshelves.

"Don't mind the place," Sir Quincy rumbled. "The woman who does for me doesn't come until Saturday."

"Does what?" Remo asked, looking around.

The professor blinked. "My domestic," he said. Then, seeing Remo's expression go even more blank, added tartly, "My *char.*"

"I only speak American."

"Oh, bother! Never mind. Sit down, sit down. Would you care for a cuppa tea?"

"No, thanks. Look, I don't have time to beat around the teapot. Are you the one responsible for this economic mess?"

"Dear me, no. It was a mess to start with."

"That doesn't answer my question," Remo said edgily.

"What *is* your question, dear boy?" the don asked.

"Are you the one who's been writing the chancellor of the checks?"

"Exchequer. A check is an instrument of payment."

"Spare me the classroom lectures. Are you him or not?"

"I am he. I trust all is proceeding satisfactorily."

"Are you crazy? Stock markets all over the world are disintegrating."

"Really?" The thought apparently intrigued Sir Quincy Chiswick, because his eyes grew momentarily reflective.

"Don't you read the papers?"

"Dear me, no. Dreadful nuisance, those rags. Not one of them worth a bent copper anymore."

"Well, congratulations," Remo snapped. "You've just wrecked the world's economy, and before I snap your stuffy throat in two, I want to know if you can stop it."

"Stop it? Why should I do that?"

"Because the British economy is going down the tubes, along with everyone else's."

"It's taking the underground?" Sir Quincy asked, perplexed.

"I mean, down the john."

"Eh?"

"The loo! The loo!" Remo said in exasperation. "Everything's going down the loo. Do you understand that?"

"No need to shout, dear boy. Would you care for a scone? They're a trifle hard now, but still scrumptious, I think."

"Why? Just tell me why you're doing this."

"Because I received the signal to put into effect the Grand Plan."

"Now we're getting somewhere," Remo said. "What Grand Plan?"

Sir Quincy blinked. "Why, King George's, of course."

"King George III!" Remo exclaimed.

"Ah, you know your history. Good. Yes, it was George III's idea. My great-great-great-great-great-grandfather was entrusted to be the expediter of the plan. I, as his descendant, have had that glorious duty fall upon my shoulders. And frankly, at my age, I had all but given up that I would ever receive the signal."

"What signal?"

"Why, the signal to effect the Grand Plan, of course. What other signal is there?"

"Silly me," Remo said distractedly. "Of course, that signal. Who gave it to you, by the way?"

"The Duchess of York—indirectly."

"Isn't she the redhead with the freckles?"

"That's the one. Good chap. Yes, the duchess. Although they all had a hand in it, from the queen mother to the relatives in the Netherlands and elsewhere."

"The royal family is behind this?"

"I do not care for your tone of voice, my good man. Now, keep schtum and let me finish my story."

Remo stood up.

"Sorry. You've told me all I need to know. It's time to go bye-bye."

"Where are we going?"

"I'm going back to America. And you're going to the nearest boneyard. Sorry, old chap. But that's the biz."

Just then, Mrs. Burgoyne's voice called up from downstairs.

"Professor. Another caller. A doctor. Says his name is Smith."

"Smith?" Sir Quincy Chiswick said, blinking owlishly.

"Smith?" Remo said in disbelief.

29

If it hadn't been an emergency, if the economy of the entire world had not hung in the balance, Dr. Harold W. Smith could never have justified it to himself.

But time was critical, and so after disembarking from the British Airways jet at Heathrow, Smith eschewed the cheaper Piccadilly Line tube and actually hailed one of the ubiquitous black London taxis that reminded him of what the British version of a mythical 1938-vintage Edsel might have been.

Smith directed the driver to take him to Victoria Station.

At Victoria Station he actually told the driver to keep the change. It was painful but necessary. He could not wait for change.

Smith paid five pounds, fifty pence for a day-return ticket to Oxford and was told that it would depart in five minutes. Smith had already known that. He had timed his transatlantic plane trip to arrive with enough time for him to catch that bus.

Smith sat in the upper deck of the CityLink bus, oblivious of the darkening British countryside as it rolled past him; his briefcase was open and he was monitoring the world economic situation via his portable computer.

In America, the Big Board was upticking, as small investors, attracted by the bargains of the century, returned to the market in droves. Activity among the pool of Crown investors had slowed to a trickle. As Smith watched, the last Crown stockholder stopped trading. Smith smiled thinly. Success.

Reuters was reporting the discovery of a long-forgotten eighteenth-century document in the dusty archives on the Public Records office on London's Chancery Lane. Details of the document were not being released; a joint statement from Buckingham Palace and Ten Downing Street was issued, repudiating it.

Smith frowned as he read this.

Too little, too late, he told himself.

In one corner of the screen was a phone number. It was the number of a house on St. John's Street in Oxford, which his computer had spat out after several agonizing hours of backtracking through the Mayflower Descendants bulletin board. As Smith had suspected, the trace had gone through several terminals throughout the U.S. to a relay point in Toronto and from there to London—and finally to Oxford.

Because the computer net operated through telephone lines, Smith was able to access the phone number. The telephone was registered to a Mrs. Alfred Burgoyne, at fifty St. John's Street. It was there, he knew, he would find the person who controlled Looncraft and the others.

It was there that Harold Smith would be forced to make the ultimate choice of his life—between loyalty to his country and duty to his father.

For the hundredth time, Smith read through the closely typed letter his father had written so many years ago.

Finally he put it back into its original envelope and closed the briefcase. He closed his red-rimmed eyes as well. The long ride from London to Oxford would be about one hundred minutes long. And Smith knew he'd need his sleep for the final resolution of this incredible matter.

30

"Sir Quincy, I am Harold W. Smith. Harold *Winston* Smith."

Sir Quincy blinked. "Of the Vermont Smiths?"

"Exactly. I received my orders today."

"Well, dash it all, man. What are you doing here? You should be going about your business. There is work to be done."

"Hold the phone," Remo Williams put in. "I have a question."

Both Smith and Sir Quincy looked to Remo.

"What happened to your wheelchair?" Remo demanded hotly.

"Not now," Smith said peevishly.

"Yes, now. I've been working for you on this because you needed me. You couldn't use your legs, you said. And here you just stroll in like a frigging stork in a three-piece suit."

"Remo, please. I have to know about Sir Quincy's operation."

"Be glad to fill you in," Remo snapped. "He's behind it, all right. Says the royal family put him up to it. He's some mastermind, too. He's not exactly up on the fine details. I was just about to take him out when you sauntered in."

"No," Smith said firmly. "You will not kill this man. That's an order."

"I don't work for you, so I don't take orders from you," Remo said, grabbing Sir Quincy by the collar. He lifted the man off the threadbare rug.

"Unhand me, you . . . you vulgarian!" Sir Quincy sputtered.

"I was thinking about a heart-stopping punch," Remo

suggested. "Say, right about here." He stabbed Sir Quincy in the chest, above the heart muscle.

Sir Quincy went white. He looked like a crow that had gotten his head into a flour sack.

"Remo, no!" Smith said hoarsely. He grabbed for Remo's hand, desperately attempting to pry his fingers loose from Sir Quincy's gown collar. They might have been cast of metal.

"What's with you, Smith?" Remo asked in exasperation. "This is the head market manipulator. We take him out and it's over."

"No, it is not over. This man knows the secret behind a conspiracy that dates back to the days of the American Revolution."

"He said something about that, yeah," Remo admitted. "How'd you know that?"

"Put him down and I'll tell you," Smith said calmly.

Remo shook Sir Quincy like a drowned rat. "I like killing him better."

"You no longer work for the organization," Smith pointed out. "Killing this man is not your responsibility."

Remo thought about that. He released Sir Quincy from his grasp. The don struck the rug like a black sack of kindling.

"I don't like being manipulated," Remo warned Smith.

"This is important," Smith said, helping Sir Quincy to his feet. He sat him down on a faded lumpy sofa near the fireplace.

Remo folded his arms angrily, but he didn't interfere.

"Sir Quincy, first let me apologize for your rude treatment."

"What!" Remo exploded.

"I must ask you this," Smith went on "Who gave you the signal?"

"I can answer that," Remo said. "The Duchess of York, no less."

Smith shot Remo a harsh glance. "That is not funny."

"It is true," Sir Quincy said as he brushed off his gown.

"What? The Duchess of York? Prince Andrew's wife?"

"Quite. It was planned all along. As the Royal Reclamation Charter stipulates, when a member of the royal family gives birth to a girl and names her Beatrice, that will be considered the signal to begin implementing the Grand Plan."

"What?" Smith's haggard face was comical in its dumb-foundedness.

"It's really quite sound, my dear chap. As you know—as you *should* know—the royal family must obtain the approval of every branch of the family, no matter how distant, before a name can be decided upon. Not only the queen mother and the queen, but the distant relatives in the Netherlands and elsewhere must be consulted. And agreement must be unanimous. It is quite foolproof."

"I see," Smith said. "And the nature of the takeover?"

"Actually, I'm somewhat muddy on the details. The Loyalists handle that end of it, chiefly Percy."

"Percy?" Remo wanted to know.

"Looncraft," Smith supplied.

"Sterling lad. Like his forefathers. The Looncraft family quartered in the Fourth Regiment—the King's Own—during the Rebellion, you know. Yes, the Looncrafts were the family charged with the duty of effectuating the Grand Plan once they received the signal from me."

"By computer?" Smith asked.

"Confounded nuisance," Sir Quincy said gruffly. "I do not like the bloody things. Refuse to have a telephone. But the mails, you know, they're so dashed slow these days."

"It's like that in the States too," Remo said sourly.

"Quiet," Smith said flatly. "Go on, Sir Quincy. What is the plan?"

"Why, dear boy, you must have an inkling by now. To compel the colonies back into the fold, of course."

"By force?"

"No, dear boy. Nothing so dreadful. We bear no ill will toward our wayward cousins. Even back to King George. He felt that the colonies couldn't survive without the protection of Mother England. That proved untrue, which he foresaw, and so he created the Grand Plan. The idea was brilliant. To force America into financial ruin, so that it must rejoin the empire. I imagine this stock-market business has something to do with it."

"Sir Quincy," Smith said firmly, "you must know that the British economy is in very sorry shape right now."

"That's an understatement," Remo snorted.

Sir Quincy cleared his throat. "I have heard rumblings," he admitted, "but every era has its lean periods. Things will bounce back, don't you fret. Everything will be all right if we simply keep our peckers up, as the young ones are so fond of saying."

"Unbelievable," Remo said, throwing his head back and staring at the yellowing ceiling. "This guy doesn't even live in the real world. He thinks it's still the eighteenth century."

Smith glared at Remo. In a calm voice he told Sir Quincy, "You must stop this. It's wrecking the British economy."

"Oh, stuff and nonsense. England will endure. You must have faith in our traditions. We are too hardy a race to perish over some minor economic hiccup."

"The global markets are in turmoil," Smith said firmly. "There is financial panic in London. The pound sterling is depreciating by the minute."

"Confound it! Have those colonists mucked this up?"

Smith stared at Sir Quincy. "You don't even know the operational details of the plan," he said in a small voice.

"The Grand Plan," Sir Quincy corrected, "and no, I do not. History is my forte, not economics. I am merely the man who lights the lighthouse that will bring the colonial ship back to home port. The details are not my concern."

"They should be," Smith said harshly. "Given the current economic situation, England will be ruined long before America if your people persist in this mad scheme. You must call them off."

"I cannot. There is no way to stop it. Nor would I. And on what authority? The word of a Yank who doubtless drinks his ale ice-cold and doesn't have the breeding to knot his necktie with a full Windsor?"

Smith touched his tie self-consciously.

"Dartmouth?" Sir Quincy asked, noticing the stripes.

"Yes," Smith said tightly.

"Worthy school, I hear. It's not Oxford, but what is?"

Smith noticed the oversize tea cozy on the writing desk. A gray electric cord snaked out from under it. He pulled the tea cozy off, revealing a computer terminal.

"This is your computer," Smith said. It was not a question.

"Yes," Sir Quincy admitted. "How did you know about that, by the way?"

"I inserted a worm into the Mayflower Descendants network. It enabled me to trace this address."

"Jove! It must be a talented worm to do all that."

"A worm is akin to a computer virus," Smith explained, turning on the machine. "I designed it to follow the audit trail and replicate at every relay point, which I see it has."

On the screen appeared amber letters:

WARNING!!!
TUBE IMPLOSION IMMINENT!
STAND CLEAR!
DANGER

"Good God," Sir Quincy gasped. "It is about to explode."

"No," Smith said. "The message is harmless. It's designed to prevent anyone from attempting to rid his system of my virus worm. And without their computers, no further stock transactions can be consummated by your people. They are effectively frozen out of the market, which is now rebounding."

"Dammit, man!" Sir Quincy said furiously. "You are one of us. Why would you do a dastardly thing such as that?"

"To save the world from a lunatic scheme hatched for an eighteenth-century political situation. You see, the British government knows nothing of this so-called Grand Plan."

"Rubbish! They have in their possession a copy of the Royal Reclamation Charter."

"Which was misfiled in 1877 and forgotten by successive governments," Smith snapped. "The signal you thought you received was just a coincidence. In a sad way, it was almost inevitable that this would happen. It was fortunate that it did on my watch. You see, Sir Quincy, the royal family has repudiated the charter."

"The deuce you say!" Sir Quincy Chiswick said in astonishment. "This would explain why the queen did not answer my letters. I was reduced to writing to the chancellor of the exchequer, who also does not bother to read his mail, it seems. This is a most unlikely turn of events, if true."

"I have one more question for you, Sir Quincy. Then I must go. Of the people who have carried the torch over these last two centuries, who are the leaders?"

"Why, Percy is paramount. I have no idea whom he has selected as his lieutenants. Those decisions were made in 1776 by H. P. Looncraft, his great-great-great—"

"Never mind," Smith said. "I know all I need to know. Good-bye, Sir Quincy."

"Good luck, chap," Sir Quincy said. "But where are you off to?"

"America. There is work for me there."

"Glad to hear it. For a moment, I was fearful that you were not loyal."

"I have always been loyal to my country," Smith said coldly. He turned to Remo. "You know what to do. Meet me outside when you are finished with him."

"Now, just a moment, Smith," Sir Quincy said. "You can't leave me here with this . . . this Mediterranean type. As one Englishman to another, I implore you. What would your father say to this? Think on that, Smith. Listen to your heritage. It is calling you."

Dr. Harold W. Smith went out the door without a backward glance.

"Wait a minute," Remo called after him. "You can't stick me with the dirty work just like that."

Smith's leaden footsteps were heavy on the staircase. Down below, a door clicked open and then shut heavily.

Remo turned to Sir Quincy Chiswick.

"What happens if I don't kill you?" Remo asked.

"I do not die," said Sir Quincy as if speaking to an idiot.

That almost made up Remo's mind for him. "No, I meant now that this squirrely scheme has gone south, are you going to try it again?"

"Of course. I have received the signal—regardless of what your misguided friend believes."

"Smith's not my friend," Remo said coldly. "And nei-

ther are you." He took a fistful of Sir Quincy's gown front
and pulled him to his feet.

"Unhand me, you . . . you rebel!"

"I'm an American," Remo said firmly. "Just like Smith.
It's the one thing we have in common."

Sir Quincy sneered. " 'Common' is precisely the word
for it. You are both commoners. Not a drop of Anglo-
Saxon blood in either of you, you Yankee Doodle traitors."

"A lot of innocent people were massacred by your Cornwallis Guard," Remo said slowly, his eyes hard. "People I
knew. What do you say to that?"

"Were any of them of British descent?"

"It never occurred to me to ask," Remo said bitterly.
His mind was made up now. He led Sir Quincy Chiswick
over to one of his dingy beds and asked, "Any last words?"

"God Save the Queen! Rule Britannia! For as long as
one of us upholds crown and country, the English shall
ever be free."

"That's enough," Remo said. He punched Sir Quincy in
the exact center of his chest, stepping back.

For a moment Sir Quincy teetered on his heels. His eyes
rolled up into his head and his face acquired a faint blue
tinge at his jowls.

Remo decided it was taking too long, so he pushed the
teetering corpse of Sir Quincy Chiswick onto the bed.

Remo took a moment to lift his feet onto the bed and
tuck him in, where, when he was eventually found, his
death would be taken for simple heart failure.

On his way out of the flat, Remo took a moment to type
the word "CHECKMATE" onto the silent computer screen.

Out on the sidewalk, Dr. Harold W. Smith waited
impatiently.

"Is it done?" he asked tonelessly when Remo emerged
from the row house.

"Yeah," Remo said unhappily. "I've got a few bones to
pick with you. First it's kill him. Then don't kill him, and
then it's go ahead and kill him. And you walk out. Not
wheel out, but walk out. And I'm still waiting for an
explanation on that one."

"My country means everything to me," Harold Smith

said, tight-lipped. "More than my heritage, more than the
memory of a father who disinherited me because I dared
to choose my own path in life. It's what I sacrificed for all
my adult life. I do not like to lie. I abhor killing. And I did
not ask for the responsibility that forces me to do one and
order you to do the other. But it was thrust upon me and I
accepted. I have had to live with that choice for many
years, and I do not regret it. Not a bit. There will be no
other Harold Smiths to take my place when I die, in the
family business or in government service. I must do as
much as I can while I'm alive, because after I am gone
there will be no one to take my place. Lying to you, even
eliminating you if it serves the national interest, does not
seem too high a price to pay for freedom."

Remo Williams stared at the man he had known for
nearly twenty years. A cold rain began falling on Oxford's
benighted spires.

"Sometimes I hate you, you bloodless son of a bitch,"
Remo said.

"But you understand me?"

"Too much."

"You were chosen for this work because your patriotic
quotient was extremely high, you know."

"I like to think I just love my country."

"Many people love their country. You're privileged to
serve it in a way no one has since the Founding Fathers."

"I never thought of it that way before," Remo admitted.

Smith opened his briefcase and logged onto his computer.

"The stock-market crisis seems to be over," he said
absently. "The Far Eastern markets have opened up. Investor confidence should stay high. There will be some
sorting-out to do, but that is the SEC's responsibility. If
we eliminate Douglas Lippincott and DeGoone Slickens,
the rest do not matter. Without leaders, they will revert
to their sleeper status, passing their heritage on to the
next generation, who will wait for a signal that will never
come. You see, Remo, like myself, Sir Quincy is the last of
his line. His landlady told me that. There will be no more
Chiswicks to activate the Loyalists."

"You want me to take out Lippincott and Slickens?"

"It's your choice."

Remo considered. "Why not?" he said at last. "I'll do it for the Nostrum employees who died. What about Looncraft?"

"He should be arriving in London for what he thinks is to be a royal audience. The British are very unhappy with him and he will be dealt with severely, rest assured." Smith snapped his briefcase shut. "Then you are back with the organization?"

"Maybe. But we won't be friends."

"We never were. I won't hesitate to sacrifice you for the cause. If you keep that in mind, we will get along."

"You know, Smith," Remo said thoughtfully, "I never knew my father. I always thought that was pretty tough. But from what I heard back there, your situation was worse than mine."

"I threw away my last chance to make amends in the flat," Smith said, glancing up at Sir Quincy's window. He adjusted his glasses. "I will never forget that, but I will never regret it either. My duty was clear. I hope that you will come to see your duty more clearly, and with less pain."

Remo smiled tightly. "Give you a ride back to London, Smitty?"

"No," Harold Smith said without warmth. "I bought a return bus ticket. I like to get my money's worth."

And Harold W. Smith walked away, looking old and stooped and very fragile.

Remo waited until he turned the corner before trudging off to his car. It started to rain, but he didn't notice this time. He had too much to think about.

31

P. M. Looncraft arrived in London's Heathrow Airport confident that back in the soon-to-be-defunct United States of America, the balance of economic might had shifted to Crown Acquisitions, Limited, and its stockholders. It would take another year, possibly two, before everything was consolidated, Looncraft reflected, but it was better than running tanks in the street. The Conscripts would be a great help once the stubborn ones were brought into line by the impressment gangs.

As the Jetway ramp was moved into position to accept disembarking passengers, he adjusted his chalk-striped Savile Row coat and patted his tightly combed hair.

The stewardess said good-bye in a homey British accent and P. M. Looncraft stepped out into the waiting room, smiling thinly.

"British soil at last," he said.

He looked around, wondering if perhaps the queen herself might be waiting for him. He dismissed the happy thought as sheer vanity. Of course not. A coach from the Royal Mews would suffice, however.

Instead of a coach from the Royal Mews, there was a quartet of stern-faced London constables. One of them stepped up to him after glancing at a *Forbes* cover. Looncraft recognized it as the one that had first proclaimed him King of Wall Street. He wondered if he would be knighted.

"Percival Marylebone Looncraft?" the constable inquired with proper British civility.

"Precisely, my good man," Looncraft said, trying to match his accent. "I presume you are to escort me to my destination?"

"That we are. A car is waiting."

"Capital."

The car proved to be a common police car.

At the sight of it, Looncraft's long face became positively sunken.

"I was hoping for something more . . . ah, ceremonial," he complained as the door was held open for him. "One does not normally go to Buckingham Palace in a common police vehicle."

"In you go," one of the bobbies said. "We'll explain it on the way."

Looncraft climbed in. The door slammed and the others entered the car.

The drive took them to the outskirts of London, and the car kept going. Perhaps they were taking him to Windsor Castle. Looncraft asked.

"You are not going to Windsor Castle, bloke," the man seated next to him said tartly. "Your destination is Wormwood Scrubs."

"Remarkable name," Looncraft said. "Is it the royal retreat?"

"Wormwood Scrubs is a prison," he was told. "For you have been detained in the name of the queen."

Looncraft's lantern jaw dropped. "Prison?" he bleated.

"The charge is perpetrating crimes against the crown."

"There must be some mistake," Looncraft insisted. "This is highly uncivilized. I understood I was to see the queen."

The bobbies broke into raucous laughter at that remark.

They were still laughing an hour later as they unceremoniously threw him into a dank prison cell.

P. M. Looncraft grabbed the scabrous bars and stuck his long nose through two of them.

"A dreadful mistake has been made!" he called. "My family has been loyal to the crown for over two hundred years. The Looncrafts billeted the King's Own regiment during the Rebellion. You must get word to the queen. She knows who I am."

"Queen?" a mincing cockney voice asked from the creaking double cot directly behind P. M. Looncraft. "You've come to the right pew, mate."

*　　*　　*

Remo Williams pulled up in front of the Morton Court Hotel, wondering where all the SAS commandos had gone.

The Indian girl at the reception desk told him that the Master of Sinanju had checked out after receiving a telephone call from a man who said his name was Smith.

"Know where he went?" Remo asked, noticing that the girl was not returning his smile.

"No, I do not," she said coolly. "And he neglected to pay his charges."

Remo sighed. "Give it here."

After Remo had paid the bill, the clerk found her smile and her memory.

"Oh, I nearly forgot," she said. "He *did* leave you a note."

The note was brief. It said:

"REMO: I AM TAKING TEA WITH THE QUEEN MOTHER. AWAIT ME OUTSIDE BUCKINGHAM PALACE GATES. CHIUN."

Remo took the underground to Green Park and walked up the tree-lined Queen's Walk to the Mall and Buckingham Palace. There was no sign of the Master of Sinanju, so he cooled his heels outside the gates until, nearly two hours and three intermittent rainstorms later, Chiun emerged from the gates, beaming contentedly.

A matronly woman in what Remo thought was a dowdy dress and a gold crown waved good-bye from the big front door.

"How did it go?" Remo asked grumpily.

"It went well," Chiun said airily. "The queen mother is a sterling woman. She accepted the Royal Sceptre with grace and without recriminations—unlike that common scold, her daughter."

"I saw Smith in Oxford," Remo said as they began walking in the direction of Saint James's Park.

"I know. He told me everything. I understand the matter is settled."

"I got the head guy. And an earful from Smith about duty."

Chiun looked up at Remo's set profile with lifted eyebrows.

"And what have you decided?"

"I haven't. I'm still pissed at Smith. But I'll string along with you until I figure out what I really want to do with my life."

"Then be good enough to string along with me for a few more hours," Chiun said. "Then we will leave this gray city of gray people and gray skies."

"An island full of Smiths," Remo remarked dryly.

"There is some good in all peoples," Chiun said, lifting a yellow forefinger. "Except possibly the Japanese."

"Don't forget the Chinese," Remo said good-naturedly. "Whom we are never, ever going to work for."

"The Thais also have their shortcomings," Chiun put in.

"I was never a fan of the Vietnamese. Or the French."

The Master of Sinanju led Remo to Oxford Street, near Oxford Circus, where he went into a store called Virgin Mega.

Remo waited outside, where he bought a copy of a tabloid which ballyhooed the realigning of the sphinxes at Cleopatra's Needle. He gave the vendor a fifty-pound note and received what seemed like a piggy bank's worth of coins in change. His pockets were already bulging with pound coins.

"Don't you have any pound bills?" Remo demanded.

"Sorry, sir. The pound note's been abolished."

"Keep the change, then," Remo said, letting the coins drop to the sidewalk. His pockets couldn't bear any more weight.

Chiun came out and crossed the street to another store called simply HMV. When he came out again, his arms were filled with plastic bags.

"Where to now?" Remo wanted to know.

"Heathrow," said Chiun. "I have summoned the Nostrum jet. Now that we are once again honored in this land, we need not leave as we entered, in secret."

"What do you mean—we? I was catching my death, as the British say, while you were sipping Earl Grey."

"Green tea," Chiun replied smugly. "The British may be uncouth, but their royalty continue to uphold certain meager standards—un-Korean as they are."

32

The next morning, Remo Williams walked into the Lippincott Mercantile Bank. He wore a fresh black T-shirt
and a businesslike expression on his high-cheekboned
face.

He went directly to Douglas Lippincott's office and
breezed past his secretary with such feline fluidity of
movement that she never noticed him, not even when
Lippincott's door opened and closed behind Remo.

Douglas Lippincott looked up from his hand mirror
with a startled expression. He had been caught trim-
ming his nostril hair with a sterling-silver rotary-blade
tool.

"I beg your pardon," he sniffed, shoving the tool-
and-mirror set into a drawer. "Are you my eleven
o'clock?"

"More like your high noon," Remo said, coming around
the desk.

Lippincott looked at Remo with sudden recognition.
"Do I know you?"

"Not unless you read the *National Enquirer*."

"I should say not."

"Then you don't know me," Remo said casually, looking
at a desktop computer whose plug dangled loose. "I hear
you took a big beating in yesterday's stock market."

"I do not discuss mattters of business with persons I do
not know socially. Please leave."

"I will." Remo said. "After you."

"Why should I leave?" Douglas Lippincott demanded,
following Remo with his eyes.

Remo went to one of the office windows. He attempted

to throw the sash up, which made Lippincott smirk to himself. Who was this ruffian? Everyone knew that modern office windows did not open. It was a design element that had come into popularity after the 1929 stock-market crash, when, but for the convenience of an open window, many fewer panicked investors might have committed suicide by defenestration than had happened.

When Remo realized the sill was locked in place, he blew on his right index fingernail and used it to score a rough oval in the glass. It screeched. He tapped the glass with a knuckle. It popped from its pane. Remo grabbed it before it could fall, and pulled the crystal oval inside.

He dropped it on Douglas Lippincott's desk, where it broke into triangular pieces.

"My word," Douglas Lippincott gasped.

"I hear you took such a big beating in the market that you're beside yourself," Remo went on in a cheerful voice. "Can't cover your margins and all that investor kind of stuff."

"I will say it again. That is not your concern." He reached for his intercom. Too late.

Douglas Lippincott stood up, his face quirking in sudden surprise. He had not given his legs the command to stand. But there he was standing nevertheless. And then he was walking. He felt the tightness at his shirt collar and the thick wad of his full-Windsor necktie knot pressing his Adam's apple, and realized that he was being led to the portholelike window opening by the scruff of his neck.

"Any last words before you throw yourself into instant and permanent bankruptcy?" Remo asked nonchalantly.

"I fancy 'God Save the Queen' is appropriate."

"Not in this country," Remo Williams said, arranging Douglas Lippincott's limbs in preparation for throwing him through the hole.

Lippincott didn't quite fit. He took most of the remaining glass with him on the way down. It made Remo glad he had checked for passersby first. Falling glass was dangerous.

*　　*　　*

DeGoone Slickens wet his lips. His typing fingers—the right index and the left middle finger—were poised over his office computer terminal. There had been no word from P. M. Looncraft since he had rushed off to England. Doug Lippincott had sounded like a broken man over the phone. That meant it was up to DeGoone Slickens to pull it all together.

If only the danged computer would work. Settling himself, he hit the "On" switch.

The amber lines were slow to appear, like a TV set warming up.

Slickens leaned forward, squinting.

The message read:

WARNING!!!
TUBE IMPLOSION IMMINENT!!
STAND CLEAR!
DANGER

"Dang!" Slickens said, ducking to escape the flying glass that never came.

When he felt it was safe, he lifted his head to read the screen again. He was no computer expert, but when a computer warned that it was about to go berserk, he took the threat seriously.

But this computer didn't look like it was going to do anything but scream its silent warning.

Slickens started to pick himself up from the floor when something changed. The warning still glowed in smoldering amber letters, but a shadow had crossed the glareproof screen. It was a face, dark, ghostly, with hollow skull-like eyes and a cruel mouth under high cheekbones.

Steeling himself, DeGoone Slickens lifted his face to the screen to see the face more clearly. His face kept on going, propelled by a hand he neither saw nor felt, because it was moving faster than his nervous system could react to it.

The screen accepted his face with unqualified hostility. The tube imploded, swallowing DeGoone Slickens' head. Sparks flew like electric spittle, and something inside the housing buzzed like a dying cicada.

As DeGoone Slickens' soft organic brain matter mingled with the terminal's hard-wired brain matter, Remo Williams unplugged the device. He didn't want to start a fire.

An hour later Remo showed up at Faith Davenport's apartment lobby. The blue-blazered security guard was only too happy to fax the joyous news of his arrival.

Under his arm Remo carried the thick paper-wrapped bundle he had brought from the car to the elevator and up several flights to Faith's door.

"Remo, lover!" Faith said excitedly. "I was so worried about you."

Remo stepped in, his face screwed into glum lines. He willed his facial muscles to hold that expression, hoping for the best. This wasn't going to be easy, he knew.

Faith threw her arms around his neck the moment the door was closed. "I missed you so much!" she exclaimed. Her nose touched his; her eyes were practically mating with his own.

Gently, with one hand, Remo unlocked her embrace. Faith's hands went to his thick right wrist, and, moving slowly, began to caress his index finger.

"I can't stay," Remo said seriously, pulling his finger away.

Faith's face went into shock. "No?"

"No," Remo echoed. "This is good-bye. I don't know how to tell you this, but we can't see each other anymore."

"But . . . but I love you."

"No," Remo said, paraphrasing Australian soap-opera dialogue he had heard in London. "You don't love me. You only love my index finger. Admit it."

Faith's expression broke like a mirror. "It's true!" she sobbed. "But we can work it out. I know! We can go into counseling."

Remo shook his head sadly.

"Give me one reason," Faith demanded, hurt.

"Here," Remo said, handing her the paper-wrapped bundle.

Faith carried it to the sofa, where she began unwrapping it. The rolled-up pelt of Bear-Man came forth.

She looked at it, at Remo, and at the suit again. "You!"

"Now you know my secret," Remo said, solemn-voiced. "Now you know why our love can never be. I am needed elsewhere." He took her trembling hand in his. "You're the only person I've told my secret to. Promise me that you'll keep it."

Faith's lower lip trembled. Her chin joined in. Her eyes began to well up and overflow.

"Y-yes," she said. "Of course. I'm so . . . honored you told me. I feel just like Kim Basinger."

"My life is too dangerous to share it with anyone. You know how financial crime-fighting is."

"Oh, I know! I know!"

"Well," Remo said, thankful his facial muscles were holding together. "I gotta go now. Duty calls. Someone has to protect the market from the greedy."

He gathered up the Bear-Man suit and stuffed it under one arm and started for the door.

Faith rushed to him. "Before you go," she said. "Do you have any hot market tips?"

"Yeah. Dump all your faxes. They cause sterility in laboratory rats. The AMA is about to blow the whistle on the whole thing."

"Oh, I will. I promise."

At the door, Faith bestowed on his lips a wistful butterfly kiss. He gave her a discolored bear's tooth souvenir in return, then left, feeling her eyes follow him to the elevator.

His pent-up laughter held long enough for the elevator to reach the lobby. He laughed all the way down the street.

It stopped abruptly when he passed a teenager in a T-shirt that read "I SAW THE BEAR!" Under the legend was a picture of Bear-Man's ferocious head. Two blocks further along, a business type carrying *The Wall Street Journal* under one arm almost bumped into him. He wore a brown baseball cap with a bear's head mounted on top. Remo saw bear-teeth bumper stickers, necklaces, and even a street mime in a shaggy grizzly costume.

"Oh, no," Remo said. He hailed a cab and raced to the Nostrum Building.

Remo found the Master of Sinanju fuming in the emptiness of his office. The trading room was still in ruins from the shooting. There were no workers to be seen anywhere.

Remo stepped over the litter of broken glass and furniture. Chiun caught sight of his worried expression.

"What is wrong, Remo?" he squeaked.

"What makes you think something is wrong?" Remo asked innocently.

"Your face betrays you, as always."

"Tell me your troubles and I'll tell you mine," Remo countered, joining him in the office.

"I have just been on the telephone with that deceiver, Smith," Chiun complained.

"Let me guess. He's taking Nostrum away from you."

"He would not dare. He says it is mine if I will assume all the debts. Nostrum is overleveraged, whatever that means."

"Search me," Remo said. "I don't understand business talk."

"It has something to do with Nostrum having borrowed money from something called the Social Security Trust Fund. They have called in the note. Nostrum must sell all its stocks to accomplish this. I knew nothing about this debt. Did you?"

"It's news to me," Remo admitted. "So what did you tell Smith?"

"I asked him who this Social Security Trust Fund was and he told me it belonged to the American government. I then told Smith that if the President wishes to sue Nostrum, I will take this to the Supreme Courtyard. You see, I have learned how these business people think."

Remo masked a smile. "And what did he say?"

"He began babbling about the elderly persons who will not be fed if the money is not returned. And then he made me an offer I could not refuse."

"He did?" Remo said. "Smith? Our Smith? Tightwad Smith? What did he offer?"

"Something more worthy than all the stock certificates in the world," Chiun replied.

"Yeah?"

"Australian beautiful dramas!" Chiun cried triumphantly. "Beamed by satellite to our very home every day. Think of it, Remo. I will once again have beautiful dramas with which to pass my declining years."

"I'd say that's worth millions of dollars any day," Remo said wryly.

"I knew that you would agree," Chiun said. "That is why I freely and with clear conscience offered him your share of Nostrum as well."

Remo's eyebrows shot up. "My share?"

"Smith threw in British dramas. How could I refuse anything so magnanimous?"

"Especially when you're not footing the bill," Remo said dryly. "What about Cheeta Ching? I thought she was number one on your wish list."

"A woman is young for a time," Chiun said loftily, "but art endures forever. And I think that when she learns of my magnificent treasure trove of beautiful dramas, she will beat a path to my very door, begging me to share these riches with her."

"Could be," Remo said. Chiun's wrinkled features broke into a pleasurable smile. "But I doubt it," Remo added quickly.

Chiun frowned. "We shall see," he said in a careless voice. "Now, what is it that troubles you?"

"I see Bear-Man everywhere I go. And he's not me."

"I know, I know," Chiun said unhappily.

"You must be cleaning up, huh?" Remo prompted.

Chiun's frown soured even more. "That lazy woman Faith," he spat. "She is ill-named. Her mother should have named her Faithless. A common shooting happens and she is afraid to come to work. I have fired her. I have fired them all."

"What happened?" Remo asked.

"She did not do as I instructed," Chiun explained. "Some bandit has appropriated the Bear-Man merchandising. Faith neglected to secure the proper copyrights or some such white nonsense, and now others are copying what should be only mine to copy."

"Great," Remo said. "I'm off the hook for personal appearances. The Bear-Man suit's out in the hall. It's yours. I never want to see it again."

"And you will not," Chiun snapped. "I have lost billions. Billions."

Chiun looked about him with the air of a Napoleon bidding farewell to Paris before going into exile.

"Good-bye, Nostrum," he said. "I will miss you."

"But I won't," Remo said.

"We will leave now. Let the new owners clean up this place." Chiun went to a file cabinet and began pulling out plastic bags.

"Come, Remo," he said. "Help me carry these away."

Remo accepted an armful of the bags. They were very heavy and bore store logos such as HMV and Strawberries.

"What's all this?" Remo asked, looking into the top bag. He saw only stacks of clear flat plastic boxes.

"My CD's," Chiun said proudly as he emptied the cabinet. "You see, I have not been completely cheated. On the advice of Smith, I have invested all my Nostrum salary in CD's."

Remo shifted the package to one arm and pulled out a box.

The label read "NANA MOUSKOURI IN CONCERT." The box under it featured Barbra Streisand's face.

"Compact discs?" Remo said, blinking.

"Now that the stock market is healthy once more," Chiun said, "I am going to redeem these for gold."

"Where?" Remo wanted to know, his face a study in sobriety.

Chiun closed the final drawer. "Smith said any bank will take them."

"I have an idea," Remo said as they walked through

crunching glass to the elevators. "Why don't you get Smith to handle the transaction? He knows lots of bankers. He can probably get you the best rate."

"That is an excellent idea, Remo," Chiun said. "It is the least that man can do after the cunning way he has tricked me. Do you mind if we do this tonight? You know these Americans and their gambling manias. Today the markets are up. Tomorrow they may crash anew."

The elevator arrived, and they stepped aboard.

"Little Father," Remo said, grinning broadly, "I absolutely insist that we rush back to Folcroft and take advantage of Smith's investment acumen."